GIRL AGAINST THE UNIVERSE

Hump slapped the off button. "Screw the teev. I'm sick of space. And you act so goddamn superior! I ought to turn you in."

But Vanity's mind was already a million miles away. The signs were too clear. Soon the Space Authority would request "nonreturnable samples from the local population." and . . .

There was only one way out. "Hump," she whispered. "How'd you like to learn to work a spaceship?"

GOLDEN VANITY

RACHEL POLLACK

GOLDEN VANITY

RACHEL POLLACK

BERKLEY BOOKS, NEW YORK

GOLDEN VANITY

A Berkley Book / published by arrangement with
the author

PRINTING HISTORY
Berkley edition / July 1980

ISBN: 0-425-04483-1

A BERKLEY BOOK® TM 757,375
PRINTED IN THE UNITED STATES OF AMERICA

TO MY MOTHER

There was a lofty ship
and it sailed upon the sea,
And the name of that ship,
It was the Golden Vanity.
And it was set upon by a Spanish enemy,
As it sailed upon the lowland, lowland, low,
Sailed upon the lowland sea.

Then up spake the cabin boy
Of the age of twelve and three,
And he said to the captain,
What will you give to me,
If I swim alongside of your Spanish enemy,
And sink her in the lowland, lowland, low,
Sink her in the lowland sea.

I will give you silver,
And gold, and much money,
And the hand of my daughter,
So very dear to me
If you will swim alongside of the Spanish enemy,
And sink her in the lowland, lowland, low,
Sink her in the lowland sea.

—English Folk Song

GOLDEN VANITY

Openers ─────────────────────────────────

1

Creaser yawned. He scratched his belly, his cheeks, and his teeth, then glowered around at the dingy cabin of his ship. You would think, he thought, that a Worker important enough to run one-man space missions directly for his chairman deserved a live-zone with a little elegance. His eyes flickered across the bare yellow floor, the "bed" formed from blue Halian jelly, the control bank, grimy from years of sweaty fingers, the tall narrow cabinet jammed with souvenirs and junk from a hundred worlds (and also with a certain platinum box, but it was better not to think about that particular temptation, not with a job ahead), the holo console and the meager pile of tapes—he wished he could stuff it all through the dumphole.

All but the cargo. The huge pilot squinted at the light-density box, sitting in all its impenetrable black glory in the middle of the floor. What was in there, anyway? Jewels? It looked small enough, about four hands square. Nonsense. The chairman owned enough jewels to melt them into a river flooding half of Center. Some sort of documents, maybe, evidence against one of the other companies. Whatever it was, the chairman wanted it enough to smuggle it off Ktaner's Planet in a very illegal three ship convoy. Creaser and two escorts, a Nirudian, and a Clickie. Creaser didn't know their names; he didn't care.

Creaser snickered. Maybe he should open the box and peek

1

2

Throughout the big ornate room robot puppets adorned the hours with repetitious actions. In a corner, puppet milk boys dressed in untanned roke leather squeezed the teats of miniature "cows," those odd chunky animals from the newly discovered humanhome, Earth. Suspended from the ceiling a puppet acrobat did constant somersaults and twists on his nearly invisible softwire trapeze; in the room's center, surrounded by a miniscule forest of living trees five centimeters high, a four armed puppet version of Lukmii, the legendary Arbolian mountain climber, scaled an exact model of Mt. Drusso, the highest mountain in the explored galaxy. Every time little Lukmii gained the summit, he leaped to the floor and started over again.

This was the chairman's playroom, and the chairman liked movement, noise, action, more and more of it as he himself slowed down with age. The very carpets rippled in time to the faint music exuded by the trembling walls. The HgH(grunt)urian carpet weavers had woven the dark threads into an archaic battle scene in such a way that the floor ripples sent the warriors constantly crashing against each other in a charge that never climaxed.

Spaced around the room six real scale, real time projection "windows" showed random scenes on some of the different worlds owned entirely, "land, sea, air, and people" as the law phrased it, by Company One, the chief of the three primal forces in a cartel galaxy. The chairman's chief assistant had urged, along with the windows, a "radiancewall" of constantly flashing channel-assessed information. The chairman had vetoed it. "Isolation, AAri," he'd said, with that infuriating half smile of his. "Being alone. Away from information, urgencies, all the little crises you offer me like sweetcakes. I need to slice the universe for just one clock a day. You can understand that, can't you? Yes, AAri, of course you can."

Sitting cross-legged on a vibrating cushion (vibrations self-tuned by the cushion's feedback "brain" to smoothpoint the chairman's body waves), the narrowly built but thickmuscled man, splendid in his nakedness, looked—at first glance—the perfect image of young maturity. A second glance showed something else. Though his skin, smoothed daily by deep massage, showed as few wrinkles as a boy's, his age and strength shone through like a fire behind a screen. Through the years his face and body had taken on a hardness, a stone-like quality that implied a great power in his most casual movements.

A girl, a teenager, sat on the floor with her back to him. Expressionless, she stared at the mouth of a giant tigerbird mounted across the room, while the chairman quietly stroked a brush down her long gold-red hair. "We'll take a holiday soon," the chairman said as he draped the hair, with more devotion than artistry, across her shoulders, then ran his fingertips down the insides of her arms.

Though the girl's insides knotted at his touch, she kept her muscles motionless, her skin smooth. Because it annoyed the chairman when she didn't react, she'd learned to control the trigger reactions—like gooseflesh or shivers—that most people considered automatic. Three "shields," narrow elliptic rings of darklight, hung suspended in the air ten centimeters from her breasts, her waist, and her thighs. Homeostatic mechanisms tuned to her body radiation moved the rings when she moved. Against her skin she wore nothing but a necklace of small glittery black stones.

"Someplace new," the chairman continued, "with unexplored territory where we can go alone in a surface plane." The girl said nothing. His hands pressed her hips, breaking through the darklight like knives. "Or would you like someplace cold, full of dead trees and filthy winds? Would that match your gloomy fants? And your cold body?" His voice carried the thinnest recrimination, the softest of warnings.

The girl said flatly, "My body hasn't gotten cold. Your fingers have. You better send to Arbol for another treatment before you shrivel up like a dead bork."

His hands moved up to squeeze her waist. "Or maybe you should remember to put on your skin cream. Asser tells me you've ignored it or thrown it out the last two weeks. That's not good for you. You know I don't like it when your skin gets chapped and rough."

She allowed herself a smirk. "It doesn't *get* rough, Jaak. I make it that way. I take baths in Luritti dust so it'll flake off on your fingers. Maybe I'll strip off the skin altogether and graft knives onto my muscles like the Nashi warrior women. Then I could cut you every time I turn around."

"You're getting morbid again, Vanity. Didn't Cixxa warn you that would happen?" Despite herself, the girl's mouth twitched and she felt the blood level drop in her face. The chairman said, "That's why I want to take you on a holiday. It'll wash your head clean."

The girl stood, twisting away from his hands. "I've got a better idea. Suppose I go somewhere alone and send you back a tape of my serene clean face glowing in the sunshine?"

He rose and walked towards her, his hands slightly in front of his body as if to grab her. "A holiday without you? Vanity, that's no holiday at all."

"How do you know? You've never tried." She walked across the room where she pretended to watch the puppet cows. "What do you get from me, Jaak? What do I ever give you? All my fants include cutting you. Every one. I built one last week, a really long one, where I dismembered you, statted all the parts, and hooked them to your head. Then I acid-etched your brain with cyclic torture memories. It was very extravagant. Beautiful in a way. But all my fants are like that. Ask Cixxa."

"I have, and I don't believe you. Cixxa tells me viciousness wouldn't feed your head."

"Well, what if it isn't true? What do I ever do for you? I just ridicule you. Why don't you let me go? You've owned me for years."

"I've owned you all your life, Vanity. That's why I'm keeping you. If I sliced you now you'd run far away somewhere, then fall down whimpering until I came and brought you home."

"Maybe. Let's experiment." He said nothing. "Oh burst, Jaak, I don't want any holiday. Take someone else. Take AAri. You can chill me in a coffin-nest until you get back."

He walked up beside her. His eyes moved along her body, the long legs, the narrow almost flat hips, the soft belly covered in fine golden hairs, the high small breasts with their deep golden nipples, up to the tight neck and the cold calm face. "You might as well not get sullen or resentful," he said. "We're going on a holiday together so why don't you enjoy yourself? In fact, I insist on it." One hand touched her chest above her breasts. She pushed away his arm, then leaped to grab the puppet acrobat's trapeze, and a moment later had swung herself up to a cushioned platform mounted halfway up the wall. She crossed her legs and grinned down at him.

"Vanity, come back here." He didn't raise or sharpen his voice, but her grin twitched away and she raised her legs against her chest. "Come down here, Vanity," he said mildly. "I want to talk to you."

She dropped cat-like to the floor, then stood straight without pushing her hair away from her face. "Now walk back to me," he ordered, and she glided towards him across the silent rippling armies.

At that moment the door opened. The chairman spun around, enraged, while the girl stopped and crossed her arms. A grin tugged at her mouth.

"AAri," the chairman grated. "This room is closed, inviolate. Can't you remember that? When I say 'no one' that includes you."

The chairman's personal assistant made a noise. "Slice the speeches, Jaak. You don't have to recite your rules for me. I'm the lackey who keeps everyone away."

"Wonderful. Then keep yourself away too."

AAri sighed. "Something's come in that can't wait."

"There is nothing that can't wait until I'm ready for it."

The girl laughed. "You're believing your fants again, Jaak. Just because you own the universe doesn't mean you control it."

AAri said, "The convoy busted. Blew up. I don't know how yet, but only one of the three survived."

"The one with the prize?"

AAri shook his head. "Gone. Exploded with the ship."

The chairman raised a fist as if to strike something, saw nothing available, and dropped his hand. "Filth," he muttered.

The girl laughed. "Vanity," he hissed without looking at her, "be quiet." He narrowed his eyes at his assistant. "Two years. Two years of searching, fighting—"

"Jaak, set yourself for a jolt. The bust-up isn't all."

"The loss of that prize is enough of a jolt. Slice the preliminaries."

"All right. The pilot carrying the prize—I don't know how it happened yet, but I suspect he might have opened the box somehow—anyway, he suffered an ego collapse."

The chairman opened his mouth, closed it. "That's how the ship blew?"

"What do you think? All over space, like a light bomb."

"The pilot who got away, he's sure about that?"

"It's a she, and she certainly sounds sure. We'll have to dismantle her head as soon as she reaches Center."

"How the burst could he have unlocked a density box? Who was it anyway?"

"Not one of our top group. A Worker who happened to be on Kap when we needed him."

"Why did Yuta trust him? Didn't it occur to her, and you, to send for someone who could handle the job? Do you know what we could have done with that prize? We could have ripped Acina, we could have cut his insides like a slice-fish."

"You know very well we didn't have time. The thing just fell in our laps. It was send it out immediately or forget it."

Jaak rubbed his forehead. "So now there's a shrieker out there."

AAri nodded. "A young shrieker, two days out from Ktaner's Planet, gobbling up space and growing like a kura-lover. And it's only a matter of what, weeks, before the SA finds out about it."

"Can they trace it back to us?"

"Possibly. Though they can't prove it."

The girl said, "Unless they go poking around Kap. Once the people there find out a shrieker's coming they'll get too scared for you to bribe or threaten them."

AAri made a face. "She's right, you know."

"Then we'll just go after this thing ourselves, send out an executioner. We'll fix up a ship with dampers, we can do it in twelve hours."

"Talk sense, Jaak. Of course we can fix up a ship. I've already started one. The Worker's the problem."

"You know the rosters better than me. Who've we got?"

AAri searched his boss's face. "You know whom we need as well as I do."

The chairman looked at him curiously a moment; suddenly his face contorted in a burst of furious understanding. "No. Absolutely not."

"We don't have any choice. Do you want to run a talent search? Or maybe Cixxa could do a topographical head survey. That shouldn't take more than a month. For burst's sake, there's a shrieker out there. We're not equipped to handle it and we can't ask the SA. That leaves one choice. Loper."

"No. I told you when he left, that filth-lover will never work for me again."

"No one'll work for you if we don't survive. We don't have anyone else. We purged our lists last year, remember?"

"And that was Loper's fault as well. Do *you* remember that? Now you want me to bring him back?"

"If we send some hack or trainee out there he'll blow his ship too, before he can use the dampers. And that'll make the shrieker grow some more, until who knows if even the SA'll be able to kill it."

"We could send out double ships. Back ups."

"Nonsense."

The chairman glanced at the girl, who was staring at the wall. He couldn't tell if she was laughing. "All right," he said to AAri. "All right. Get him. But you arrange it. I don't want to see him or hear him or even know he's here."

"We'll have to offer him something."

"I hardly thought he'd do it to help humanity. You bargain with him. Just keep me out of it."

AAri half turned, stopped. "There's something else. You might as well face it now." Jaak nodded. "Loper'll want his old ship back."

"No!"

"We can't help it. I'm fixing up one of our other ships, just in case he'll accept it. But you know him as well as I do. He won't do it otherwise."

"That filth isn't going to work my ship."

"It used to be his ship."

"It was never his ship. I built it and I run it, no matter who sits hitting the switches. He worked it when I ordered him, that's all, and he's never going to work it again."

"Then he'll refuse."

"We'll find someone else."

"We can't find someone else. We're too depleted. Loper's the only one outside the SA and the other companies who's good enough for that kind of work. This isn't cargo hauling." AAri's voice was rising; he bit his lip.

"He will not work the *Golden Vanity*."

"Stop the idiot act, Jaak. You've got no choice. You can't throw away the whole company just because this Worker once—" He stopped at the sight of his boss's twisted face.

For several seconds the two men glared at each other. Finally the chairman looked away. "If I've got no choice, I've got no choice." He pointed to the girl. "She's got to leave. I don't want her anywhere near here when he comes to take the ship." He tried to smile as he looked at her. "It looks like you'll get your holiday alone after all."

"I've decided I'd rather stay here," she said.

"Really? I didn't think you'd relish his return any more than I do. But it doesn't matter. You're going somewhere safe until we get this finished."

"How about Ktaner's Planet?"

"You'll go where I want you to go." Softening his voice he added, "I'm only trying to protect you." He stood over her; when she looked away, his fingertips on her chin pulled her head around. "Vanity," he said, "give your father a kiss."

She didn't move. While his cold lips pressed her mouth she stared over his shoulder at the puppet Lukmii doggedly climbing its miniature mountain.

Part One

Chapter One ───────────────────────

Humphrey Chimpden Earwicker McCloskey wasn't drunk. He certainly had been earlier, he knew, when he'd left the robot bar and the witty somewhat pedantic woman who turned out to be an android. He must have been very drunk to wander into this neighborhood on a Saturday night. Or any night. But now that he'd found himself here—too far inside to simply scurry out again—fear had sobered him.

Luckily the streets were dark, the lights all burnt out or broken, particularly away from the avenues. More important, most of the kids who lived in the crumbling brick five and six story buildings were out prowling the border where they hoped to find some man who didn't know enough to keep to safe territory on a Saturday night. Judging by the emptiness it never occurred to rat fems that some drunk might actually stagger inside their own territory. No lights and empty streets gave Hump a thin hope; if he went north rather than east, the way he'd come in, he might make it to the spaceport.

The spaceport. "The great glory of our age," as the government called it, the "monster" as everyone else called it, covered half of what used to be the Bronx (how eagerly the army had tossed out the people), filling the razed streets with wonderful searchlights, shiny new buildings—and four separate police forces marching along the borders like hunters protecting a settlement from wolves.

A piece of blackened glass scrunched under his feet and he leaped for a doorway; when no one came he let out his breath and started walking again. Glass and rubble filled the streets; oily sewer water ran through the garbage that lay next to the overturned empty flower pots. "What a goddamn shame," he whispered. He remembered the women, his Aunt Marilyn among them, who had originally bought, rented, or occupied these old buildings years ago in the hope of building a "liberated community."

"We just want some peace," Marilyn had told him. "We just want to be left alone."

For awhile it almost worked; when the government saw the buildings restored, crime lower than anywhere else in town, and the sidewalks adorned with red and yellow flower pots, it eagerly offered money and technical help in the hope the women would establish a peaceful alternative to the feminist bombings and assassinations of the late eighties.

The women were still arguing whether to accept when the first spaceships arrived and all such programs ended. Abandoned. They still might have survived on their own if the government hadn't decided that a "liberated" zone of any kind threatened negotiations with the aliens; especially since Marilyn and some of the others had already joined the Earth Resistance Movement. When troops failed to clear the area, the government simply cut off all services. Without water or electricity the women finally left, in twos and threes, until the last holdouts got picked off in a dawn raid.

For a while the buildings stood empty, gutted, useless. So the government thought. Then the kids came in. Rootless, valueless, cut off from history by the arrival of the aliens, scornful of any recognized emotions, even hate, they drifted in one by one, joining together to scavenge food and victims. Apolitical, they didn't threaten anyone who didn't meet them face to face. If they wanted to live in buildings without floorboards or water, the government would let them stay.

Their apoliticism came through also in their attitude to the area's previous occupants. Though they parodied the radical feminists' name and always chose men for their "knifey-toys," the rat fems, girls and boys both, cared nothing for any ideology. You couldn't even describe them as anarchists or terrorists, only

as a ragged gang stealing food, water, clothes, living for flashes
of violence to light up their faces.

Hump remembered news stories about men who'd survived
rat fem parties. He wasn't sure he'd want to. How many blocks,
three, four? He began to hope he might actually make it. He
could write an article, "I Entered Rat Femland and Lived."

He could go home and kiss the locks on the door.

The street ended at a t-shaped intersection filled with garbage
and old junk, mattresses, chair arms, oil heaters, some of it
originally thrown from windows in the riots that greeted the
government's decision to cut off services. Which way to go? To
the right, he thought, it looked narrower.

He was halfway down the side street and smirking at his
nearly consummated escape when he saw the girl. She sat on a
stoop, her elbows on her knees, a bottle perched in front of her.
She was staring at him. And grinning. As he turned to run,
Hump's throat made a noise between a gulp and a gag. The girl
laughed. "Hey," she called, "come back here." He stumbled as if
she'd thrown a knife in his back. "Come on, it's simple," she said.
"Turn around and walk back to me. First one foot, then the
other."

Was she safe? Was she possibly safe? Her giggling laugh
hardly sounded sinister. And what could he do? If he tried to run
she could make so much noise the other rat fems would rise from
the sewers. His mind jammed with prayers as he walked back to
stand in front of her. Arms crossed, she looked him over.

Hump didn't know what impression he made, but the woman
certainly didn't fit his picture of a snuffer. Slim, relaxed, with a
sharp yet pleasant face—streaked in dirt—with long gangly legs
and arms, thin shoulders, high breasts, and long matted hair (he
thought dull blonde), she wore loose shiny trousers belted at the
waist, an over-large collarless shirt of translucent green with
wide black cuffs, and boots made of some grainy leather. Too
good. The clothes were too good for a rat fem. He guessed her
age around sixteen.

"You look as if someone just chewed up your stomach," she
said cheerfully, obviously delighted at the sight of him. Like
someone at a circus when the clowns come in. "Would you like
some of this filth?" she asked, and held up the bottle of colored
water.

He shook his head. "No. No thank you," he croaked.

She held it up to the moonlight. "It is pretty slime-face," she said and threw it across the narrow street to smash against a building. The way Hump jumped it might have hit him in the head. He watched the tiny river twist down the gutter, and when he turned back she looked as if she waited for him to balance something on his nose.

He wondered how he looked to her. A good target? Tender? About five ten, stockily built, with a slightly hooked nose, wide lips, a strong chin ("Your chin's the best part of you," Kate used to tell him. "I love it."), and big dumbo-like ears. Hump thought his not quite flabby body would melt like heated jelly and run down his green sherpa-pants (shaggy cotton, wide legs tied at the cuffs) into the street.

"Are you . . . ?" he tried to ask.

Her eyes narrowed. "Am I what?"

He swallowed. "One of . . ." he waved his hand, "a fem?"

The woman let her shoulders drop and leaned back, relaxed, against the stoop.

She's not, Hump thought. *She's not a rat fem. She's another outsider.* He became suddenly aware that her bravado hid a great strain. Whoever she was, she was fully half as scared as him. "Fem," she said. "Is that what they call the people here in filth town?"

He nodded. "Rat fems. Listen, can I go now?"

She laughed; Hump winced at the loud sound. "No, stay with me. Rat fems. I like that. You know, they're totally crazy. They wanted me to go with them on some escapade. I told them to let me sleep and do you know what they did? They hit me on the back like I was a bork—" She bit her lip. "A horse, and then they showed me these skinny knives they all carried inside their shirts. Here." She pointed between her breasts.

"Look," Hump whispered, "I've got to get out of here, before one of those knives ends up *here*." He pointed to his stomach.

"Is that what they do?" she asked, as if he'd told her they gave dance recitals.

"Goodbye," he said and spun around.

"Please don't go." She grabbed his arm.

Before Hump could answer, a high nasal voice cut through the damp air. "Well, grandlady bitch. A jerker. Right here at home."

Hump spun around; a whimper escaped his throat. A boy and a girl, each about thirteen, were standing in the gutter, holding hands like schoolkids. Their dirty leather pants, ruffled shirts, and steel tipped shoes looked too big for them, like clothes worn for a masquerade. The boy had circled his eyes with thick red lipstick and painted his nose and ears black. The girl had whitened the area around her eyes and wore a long false mustache. Their teeth gleamed with glitter paint.

The boy gestured gracefully to the girl sitting on the stoop. In an artificially deep voice which threatened to break, he said, "Thank you, sister straight, for finding him. The goddess will eat you when you die."

The girl laughed as she got to her feet. "You see," she said to Hump. "They're crazy."

"Shut up," Hump grated. "Will you shut up?"

The female rat fem laughed. "Jerker's giving orders, here comes jerker the order-giver. That's how come he's got a tongue, thinks jerker, he can give everyone their orders. That's a disease, jerker, a sad sickness. Goddess finger's gonna cure you." Simultaneously the two rat fems reached into their shirts and lifted out long stiletto knives in graceful arcs that left the pin-sharp points aimed at Hump's face. As Hump stepped backward the girl made a sharp sucking noise. Light flickered from her teeth to the knife.

From the corner of his eye, Hump saw the blonde from the stoop pick up a chunk of concrete. He forgot her immediately as the two circled sideways around him to make sure he couldn't run. The female worked her lips to juggle the fake mustache.

"Are you thirsty, jerker?" she asked. The two of them spat on their knives. "Goddess offers you a drink."

The other drawled, "Stick out your tongue, jerker." Hump didn't move. "Stick it out," they both whispered, and then laughed, their voices shrill and piercing.

Forgotten by all of them the girl from the stoop suddenly sprang at red eyes. The chunk of concrete slammed clumsily against his head, then the two of them rolled in the dust, fighting for the knife.

With a scream the female leaped on top of them, but a miracle enabled Hump to kick her cleanly in the stomach, once, twice, before she could roll away. When the bodies separated, Hump's new ally had somehow gotten the knife. He yanked her to her feet. "Come on," he yelled. "Let's get out of here." He started to run, pulling her behind him.

She tried to break away until the two rat fems jumped up screaming and snarling, and then she took off behind Hump, pumping her legs (though Hump couldn't hear anything but his own hysterical feet), while her matted hair flapped like rags against her neck and shoulders.

Shrieking, the rat fems threw bricks, chunks of concrete, pieces of glass. "Bitch!" screamed the female. "Jerker-loving bitch!" Hump got hit in the back; he hardly noticed.

His new found savior hollered over her shoulder, "Bork mother filth. Slime fingers."

"For god's sake," Hump gasped. "Keep going."

Laughing, the girl waved the stolen stiletto and stepped up her pace.

They'd almost reached the spaceport with its well lit streets and quadruple police—city cops, US army cops, UN observer corps, alien space authority—when the girl suddenly stopped short and grabbed Hump's arm, spinning him into a wall. "What are you doing?" he pleaded. "We're almost out."

"What's that?" She pointed down the block at the patch of light.

"The spaceport, for god's sake."

"No." She shook her head. "Can't go there."

"Why the hell not?" he whispered. "And keep your voice down." He looked back down the block.

"I can't, that's all. Can't we get out some other way?"

"Yeah, sure. After nine or ten blocks."

She bit her lip. "That's not so much."

"It is for me. You like it here? Fine. Goodbye." He patted her on the cheek and turned. He turned back with a sigh. She looked confused, scared, miserable, like a kid deserted by her only friend. Hump said, "Look, we'll get killed if we stay here."

"You'd be dead already if it wasn't for me."

"Yeah, I know." He made a face. "Look, suppose we do this. There's usually plenty of cabs roaming the spaceport. Suppose we hail the first one we see and go to my place. It's all the way downtown, and I give you my word I'm not hiding any aliens. Or cops." She looked doubtful. "Please?"

"Hey okay," she said and grinned. They took off at a trot for the bright streets.

Chapter Two ───────────────────────

Sitting in the cab Hump studied his rescuer. An odd face; nice. The thin longish nose looked excessively sharp against the round cheeks and full lips. Long neck, like her arms and legs. Cat-like? No, some kind of bird, graceful. Nice. Odd complexion, a kind of clear yellow, like sunflower oil. Her eyes didn't look Oriental at all. For some reason he felt disoriented, almost queasy, looking at her. But nice?

Age—he guessed around sixteen. He hoped. If she was fifteen or younger, and a runaway, he could pull some real scab. Not that the police or even most parents cared about the thousands of kids who ran away every day. If the children could find some place that wasn't falling apart in the world-wide obsession with the aliens, then the parents wished them luck. But this one's clothes looked rich under the dirt and smell, and somewhere a powerful mommy and daddy might be sending out private cops to look for her. "How old are you?" he asked.

"What?" She calculated something. "Sixteen."

"Are you sure?"

"Of course I'm sure. What a stupid question." She turned back to the window.

Runaway or not, she was certainly a tourist. She gaped at the buildings and lights, she laughed every time the cab nearly sideswiped a ped or some other car. When two truck drivers started a fight with a cop, she cheered (he wasn't sure whom), and at one point Hump had to yank her head back in the car as she tried to see the tops of some old buildings.

It didn't bother Hump at all if she didn't want to talk. For one thing his heart and lungs hadn't settled down after the escape, for another he didn't think they should talk much with the driver sitting there. All spaceport cabs ran robot now (one of Earth's gimmicks to impress the aliens), but the union had demanded human "drivers" sitting in the front seats. A lot of the bored drivers moonlighted by working for one of the eight hundred or so intelligence agencies which spied on the port and visitors. Ridiculous, Hump scolded himself, straight from the teev; the florid-faced pudgy-fingered driver with his marbly eyes fixed on page 104 of "Great Erotic Science Fiction of the Twentieth Century" hardly looked like a secret agent. But Hump was too schizzed to make sense.

While the cab lurched down the rotting cement of Second Avenue, the girl gawked at the drunks, the ethnic restaurants, the motorcycle graveyards, the bombed or burnt out buildings. So she's a tourist, Hump thought. From where? He remembered her rigid fear at the spaceport and a certain suspicion pecked at his mind. No, no, he told himself. Don't be ridiculous. People like the president got to see *them*, and then only with difficulty. A useless hack writer, teacher, and bar cleaner only got to see other useless people.

So why did the spaceport wig her like that? Oh no, he thought. No. Not a terrorist, not one of those nuts who thought they could restore the social services by blowing up toilets in the spaceports. Maybe he could dump her on Marilyn and the ERM. Maybe she already knew Marilyn.

He glanced quickly at his peculiar neighbor. She looked too young, too innocent, not nearly sly enough for a terrorist. Well, maybe she just hated the place. Lots of poeple did.

The moment the cab pulled up in front of Hump's dirty red brick house the girl bounded out as if she'd waited for years to see this historic site. "Let's go," she said impatiently, while Hump undid the secret compartment in his jacket and took out his wallet.

"I've got to pay the bill," he told her.

"What?" She sounded annoyed.

"Money, you know. Makes the world go round."

"Oh, of course. Legal tender." She stroked his cheek as the cab jerked away.

On the stoop of Hump's house, Gari, the resident drunk, hoisted himself to let them pass. For fifteen dollars a week you could hire a drunk to live on your stoop, clean the steps, and chase away the other drunks who wanted to sleep or puke in your doorway. "Hello, Hump," the bearded old man growled. He tugged his threadbare black and silver tunic. "Everything quiet tonight." Down the street they could hear shouts as police grabbed two women and slammed them against a wall. Hump's guest stared for a moment until she noticed that the two men hadn't even turned their heads.

"Thanks Gari," Hump said; he gave him five dollars in joy of getting home. Smirking, the drunk waited for them to get inside so he could scurry for the all night super-liquor-mart. "Gari" was short for "Garibaldi"—the bum claimed to be the nineteenth century revolutionary gone downhill in his old age. "If it wasn't for guzzlejuice," he'd once told Hump, "I'd be king of Italy today." In vain, Hump had pointed out that Garibaldi was a republican.

As soon as he'd closed the electronic and manual locks, Hump collapsed onto the old hallway chair where he watched the girl examine the carpet, the crummy little table, the stairs, even the door hinges. "It's not for sale," he said.

She raised an eyebrow. "I'm not buying. Anyway, if I were—" She stopped herself.

"If you were, what?"

"Nothing." She sat down on the thinly carpeted stairs.

"If you were, you wouldn't buy a dump like this, right?" She shrugged. "As a matter of fact, this rates a very nice dump. High class. I happen to own it, toto, which means I get the whole house to myself. Whatever you're used to, that goes as a rare commodity in Appletown."

"How precious."

"I got it in the last months of the squatting act, during the second bankruptcy. You see that?" He pointed to a patch of chipped wall before the stairs. "That came from a shotgun blast during the housing riots. I defended the whole mother house myself for two hours, until the goddamn police finally finished their dinner and swept the streets." He took a breath, conscious of how ridiculous he sounded, yet unable to stop. "And as for the condition, I've just painted the whole place. By myself."

Her eyes fixed on a blotch of paint staining the carpet. "I see."

"And I could also add that it ranks a hell of a lot higher than that garbage dump stoop you were perched on when I came along and invited you to come home with me." Hump's irritation collapsed as suddenly as it arose; he fell back in his chair, laughing and shaking his head.

"Is that what happened?" she said. "I remembered it a little differently."

"What should I do with you? I don't know a damn thing about you. Maybe you're a former princess and part-time terrorist."

"You could let me stay here for a while. I won't bother you. I promise I'll go out every day and not come back till late at night."

"Do that and you'll come back dead." He added, "I don't even know your name." As usual, the thought of names made him brace himself. Hopefully, he thought, she would just take the first name and let the others go.

To his surprise she appeared as flustered as he usually got whenever names came up. Finally she shrugged and said, "Vanity."

His lips twitched. "Vanity? Do you have three sisters named Faith, Hope, and Charity?" She shook her head as if he'd asked a normal question. "Vanity what?"

"Not Vanity what. Just Vanity."

"Dummy. What's your last name?"

"Van-i-ty."

"Oh. What's your first name, then?"

"My whole name, start to finish, is Golden Vanity."

"Wow. That's worse than mine. Your folks were *really* crazy."

"Whatever Father Filth is, he's not crazy."

Though Hump raised his eyebrows at the tender nickname, he decided to ignore it. "Then why did he name you Golden Vanity?"

"He named me after—after a boat."

"Do people call you Goldie?"

She shook her head. "Vanity. What's your name?"

For once, Hump decided to reveal his whole name. "My name," he said, drawing himself up proudly in his old saggy chair, is "Humphrey Chimpden Earwicker McCloskey. People call me Hump." She roared with laughter. "Well, it ain't no worse than Golden Vanity."

"How did you ever get a name like that?"

"You sound like I don't deserve it."

"I thought all the names here were so simple. Robert Regan. Huan Ko Li. Sharon Hume."

The names struck briefly in Hump's mind as if he'd heard them before. "It happens my parents were ints. From the Fourth Irish Renaissance."

"What's an int?"

"Short for intellectual. Where did you come from anyway? You talk about 'here' like Cristoforo Columbo." She met his gaze with a mask of calm patience. "All right. Forget it. At least I know your name."

"So I can stay?"

"Hold it. Just because I know your name?"

"I saved your life."

"Only after you'd endangered it."

She touched his knee. "Come on, Hump. Let me stay. Hey okay?"

He glowered at her hand, then grinned. "Hey okay. What the hell, how often do I meet another crazy name?" She sprang to her feet as if she'd plant a flag of conquest. "Anyway," he added, "the place is too big for one person. I should take in mystery loonies all the time."

"Too big?" she blurted, "it's so small."

He stood up. "Doubtless you live in the Taj Mahal. Pay attention." He pointed to the two doors off the hall. "Living room, sloppy room."

She eagerly opened both doors. "They both look pretty sloppy."

"Wonderful. You can start cleaning immediately." He pointed at the end door. "Bathroom. Each floor's got one, but the one upstairs has the only working shower. Downstairs is the kitchen and a storage room. Upstairs are the bedrooms, two of them. The majestic one on the left is mine, the other one you can use." She started upstairs. "Oh, if you see little black pellets along the floor edges they keep away rats, roaches, elephants, spacemen, everything. They work, so please don't move them. I sound like a hotel manager."

"I won't even touch the floor."

"I bet you won't. Listen, do you have any money? For food, I

mean. I can hardly afford to feed myself." One of the last people
to get on welfare before the government closed the rolls like St.
Peter slamming shut the doors of heaven, Hump received
subsistence money each month for a faked "mental instability."
A few years ago the investigators would have found him out and
shoved him off; now, however, the government had fired most of
the investigators. Hump supplemented the meager checks with
bar cleaning, message running, part time teaching, hack writing,
bit parts in suburban sex fantasies (the agency he worked for
specialized in rubber and animal acts), and occasional begging.
All of it never came to much.

Golden Vanity reached into her wide shirt for a small bag
that must have fixed itself to her midriff in some way. "Here,"
she said, and tossed down a few bills that fluttered at Hump's
feet.

"Hey, I don't want your money," he hollered after her. "I
just wanted to know you had some."

"That's all right," she called from the top of the stairs. "I can
get more tomorrow."

"How nice for you," he muttered. Louder he said, "I'll be in
the kitchen," and turned around. He left the money on the floor.

Halfway down the steps he stopped. His arm reached out
wildly for the banister and he would have fallen if the—the
hallucination?—hadn't left him almost as quickly as it struck.
For just a moment he'd been upstairs, in the spare room (Kate's
room, crazy Kate), staring in horror at—at what? He didn't even
know. He didn't care. What really wigged him was that it wasn't
him, it wasn't *his* eyes he was using, *his* body hadn't left the
stairway. And yet his *mind*—consciousness—something—had
looked out through someone else's eyes. Golden Vanity's eyes.
The hallucination faded. Hump was back on the stairs, back in
his body; white-fingered hands gripped the chipped banister.

Then the scream came.

"Vanity?" he called. He spun around and dashed upstairs.

He found her in the spare bedroom, backed against a wall,
her shoulders hunched up as her long fingers curled around her
arms. His eyes went to her, then flicked away. She stared straight
ahead. At the closet. Hump realized with a thrill that the closet
was exactly what he'd seen in his brief burst of telepathy.

"What's the matter?" he asked. He tried to take her arms, but
she snapped away. "What's wrong?"

She watched him warily. "Didn't you feel it?"

Some strange fear swept through Hump. "Feel what?" he lied. "I didn't feel anything." Vanity let out a breath. "What's going on?" Hump asked.

Vanity gestured at the closet. "That door."

He looked at the red closet door. Old and garish with its cracked glossy paint—he'd meant to paint it for months—it looked so ordinary. "It's just a closet door," he told her. She shook her head. "Look, I'll open it myself."

"No!" She turned her face away. And yet, he could hear relief in her voice, as if she knew he was lying, and was grateful for it.

"Hey, calm down. Look, nothing but old clothes." When he touched her arm she shivered but didn't push him away. "Come on, Vanity," he said softly. "Turn around."

"I can't."

"Sure you can." Gently he turned her shoulders and then her head until she saw the dirty closet with its few old jackets and pants drooping on plastic hangars. "See?"

With a soft moan she fell against him. "Burst of slime," she said vehemently. "Borkson filth mother."

Hump discovered himself holding her, stroking her back and arms. Her skin felt very smooth under the thin shirt, while her breasts against his chest made him breathe very shallowly to keep from panting. He worried she could feel his erection pushing at her. "Why did you get so scared?" he asked.

"That door," she began.

"It's just a door.

"No. Yes, but it looks like another door. In a—" She paused. "In a dream I once had."

"Was it a closet in your dream?"

"No. I mean, I don't know. I didn't open it."

"Anyway, why worry about a dream? Dreams don't count in real life, unless you're a neo-Freudian, and everyone knows how ridiculous they are."

She gave him a frozen look. Contempt? He couldn't tell, but he wanted to swat her. A moment later, she leaned her head against his shoulder again. Her hair fell across his fingers.

"Listen," he said quietly. "If this room scares you, you can stay in my room. If you like, I'll even stay there with you. The bed's big enough for both of us."

She didn't twist or push, yet somehow they were standing apart. And then she did something that twisted Hump's stomach around like a Brooklyn Menco dancer. Deliberately, slowly, she moved the muscles of her face into a sneer. It wasn't the expression that shriveled Hump's sexuality; it was simply her complete control of her face and body. *Jesus*, he thought, *what have I taken home with me*?

"Sorry," he murmured. Instantly he got angry. "Look, so I threw a junior high school pass. And at the wrong time. You don't have to crucify me."

A grin replaced the sneer, as if she'd spun a dial. "I'll stay her," she said, adding, "I want to wash."

"Yeah sure. Scrub it all way. The towel's in the bathroom, hanging up. If it looks too dirty you can wash it." She marched past him. "Come down to the kitchen when you finish." She nodded.

Hump was lighting the stove for coffee when his hands started to shake and he fell back into a chair. Bright Mother, he thought; would he have to cope a real loony? Part of him tried to say, "Come on, Hump, she didn't wig you, your own little vision on the stairs did it." He pushed the thought away.

The whole thing reminded him too much of Kate, the woman who used to live with him. She ran away one night, thinking Hump would mutilate her into a monster. Like millions of others around the planet, Kate had schizzed when the aliens arrived.

Aliens. Hump sat up. Robert Regan, Huan Ko Li, Sharon Hume. Now he remembered those names. They were all members of the UN team appointed to negotiate with the aliens.

Chapter Three ——————————

The chairman met his hated ally on a bare moon, in a stone and plaster house that consisted of an underground service plant plus seven wide rooms once decorated with the pickings of a hundred worlds. Now Jaak had ordered it stripped bare of any decoration or furniture beyond the "live stone" columns in the hallways and the Galul hook rugs growing out of the floor. "I don't want that kura-lover's comfort contaminating any of my galaxy."

He hadn't wanted to meet Loper at all, of course. But the Worker had killed Jaak's shrieker, and he could still tell the story to the SA. Loper himself had suggested the meeting place. Years ago he'd now and then ferried Jaak to this barren rock where the chairman could retreat from the hysterical demands of empire. Loper remembered it when he had sought a place he and Jaak could meet on something close to equal grounds.

The chairman stood by the window of the empty anteroom, eyes narrowed, one fingertip rubbing the line of his jaw, while the snubnosed delta ship with the special clump of instruments hidden under its sleek back, landed along the slideway. He was really a simple man, this Jaak. He knew his desires and never learned to tolerate any opposition to their satisfaction.

The man next to him was more complicated. Shifting nervously, AAri looked from his chairman's golden brown face to the golden hieroglyphics adorning the ship's side. Despite the years together, AAri didn't really understand Jaak *or* Loper. Their violent possessiveness, their wild hatred of each other, their love of risks made them forever alien.

Practical, calculating, always a businessman, AAri took chances only when the situation demanded it. He didn't mind gambling; it just didn't excite him. Very little did. He didn't let it. Coming from a passionate romantic culture on a world far from Center, AAri had molded himself into a realist, or at least the perfect image of a realist.

For now something had begun to break apart in this immensely practical man. Under the pressure of the last weeks, with the shrieker, Loper, and now this thing about Jaak's daughter, some of AAri's carefully constructed mental shelters had begun to crack. Thoughts of his home world, of the choices he'd made, had risen up in him for the first time in years. And other thoughts, even more disturbing, burst upon him. He would suddenly believe that all the factions on Center had secretly gathered against him. Though he shook off these notions, it worried AAri that they came to him at all.

He turned his mind to Loper. Something cold, the opposite of Jaak's emotionalism, radiated from the Worker even during his wildest furies. He could do passionate things, or things that seemed passionate, though always cruel. Once, he'd bought a primitive market world at an SA auction, then devised intricate ways to kill off the inhabitants, from food that sometimes, but not always, exploded in the stomach, to a wind that could smash stone cities. And AAri remembered the time Loper had turned on Vanity, alone in Jaak's ship. Even AAri had shuddered at some of the things Vanity had recounted under hypnosis. And yet, if Loper did wild things, he did so coldly, almost uncaringly, and for no reason anyone could understand.

The Workers feared and hated Loper. They claimed he loved non-space and could leap in and out for days without stopping to build up his psychic strength. They even suspected that he spurned ego fantasies and worked the ship's mind by sheer force of will (whatever that might mean), despite the theoretical impossibility. So the Workers said.

AAri watched Loper drop to the ground from the delta ship, then walk in that loose bouncing stride into the house. In high or low gravity, in or out of a spacesuit, Loper remained the most graceful man AAri had ever seen. Yet again, something nonhuman lurked in those loose movements; someone had once said that Loper leaked the frigid perfection of non-space into the real world.

While the figure vanished into the air lock, Jaak stayed by the window, staring at the ship, his ship, the *Golden Vanity*. AAri glanced at the instrument panel built into the wall. An orange light came on. "He's wearing an energy dispersal pattern," AAri said.

Jaak grunted. "Does he think I'll blow him up the moment he steps through the door?"

AAri shrugged. "Why not? You've tried." Jaak laughed.

The doors sighed as they opened, as if the house had resigned itself to violation. Helmet under his arm, Loper took two steps into the room and stopped. Head turning side to side, eyes rolling from the ceiling to the floor, he made an elaborate show of searching the empty room. "I don't see my salary," he said. "You wouldn't hide her from me, would you?"

AAri raised a hand. "Loper, slow down."

"Of course, she could be in another room. Or maybe on that lurching garbage you call a ship. She'd better be close, AAri. Dressed up, packaged, and ready for her new life."

"Abrupt, aren't you?" Jaak said.

"I certainly didn't come to hear a beaten old man gossip. I came for my salary. Have you got her here or not?"

"Wait a moment," AAri said. He wished fervently he hadn't come.

The huge head grinned at him. The hard brown face, the thick jaw, the sharp nose and thin elegant lips, all of it framed by masses of curly orange hair, gave him the look of some creature from the endless dream catalogues of G'GaiRRin, AAri's home world. He said, "I expected some slime from you two. But something a little more creative. A clone or something else, dangerous perhaps, something sweet and killing. But nothing? Nothing at all?"

"Loper," AAri tried to interrupt, but the slow mocking voice cut him off.

"Maybe I'd better explain something to you. It's so obvious I thought it might offend you if I mentioned it, but I can see that nothing's too crude for Jaak. The *Golden Vanity*'s 'mitt holds a message primed for send off. In two ship standard tenths it'll code out to SA headquarters, unless I return, with her, to stop it.

Do you want the SA to know about your shrieker? And the reasons for it?"

Jaak cocked an eye at him. "What do you know about those reasons?"

"Enough, old man. I've got my stoops on Center. *And* on Ktaner's Planet."

"And the shrieker?" Jaak continued. "Did you kill it? Or leave it hanging there?"

"Your tenths are trooping. You know what I did with it. If your stoops hadn't reported clear space you would never have come here to meet me."

AAri said, "Yes, of course we know it's clear."

"Then where is she?"

"You don't understand."

Loper's fingers pushed back his hair. "I'm not trying to understand. I just came to get my salary, just like a good Worker. Mindless. Do the job and pick up the pay. Do *you* understand? I want Golden Vanity. I've got one and I want the other." He paused to look Jaak up and down. "Or else that message flies straight home to the SA. So you better find some good excuse, Jaak. Because they'll break you. Don't think they won't. I've got two other messages lined up in the 'mitt, one to C2 and one to C3, with everything I know and can guess about you." He suddenly laughed. "Together they'll pound so hard on the SA that all your bribes and backdoor alley murders won't stop them scattering you all over the galaxy."

Jaak said softly, "you've wanted to break me ever since you've known me, even when I let you work my ships for me. You couldn't then and you can't now."

Loper laughed again, a barking sound. He began to pace with a light almost dance-like step. "Would you like me to try? What do you say, old filth? Do we fight it out in the 'mitt?"

AAri said, "Loper, nobody wants a fight. Will you please just listen to us?"

Jaak cocked his head towards his assistant. "What's between me and this slime you'll never understand. Be quiet."

"For burst's sake, Jaak," AAri said. "Don't make it worse than it already is." Trapped between two madmen, AAri thought. What if they turned on him? For an instant an idea claimed him—the two of them had arranged the entire incident just to get him, AAri, alone on this empty rock. The thought went away as quickly as it came, leaving only a frightening aftertaste. He turned to Loper. "You don't understand. Jaak isn't trying to cheat you."

"No, of course not," Loper said. He tossed his head. "She's really not here, is she?"

AAri nodded. "But it's not our fault. I'm telling you the truth."

"Yes? You know something, Shadow-Jaak? I think I believe you. You wouldn't look so desperate if you were spouting one of Jaak's weak little fants. And you would have rigged *something* up. For your sake, you get a reprieve. Just a short one. I'll stall the message and maybe you can convince me this isn't one of Jaak's lies." He turned and strode lightly out of the room.

AAri didn't think Loper believed him; the Worker wanted to stretch out his triumph, in the hope that Jaak might squirm or plead. For the two minutes of Loper's absence Jaak stared at the bleak rock outside the window, while AAri leaned back against a wall and rubbed his forehead with his fingertips.

I shouldn't even be here, he thought. It hardly mattered to him who owned Jaak's daughter. He had his own responsibilities, and not just to the chairman. Right now he should be working out the company's contribution to the "Event" the SA was staging on the new humanhome... what was it called... Earth. AAri shook his head. He didn't like Events much more than he liked runaway daughters. He'd seen too many of those subtle demonstrations of Center's superiority, designed to instill shame and weakness in the leaders who would negotiate a market world's relations to the companies. Always the same, he thought. He suddenly felt very tired.

Loper returned still grinning. "You get five-tenths, Shadow-Jaak."

AAri took a breath. "Vanity is gone. She's disappeared. Jaak and I don't know where she is any more than you do. When you went after the shrieker we decided—it was my idea actually—"

"Faithful AAri. Why don't you let him take the blame for his own slime?"

"—that maybe Vanity shouldn't be around company center. In case the SA found out and raided us for documentation. You know what that's like."

"Or in case I came back too soon looking for her?"

"We did it as a safety measure."

Jaak said, "Oh, tell him the truth. Of course we sent her away. You think we'd actually let your slime fingers get within a pulse point of her?"

AAri snapped, "Jaak, be quiet!" He bit his lip. They *were* provoking him. No, of course not. What was he thinking?

Loper said, "Let him talk, AAri. Maybe he can make it sound like the truth." He looked at Jaak. "You think about that a lot, don't you? My fingers stroking Vanity's skin, crawling up her legs—"

AAri broke in, "What's the difference why we sent her, anyway? She's gone, that's what counts. We made up a convoy, a small one, to send her someplace safe."

"Where?"

"Don't tell him," Jaak ordered.

"We've got to tell him. Why not, anyway? Do you think he'll find her there? We sent her to Ruuizin, an underpopulated planet—"

"I know the place. Go on."

"All right. Halfway there—"

"How far out?"

"Point seven two standard days."

"Direct from Center?"

"Yes."

"Maximum jumps?"

"No, median. You know Vanity can't take the max."

"I want the pulse points." Loper was enjoying this, testing what he thought was AAri's preparation.

"All right. Later. They certainly won't tell you anything, but I've got them recorded on our ship, and I can code it through your channels. Anyway, the convoy leaped into non-space. It was the start of the second cycle."

"How many were they planning?"

"Four. The last two very short. Anyway, when they leaped out again, Vanity was gone."

Loper stared. "You mean she didn't come out?"

"No. She just didn't come out with the convoy. We're assuming she must have overrode her program, taken some out point totally at random and then kept leaping in any direction at all, figuring that once she'd gotten away she could find a pulse point and guide herself to a place where she could hide."

Loper's eyes danced from one face to the other. Something was wrong here. He'd expected a slick lie with all the corners smoothed. "You're not making sense. How could she get the pilot to break convoy? That's insane. Who did you send, anyway?"

"No one. That's the problem. Vanity worked her own ship."

"What? Why?"

"How could we know she'd break? I told you, she would have had to override the printed destination. Going at random like that, into nothing. She could only hope she'd find herself somewhere recognizable. Burst knows where she ended up." He thought, *Maybe on H'Hain*, the stinging cold underworld of his parents' planet.

"I know," Loper was saying, "but I still don't see why Papa would send her away alone when he could just shove in a stoop." He suddenly laughed. "Unless, after a certain day, with a certain non-stoop Worker, the worried father couldn't bear to send his sweet slab of flesh out alone with anyone." He laughed again at Jaak staring rigidly out the window. "This is the truth, isn't it?"

AAri nodded. "She's gone."

"Then whoever finds her first—" Abruptly he spun around and pushed the switch to open the air lock. He stopped in the doorway. "Your reprieve is extended. I think I'll keep the SA out of this for awhile." The door slid shut behind him. Soon AAri could see him running in long low gravity leaps back to the ship. His ship now. Jaak hadn't even contested it.

The chairman watched motionless as the ship lifted off the slide. For nearly a minute Loper taunted them, circling the house so close they could see the ancient hieroglyph, a gold stick picture of a woman singing without a harp. Golden Vanity. AAri wondered if Loper or even Jaak knew that the hieroglyphics used for ship identification had originated in the ancient deserts of AAri's home planet. He shook his head. It didn't matter.

After the ship had lifted beyond their sight line, Jaak scanned the blank walls like some beast who's woken up in a cage. His eyes fixed like grappling hooks on AAri's face, ignoring the fear seeping out from behind the practiced calm. He said, "Get me my daughter back. *Find her.*"

Chapter Four ——————————————

Hump and Vanity sat in the sloppy room, watching the news on television. At least Hump was watching it, slumped down sourly in his old red chair. Vanity sat cross-legged against the wall, eating her fifth bowl of Vita Flakes for the day. Every day another food, Hump thought. All that money and she eats garbage. The day before it was micro-egg rolls and kelpweed dogs, the day before that pizza balls.

The man on the teev droned on, summarizing Senator Farmer's latest dreary speech promising to lead America and all Earth into the universe as soon as the country elected him president. The incumbent president, meanwhile, had made a speech in Ohio, where he told an organization called "Businessmen for the Galaxy" that under the current admin Earth was "striding forward to meet the stars on two fronts." A master of relativity. The usual other news followed. Food riots in Boston, Kansas, Miami—he lost track. Half the farms in America had lain fallow since the aliens came because the farmers refused to plant until they could count on a market. Although the government had talked of buying the food or even drafting the farmers, by the time they finished talking, planting time had passed. You couldn't blame the farmers; suppose the aliens introduced some miracle star food that would do away with beef and wheat forever?

Like Vita Flakes, Hump thought nastily. Golden Vanity—a

golden consumer sucker. Just last night, his old feeble teev, with its jelly faces and swampy colors, had run that idiotic cereal ad. Blackness, beep beep noises, and then a stars-at-night shot with a loud whoosh, followed by a shot of two men in aluminum foil uniforms sitting up on glass tables. The first says, "Man, hyperspace really knocks you out." After a flash of lights two trays slide forward with bowls of green tinted soya flakes. As a metallic female voice drones, "Your Vita Flakes, sirs," the two men eagerly snatch the bowls and start gobbling. Cut to empty bowls and satisfied faces. The two men leap to their feet. "Come on," one says, "We've got a lot to do before we hit that next galaxy." Another whoosh and more stars as a male voice confides, "Vita Flakes. Food for the universe." The very next morning Vanity had run out and bought three boxes.

"When do we hit the next galaxy?" she called merrily as she dropped the bowl on the rug. Hump growled at her. Since her arrival the sloppy room had gotten a lot sloppier. Though she didn't like the dirt or the mess—she complained about it enough—Vanity apparently lacked the concept of "cleaning up." Hump insisted only once. His guest had spilled the bleach on the stairs, broken a window and a vase, and tipped over a bag of garbage on the kitchen floor.

The news ended with an item about a Russian charge that the US reps to the UN negotiating committee consisted entirely of CIA agents hoping to steal a star ship. Lots of luck, Hump thought, they can keep it if they get it. Disgusted, he jabbed the *off* button.

"Hey," Vanity protested, reaching for the switch.

Hump slapped her hand away. "Leave it off."

"Rocky Jones, Space Ranger's coming on. You must have forgotten." She quoted from the teev mag, "A prophecy rescued from the archives of television."

"Screw the archives of television. I am sick of space."

She laughed. "What has Rocky Jones got to do with space?"

"That's it. That's the whole point. None of it's got anything to do with space at all. You know why the aliens won't give us starships? Because we're so stupid. The most staggering event in history happens and we respond with infantile fantasies. And *you* lap them up."

Vanity said, "Has it ever occurred to you that maybe the reason has nothing to do with Earth at all?"

"What? What are you talking about?"

"Everyone assumes the aliens won't give up the ships because of something Earth has done or hasn't done. But maybe they've got their own reason. Doesn't that make sense? Maybe it's alien policy. Maybe they don't even notice what Earth does."

Hump sat up in his chair. Grinning, he asked, "Vanity, are you an alien?"

She flipped a hand. "Sure. Don't you see the deep pools of starlight in my eyes?"

"No, I mean it. You're the first person I ever met who's even trying to see things from those bastards' viewpoint."

"I'm just open-minded."

"You? Hah. Anyway, I've got lots of other evidence."

"Oh good, let's have a trial."

"Look at all the stuff you don't know about Earth. Sometimes I think you'd never even heard of *money* until last Wednesday. You're such a tourist. And you talk funny."

"Hah to you. I talk real good."

"Don't dodge the evidence."

She put a hand on her heart. "Yes, Hump, you've got me. A refugee from the stars. 'Born inside a nova'" she quoted.

"See? You even like that disgusting song. Only an alien would like Johnny and the Galactics."

"What do you mean? They're number one."

"You and the other aliens probably rigged the ratings."

She strolled across the room to sit on the chair arm and stroke his face. "Listen darling," she whispered, "if I came from the stars do you think I'd hang around with you?"

"That's what I keep telling myself. But think what a great cover I make? Who'd ever think to look for an alien agent on Second Avenue? And what about the spaceport? Why did it scare you so much if you're not an alien?" The question sounded so ridiculous he almost blushed.

She waved a hand. "More conclusive proof. The fact is, I'm a sex pervert. I pop a climax every time I see a cop."

"More dodges. That's another thing. Stop laughing. I mean the way you absorb things, like everything's brand new. Yesterday I show you an Amazing Perverts comic book, which, I might add, you'd never seen, and today you're Kraft-Ebbing. You're just not jaded enough."

"But Hump, I mean it. Two minutes in that spaceport, with all those coppies, and zappo, I'd have used up my life's supply of orgasms. You want me to shrivel up like a peanut?"

"Peanuts don't shrivel. I think."

She took his hands. "If you hadn't taken me home—I can't

bear to think about it. You saved my life, Hump." He growled and snatched his hands back. "Why don't we go play tourist?" she suggested.

"Changing the subject, huh?" He stood up, just as happy to leave the house. "Have you got money?"

"Of course."

"Of course. If that doesn't make you alien—" But she was already opening the several locks. What the hell, Hump thought. Alien, runaway, tourist, champion pain in the ass, whatever she was, he liked her. He knew he did. She generated an excitement, a sense of adventure that his life, that everyone's life, had lacked for much too long.

He would have liked her even more if she hadn't made it plain she liked to sleep alone. What's the use of a lady guest— The thought suddenly struck him, suppose she *was* an alien. Galactic sex. Would it work? A sudden shiver made him decide he'd rather not find out.

Outside, Gari jumped up to tip an imaginary hat to Vanity. "Good morning, radiant lady," he slurred.

"Good morning to you, jewel of the revolution," Vanity said. "Long live the king of Italy." Hump glared at Gari who squatted down again, a silly grin cracking his crusty face.

"Where to?" Hump asked on the sidewalk. The late Autumn sun made him glad she'd gotten him out. Even the oily street looked good.

"You guide me, my prince. Someplace exciting."

"Every place I go is exciting. I don't know. I guess we could tour some robot bars."

"What're they?"

"Hah. More telltale ignorance. They're places where the bartenders and a lot of the customers are really androids planted by the management, while a lot of the humans pretend that *they're* androids. The other humans try to guess who's genuine."

"A genuine android. Wonderful. How do you pretend to be an android?"

"Oh, you sort of act too perfect, too smooth. Like nothing bothers you or even could. A friend of mine once said that you can tell an android because they haven't got subconsciouses. They've got egos, personalities you know, except that without any sub the ego's a propped up fake."

Vanity raised her eyebrows as if the concept intrigued her. "Wasn't that a robot bar you went to the night I rescued you?"

"Yeah, up in the Bronx. I was hoping I could make some

contacts for some work. A lot of pop editors go there. But we can find plenty of robot bars in Manhattan. Better ones, actually."

"All right," she said. "You pretend to be something, and I'll guess if it's android or human."

"Thanks."

She laughed. "Right or left?"

"Left." As they started towards Third Avenue Hump said nastily, "Another fun thing about robot bars, a lot of the aliens go there."

He saw her miss a step but before she could answer, a long-haired drunk in an old blue sweater and navy pants stepped in front of them. "Can you help me out with a little bread?" he asked Vanity.

Vanity looked at Hump. "Bread?"

"Split," Hump said, picking up the old slang.

"Come on, man, help me out."

Gari scuttled forward. "Get lost, creep," he growled. "She's protected." He turned to Vanity. "The younger generation," he said scornfully. "They don't understand. How can you make a society without rules?"

Vanity touched Gari's arm. "It's all right," she said. She took out a little book from the soft bag (leather? plastic?) tied around her waist. "What's your name?"

The drunk squinted suspiciously at her. "Alan," he said. "Alan Jacobi."

She leafed through the book. The wind stirred her gold hair and the loose shiny sleeves of her blouse. "Exactly," she said. "Alan Jacobi. Didn't I loan you three dollars two days ago?"

"Yeah." He grinned. "An interest-free loan, you said. But you know the cost of living these days."

"Of course," Vanity said. "I would like to help you, really I would, except you haven't paid me back yet for the other loan."

"What?" Jacobi said. Gari's squeaky laugh followed Vanity as she pulled Hump down the street. Looking back, Hump saw Jacobi shuffle away. Something about him looked odd, not like the others; why didn't he argue? He didn't even try to wheedle fifty cents out of her. Hump imagined Jacobi as a neo-rock guitarist whose career had collapsed, maybe because he'd heard some ethereal alien music—"

"Let's skip the robot bar," Vanity said casually.

"Don't want to meet any other aliens, huh?"

"Don't be silly. I just think you shouldn't visit a social establishment dressed so shabbily."

"Shabbily?" Hump wore an old shirt, the collar only slightly frayed, and a pair of faded white pants, with sandals and socks. "I'll have you know I got these clothes from Baron Rothschild. Besides, look at that outfit of yours. You haven't changed your clothes since I met you."

"You're right. Oh, Hump, I'm so ashamed. You'll have to take me shopping."

He rolled his eyes. "Sneaky bitch. I'll get you to a robot bar yet. Come on, let's find a cab."

They traveled up to Fifth Avenue, that former swank arcade now reduced to a decaying mixture of mercantile styles. You could walk from department stores constructed in the corporate boom just before the aliens arrived, straight into a sex shop or pinball cave or junk clothing store from the property collapse just *after* the arrival. A few doors down you could find some old luxury shop whose sentimental owner had refused to give up his traditional site. Those few islands of past elegance looked out of place amidst the pushy resentful crowds and the flashy shop fronts.

Depression slumped Hump's shoulders. The sun had vanished, replaced by a gloominess that settled heavily on the frenetic crowd and the once glamorous buildings.

Hump stared sadly at the casino. The dark blue windows, two stories high, with their delicate steel piping, still gleamed in the afternoon light, but the glass was no longer spotless, and a neon roulette wheel rotated above the oak and leather door. When Hump pressed his nose against the glass he saw the once open floors cluttered with cheap painted tables, so many that the huge crowds—gambling becomes popular when the future vanishes—had to shove and squeeze to get their bets down. Hump remembered the old clientele from the 80's, quiet, intense, their emotions heightened by restraint. And by respect for the house. The people now shouted and pushed, constantly fighting as if they came for the violence rather than the gambling. Something else to blame on the aliens, Hump thought.

The doorman's huge finger tapped his shoulder. "Get away from there," he rumbled. "No dirtying the glass."

Hump didn't move. "It's dirty enough already," he said.

"Come on, sonny, move when someone tells you." He yanked Hump around.

Hump stared wildly at the doorman's wide face and thick chin; all the resentment and frustrations of the past months settled in those heavy jowls and broken nose. He remembered the original doorman years ago, as elegant as a Russian dagger. Now this bouncer had taken over. All because of those spaceships sitting across the Harlem River. Hump's hands curled into fists.

Vanity slid in between them. "Don't listen to him," she told the doorman. "He forgot to take his medicine today. It's not his fault. Those little bugs crawl inside his head." The doorman stepped backwards.

Infuriated, Hump stared wildly at the doorman's dingy yellow braid. He wanted to grab it and swing him into the thick window. He only stood swallowing and clenching his fists, like a puppet, while Vanity urged the guard back to his post. She pulled Hump away through the crowds.

At the corner he jerked back his arm. The ludicrous scene had left him chilled and depressed. "Leave me alone, okay? You don't have to go around rescuing me everywhere. One thing I don't need is a fastmouthed bodyguard."

"No? That borkson could have pulled off your legs and stuck them in your ears."

"You could use something stuck in your mouth. You're so damn conceited— What the hell is a borkson anyway?"

She looked briefly startled before an arrogant mask dropped over her face. "An ugly filth that stands on street corners and shouts like a slime-faced idiot." The people walking by grinned.

"Aren't you smart? Always on stage. I'm sick of it. I'm sick of you. I've seen you scared, remember? And of what? A closet door, for god's sake. And a bunch of tinny cops hanging around the spaceport."

"You shut your filthy mouth," Vanity said. She looked nervously at the small crowd gathered around them.

"Got you that time, didn't I?" Hump crowed. "Slipped a little truth under that armor-plated hypocrisy of yours."

"Hey," called a pretzel vendor from behind his pushcart. "Cut out the big words. We can't hardly follow you."

"Yeah," added a teenager, "argue so we can understand you."

"You shut up!" Hump yelled.

Vanity laughed. "Rocky Dignity, street ranger. Don't like it when someone makes you leave your dirty house and takes you where people can see your pinny little eyes and funny blubber mouth."

"For God's sake I didn't ask you to move in with me. You've wrenched up my whole life. You've even organized the drunks."

Suddenly, instead of answering, Vanity stared across the street at two men in bright zipper jackets who were pushing their way towards Hump and Vanity. Hump squinted at them—something about their faces— Vanity. When he looked back Vanity was slipping away between the crowds of people.

"Hey, where are you going?" he called after her.

"What do you think?" a woman said. "You chased her away, bigmouth."

"Me?" Hump swallowed a protest. When he tried to follow Vanity, however, the woman and the pretzel man grabbed his arm.

One of the two men cried out in the universal cop voice, "Somebody stop that woman. The one in the shiny green shirt. Stop her."

Hump shoved the woman holding him at the two men. To their surprised annoyance, the woman pretended to fall and grabbed their jackets to hold them back for several seconds. Like a team, the four teenagers linked arms across the sidewalk, and even the pretzel vendor shoved his cart at their feet when the two managed to escape the rest. Cops of any kind weren't too popular in Appletown.

Hump ran in the road where the people thinned out and he only had to dodge the cars. As he chased Vanity his mind saw, like a bright painting, the two men's faces, their saffron skin—*like Vanity's*—their gold-red hair—*like Vanity's*. A voice boomed inside his head, "The real thing. She's the real thing."

"Get away," Vanity snapped at him when he caught up with her. Fear ignited her eyes.

"I'll help you get away," Hump gasped. He looked back. Half a block back the two men were using their weight to move the crowds.

"I don't need you," Vanity said. Neither of them had stopped. "Leave me alone."

"Quiet. You'll waste your breath." Panting, he grabbed her arm and yanked her into the huge toyshop on the corner of 58th Street.

"No!" she shouted, "they'll trap us in there."

"Shut up. There's another door." He dragged her through a mob of people watching toy spaceships fly around a plastic replica of Saturn. On 58th Street they emerged to a piece of luck: an empty taxicab. Before Vanity could protest, Hump had hailed the cab and pulled her inside with him. "Second Avenue and Third Street," he told the microphone and the robot car slid into traffic.

"No!" Vanity cried; the cab swung back again.

The human driver jabbed the override button. "Well?" he asked.

"Just head downtown," Hump said, looking through the window. The two men hadn't appeared.

"Okay lady?" asked the driver.

"I guess—all right," Vanity said. As the cab moved into traffic Hump looked back again to see the two men standing on the sidewalk looking for a cab. Or a spaceship.

Hump slid shut the thick window that separated them from the driver. "Goddamn it to hell," he whispered fervently. "What the hell is the matter with you? Why didn't you tell me?" She didn't answer, only sat slumped forward, staring at the robot mechanisms. "Do you have any idea—can you *imagine* the kind of scab I can pull because of you?"

She said flatly, "Where shall I get out? Here? The next block?"

"Don't act so goddamn superior." He stared at her, her face, her skin, her hair. *She was living in his house; he'd held her in his arms.* Little fingers crept over his skin, and he shrunk back against the door until Vanity's smirk jerked him upright. She laughed. "You know what I should do?" he said. "I should turn you in somewhere."

He tried not to cringe as she touched his arm. "You know you like me too much," she said.

"I can't stand you." Actually, the return of Vanity's bravado relaxed Hump slightly; at least she was herself again. Obnoxious. "And don't think I owe you anything because you helped me out in ratfemland. I would have gotten out easier without you and your loud mouth."

"Hey, sorry to interrupt," the driver interrupted through the mike, "but how's about you let us know when you decide where you want to go. Huh?"

Hump jumped. He'd completely forgotten the driver, the cab, even the city. He might have been inside a spaceship. He asked Vanity, "Why don't you like my house any more?"

"I thought you didn't want me."

"I never said that. What I do want is some honest answers."

Her eyes flicked to the driver. She's right, he thought, shouldn't talk so much. "Well?" he asked, "my house or not?"

"Suppose they're waiting there?"

"Oh hell. Let me think about that." Some hero, he thought. "You know, I must be crazy even making a guess, but I don't think those two guys knew you especially. There's been a lot of fights recently between—" He finished lamely, "your kind and mine."

As hope flared in Vanity's face, Hump wondered what had scared her so deeply. She was "their kind," wasn't she? She mumbled, "I don't know." She looked out the window. "All right. We'll go to your house but I can't stay."

"Good."

"But I have to make a stop first." She said into the mike, "Grand Central Station." As the cab turned right Vanity settled back in her seat, her eyes closed, her head turned away from Hump's confused stare.

The big old station, like a spiderweb with its central hall and radiating tunnels, stood half empty that afternoon. Since the aliens' arrival, land transport had near collapsed along with most other domestic services. People took planes whenever possible, while the buses and trains, already deteriorated, had become dirty, broken, and scarce. The stations too—dirt streaked the Grand Central walls, nearly half of the lights were broken, dust and bits of garbage covered the floors; the tracks that hadn't been closed were dark and full of smoke. Along the concourse all the shops had closed except a few tourist stands and some greasy hotdog joints.

Hump shook his head as he followed Vanity's arrogant stride through the thick smoky air. He thought, I used to love this place. Damn them, they've got no right. The whole planet's rotting, and all the superior star beings do is act like it's all a zoo or a clown show in some robot circus. But will they give us their precious spaceships? Oh no, can't do that, we might stop worshipping them. Who wants a spaceship anyway? Goddamn bork— He stopped, raised his eyebrows. "Hey," he called and ran after her. "What's a borkson?"

She smiled. "The male offspring of a very stupid animal about so big—" she held her arms about two feet apart, "with a long thick snout, a round striped belly, and floppy feet. They live in swamps where they make the smell ten times worse."

"Do they live—back where you come from."

"Ugh. No. They live on a world half covered in yellow slime, like mucous." She added, "Can we talk later?"

"Oh yeah," Hump said. Embarrassed, he looked around for

pursuers, then followed Vanity to a bank of luggage lockers set between the locked entrances to two unused tracks. With a key from her bag Vanity opened one of the lockers.

Hump looked inside. Nothing. She grinned. "What did you expect?"

"A bork leather suitcase."

Vanity stuck her hand deep inside the locker. A flash of light followed a faint click, and when Vanity removed her hand ten seconds later she held a small rectangular package wrapped in brown paper.

Hump stared. "That's not—"

"Shut up." Hump glanced once at the few people straggling by and closed his mouth. But when they'd got away from the lockers Vanity whispered, "It sure is, honeypoo." She'd picked up the last word from a television show about a nightclub singer who moonlighted as a private detective.

"How much?" Hump whispered.

"A thousand," she said nervously. "Different demoninations."

Hump whistled. "I never could see the point of a spaceship but I sure can see the point of that."

"Will you be quiet?" Her pleading tone reminded Hump that if the alien cops patrolled the city they might keep a permanent stakeout on their money fountain. Shaking a little he followed her out.

When they'd found a cab and told it Hump's address he whispered to her, "How about letting me make a copy of that key?"

"It wouldn't work for you. The light's triggered by a chemical in the skin."

He sat back. "It figures. Just like all your other tricks. Good for you and no one else."

"All my other tricks?"

"You know what I mean. All of you. You come down uninvited, show us your great marvels of the cosmos, and then chuckle when we stick out our hands. Oh, screw it." The seat squeaked as he sat back. Pretending to stare ahead, he examined her from the corner of his eye. Fear and depression stiffened her body like a coating of wax.

"Don't worry," she sighed. "Most of the package is for you."

"How did you decide that?"

"I got you into trouble. I didn't want to, I suppose I just didn't think about it."

"Habit of yours, huh?"

"If you say so. Anyway, I'm going to slice as soon as you get home and I thought I should give you something. I'm sorry it's not more."

Hump slapped the seat. "That's it. That's absolutely it. With luck and a good lawyer I could pull a thousand years in a slave labor camp and you casually throw your small change at me. Keep it. Stuff it up your spacehole." He bared his teeth at the driver who'd adjusted the rearview mirror to watch them better. In the movies the hero never talked in cabs. Screw movies.

"I said I'm sorry. I can only get one package at a time."

"Rich people. You're all alike, whether you come from New York or Betelgeuse. Try to comprehend. I don't want your handouts, no matter how much. I just want that you don't flick me away like a cockroach. I want that when we get to my house you come inside and you talk to me. True genuine facts. The certified article. Okay?"

Desolately Vanity looked at the floor. A long moment passed, then she let out a breath. "Hey okay."

Hump collapsed against the squeaky seat, exhausted. "Anyway," he muttered, "it's probably counterfeit."

Vanity grinned. "Of course it is. You don't think we can reach into bank vaults with invisible fingers. They're molecular copies of two hundred real bills. The copier randomizes the serial numbers."

"Wonderful. How easily we wreck the economy."

"It won't wreck anything. We just use it for spending money. There's not very many of us, you know."

"There's enough. Oh God, is there enough." Suddenly he started to laugh, shaking his head. After a moment Vanity started laughing also, and the two of them leaned back, holding hands and laughing. Outside, in the street, the angry confused citizens of Earth rushed back and forth, up and down the block; others slouched against buildings and dirty storefronts, breathing the sour air, staring at the grey sky as if a fleet of starships would swoop down and crush them; inside the cab the driver squinted into his rear view mirror at the two maniacs yelping in the back seat.

Chapter Five

"You could help me out," Hump said angrily. For the past three or four minutes they'd sat by the old wooden table in Hump's kitchen while Hump had done nothing but stare at his coffee until he could count the oil drops. Every time his mind had formed a question he'd looked up at her sharp nose and round cheeks and the words had tangled up in his throat. An alien; a creature from another planet, a different *sun*—drinking coffee in his kitchen. What could he possibly say?

"Tell me how to help, dear Hump. I throw myself at your feet." It didn't sound much like "Take me to your leader."

"I just want some information." She flashed him a smile, nasty in its pretended sweetness. "Well, what are you *doing* here?"

"Holiday. I wanted a vacation."

"Oh sure. That's why you run in terror whenever a cop appears."

"It's true, Hump. It's just—well, I wasn't supposed to take this vacation."

"In other words, you ran away. From your family?" She shrugged. "Terrific. What's the law back home in Andromeda?"

"Law?"

"Yeah. Here on primitive Earth I don't break the law as long as you're over sixteen. Do you people have a law like that?"

"No."

"But the law says you can't run away?"

"Of course not."

"Then why did those cops wig you like that?"

"I just don't want anyone to come between us."

"Knock it off. Let me guess. Mommy and Daddy want their little darling back, and they're so loaded they can recruit the space cops to search for you."

"No mommy. My father sliced my mother as soon as I was born."

Hump winced. "'Sliced' means got rid of?" She nodded. "Can I ask how he sliced her?"

"He did something to her face—so she wouldn't want to come back—then ported her to some filthy market world to entertain the dust miners. She was an orgy dancer."

"Lovely father you've got. No wonder you ran away."

"Thank you for your approval."

"Climb down, huh? I'm sorry your father's a bastard, and I hope I never meet him. But I've got to know what's going on."

"Ask me some more. Go ahead. My mouth is yours."

"Horrible thought. Let me see if I understand. You ran away and now Daddy's after you and he's got the cops to do his looking for him. And he's probably got a private army besides?"

"I don't know for sure about the cops. He might not have told the SA."

"SA?"

"Space Authority. The port police work for them."

"But he's definitely sent out his own people."

"Yes."

"Do you think he's brought in the Earth cops as well?"

"He might. If he knew I'd come to Earth."

"Oh. That's right. Wow. Vanity, this is too much for me. Do you know that? It's too much for me."

"I said I'd leave."

He stared. "Leave the *planet*?"

She giggled. "Actually, I just meant leave your house."

Hump laughed. "Do you know I haven't even been out of New York for the last two years?" He suddenly felt glad to see her there, perched on top of his battered old kitchen stool.

Hump was about to speak when Vanity abruptly pressed her mouth against his and threw her arms around his back. Hump went rigid for a moment, then his hands moved down her back as his mouth tried to nudge open her lips.

The kiss ended as suddenly as it began. Vanity twisted free like an angry cat, then jumped back on her stool. She folded her arms and looked at him, her eyebrows slightly raised.

"A major historical event," Hump said lamely. She didn't answer. "I'm sorry."

"For what?"

He shouted, "For kissing you. What do you think?"

"But I kissed you. Don't you remember?"

"All right, all right, for bearing down too hard. For pushing it." Panic pushed him to his feet. "I've got to go piss. Promise me you won't warp into the next galaxy before I get back."

"Space cadet's honor."

Hump stayed an extra two minutes in the locked bathroom, clasping his hands together until they stopped shaking. When he returned, Vanity had made him another coffee. Back to the questions, he ordered himself. His mind blanked. After a moment he said, "Hey, what's your real name?"

"Golden Vanity, I didn't lie."

"But that's English."

"Oh, I see. I was translating. My name is—" She pronounced an exercise in grunts and whistles.

"I'll stick to Vanity. Does your father have a name I can say?"

"His is easy. Jaak."

"Jack?"

"No, no. Jaaak." She drew out the flat "a."

"How come your name sounds like a broken computer and your father's sounds like one of the drunks on the corner?"

"He wasn't actually born on Center. He moved up years ago from one of the market worlds."

"What are they?"

"You know. Like Earth."

"Why do you call them Market worlds?"

"Because the companies use them as markets. That's what they're for."

"What? Wait a minute. Do you mean this Center, as you call it, sends its starships to places like Earth just so it can open up a new market?"

"What did you think?"

"I don't know. I didn't, I guess. The government, of course, hasn't told us anything." He grunted. "I guess I thought something like furthering galactic knowledge. Interstellar brotherhood of man." Vanity giggled. "All right, all right, so it's just oldfashioned colonialism. We should have guessed. Anyway, your father's an immigrant, then."

"A lot of people on Center are immigrants."

"Center's the home world?"

"Uh huh. The SA insists we keep the population low so people on the market worlds can move up to fill the gaps."

"The star man's burden." He gulped the coffee. "Do they keep the populations on the market worlds low too?"

"That's something the companies decide."

"And suppose they decide to lower the population somewhere? Earth, for instance. How would they go about it?"

"Whatever way seems easiest, I suppose."

"Oh Jesus," he whispered. He stared at her, cool, selfcentered, and he thought he'd faint, or scream, or throw up. Her people, her own father, could starve or sterilize half the people on the planet and she wouldn't even bother to read about it in the newspaper—if the newspaper bothered to print it. He sat for a while softly shaking his head before another question rescued his mind from its terrified ruts. "How come you speak English?"

"I learned it. Obviously."

"How? Swallow a pill?"

"Don't be silly. All spaceships carry deep learning sets, but a language doesn't take much. It's just a local use of deep speech."

"Oh of course. What's that?"

"Basic language structured into human brains. Any real language is derived from it."

"Some people here used to believe that. The idea went out of fashion."

"Too bad. Since they were right."

"Obviously." Hump sat back, maddeningly aware of the great gulf between himself and this frightened, arrogant—kid. A kid from another planet.

"What's wrong?" she asked, and Hump saw a genuine concern on her face; probably a new experience.

"There's too much of you."

She made a show of looking at her body. "Shall I cut off my legs?"

"You know what I mean. You toss things at me, market worlds, deep speech, money machines— Don't you see, to you they don't mean anything, your people have used these things probably hundreds of years. But down here we never heard of them. How would you react if some creature from space suddenly appeared on your planet—before you'd developed spaceships yourself—and started flashing around things no one had ever thought of?"

Somehow, he didn't know how, he'd scored a hit. A disturbed look flicked across Vanity's face, and she actually paled before she answered coldly, "Delighted, I suppose."

"You think so, huh?" Stupidly he stared at his empty cup; he could feel her eyes pinning him. "Hey," he said suddenly, "How did you get here?"

"Where?"

"Here. Earth."

"By subway. What did you think?"

"No, I mean it. The big question we've got is whether or not Daddy can trace you here. Now, if an Earth kid runs away he can hitch or maybe ride a train or even steal a car, and nobody knows where he's gone. But the only way you can reach Earth from another planet is by space ship. And all the ships that come into the space port get checked by three thousand cops. So what did you do, hide in the toilet?" She looked at him sweetly. "All right," he grumbled, "keep your damn secrets."

Vanity laughed. "I'm sorry."

"For what?"

"You looked so hurt."

"I haven't turned you in, have I? Why don't you trust me?"

"I want to—"

"It's just a habit not to trust people?"

She nodded. "Call it experience."

"Let's do the question again. How did you get here?"

"In my own ship, of course."

"What?"

"My own ship. Whoosh. Since I didn't land in the space port no one knows I'm here."

"Where did you land then? A spaceship is gigantic. Huge crews—"

"Not necessarily. You only see big ships because you only see cargo and passenger ships. Most of their crews *only* handle the cargo or the passengers." He looked skeptical. "Does a car have to be gigantic? Why should a ship? In fact, a lot of the minimum bulk comes from landing and taking off in an atmosphere. You should see some of the ones that operate only in space, they look like big bubbles. And most of the things inside a ship are for the people. Air systems, food, places to sleep. If they didn't carry people the ships would really be tiny."

"I refuse to believe one person can work a spaceship."

"Wrong again, dear Hump. Only one person *can* work a spaceship. The ship connects to the pilot's head—"

"His head?"

"Well, you would say his 'mind', though I don't understand the difference."

"I'm lost."

"The important thing is, the ship can only work with one head at a time. So one head, one pilot."

"Naturally. I should have realized that right away. If you grew two heads you could fly two ships at once. Listen, I'm going to be stubborn and try another question. You claim a space ship doesn't need much space. But if it basically flies itself wouldn't it need a lot of computers?"

"Sure. The channels on a space ship can get nearly half as complicated as a human brain."

"Well, don't computers take up whole blocks?"

"Only the funny ones built on Earth." He stuck his tongue out; she tried to pinch it and failed. She said, "That lumpy grey stuff in your head doesn't take up so much room. Why should a ship channel?"

"That stuff in my head is alive." Vanity raised her eyebrows. "Now wait a minute. Wait a minute. Don't tell me you slip in a little number that space ships are alive?"

"Not the ship. Just the channels."

"What happens if these channels get cranky? Or emotionally neglected?"

"Funny Hump, I didn't mean alive like you and me. It's just organic channelwork."

He snickered. "Sounds like the flip side of *Born Inside a Nova*."

"Flip side?"

"Local saying. Forget it." He rubbed his face, then got up to pace around the room, scowling at the sinkful of greasy dishes from the spare ribs three nights ago. "Look," he said at last, "suppose I just accept that you came here in a very small space ship and leave it at that."

"Your choice."

"Anyway, if you didn't park your mini compact in the space port where did you stash it?" She stared at the floor. After a moment Hump sighed. "All right. Don't trust me. Can I ask one more question? You don't have to answer it. What were you doing in ratfemland that night? So close to the space port?"

"Oh. I . . . I guess I was lonely."

"Lonely. You?"

"Don't be nasty. I'd been here—how long—four and a half ship standard days; that's six of your days. You can't imagine, by the way, how hard it was to tune my body to your filthy diurnal rhythms. This planet rotates too slow."

"Space lag."

"Huh?"

"Go on."

"Anyway, I'd wandered around and tried some things, but it all looked so strange. So alien. I couldn't talk to anyone. I kept telling myself, 'Keep away from the space port' but then I'd think, 'Oh, you can go, nobody knows you, no one even knows you're on this planet.' Finally, one night I found myself not too far and started walking. But when I got as close as ratfemland I got scared again and when those crazy people gave me that horrid drink I sat down to think about it. And then, happy winds of the stars, you came along. And you were so funny I knew I could never leave you."

"And now that the joke's over we're struck with each other."

"I told you I'll go."

"If you do, I go with you."

"Why? Jaak won't care about you."

"How do I know? If he catches you he might decide to look me up and teach me a lesson. And if he can't find me he might blow up the planet or suck up the atmosphere or turn all the children into maggots." He looked sideways at her. "Can he do stuff like that?" She turned up a hand. Hump made a noise then said, "That settles it. You and I stick together. At least I'll know what happens."

She bounded up to sit beside Hump on the counter next to the sink. "We'll swing a nova time together, dance with the quasars, swim in the nebulas—"

"The nebulas are probably polluted. If you don't stop reciting that song—"

"What will you do?"

"I'll sell you as a prize in a box of Vita Flakes." He took her wrists and crossed them over her heart. "We still haven't settled the main issue," he said.

"What main issue? Explain it to me."

"Do we stay here or do we go? In other words, what about those two space cops today?"

"We got away, didn't we? I think you're right that they weren't looking for me."

"Me? What do I know?"

"No one'll notice me. I'm so ordinary next to you."

Hump sighed. She wanted so much to believe everything was all right. Well, so did he. "What chance is there that your father knows you came to Earth?"

"Just about none. From where I got away I could have gone just about anywhere. Earth isn't even very close. There's at least twenty places much closer."

"Will he send your picture around, things like that?"

"He could send a real scale hologram a week long, but what would that do? Think about it. Think how many people live on this planet alone."

"I guess so. If you don't go around shouting on the street all the time."

"Me? I was trying to shut you up."

"And you've got to change your clothes, maybe even wear some makeup."

"Animal grease? You really want me to look like an Earth woman?"

"Listen you, the day will come when Earth beauty will set the standard for the whole galaxy."

"I hope I'm dead."

"You will be if you don't disguise yourself."

"We could both dress like ratfems. You'd look great with a bright yellow plastic nose."

"Wonderful. No one'll notice us at all." He paused. "Maybe we should change your name."

"Why don't you cut off my head? Then no one will recognize me."

"Good idea. How do you like the name 'Vicki'? It's short for 'Victoria'."

"We could just leave. Instead of all this disguise."

"Leave? What do you— Oh no. Oh no. Forget it."

She waved her arms. "Whoosh!"

"Scram it, Vanity. Earthman, stay home. See Terra first. For god's sake, didn't I tell you I don't even like to leave New York?"

"Don't be so scared. Imagine gliding through the darkness of a strange planet. The fires of a thousand suns glow in your eyes. Beep beep beep. Rocky Hump, space ranger."

Hump leaped to the door. "I'm going upstairs for a shower.

Probably back home you lase the dust away. Here we're happy when the plumbing works." He slammed the door, then opened it to stick his head back in. "Don't you leave the house till I get you some clothes." He slammed it again, louder this time.

Alone, Golden Vanity crossed her arms against her chest. She hated being alone. It scared her. Look what happened to old Workers after so many years alone in space. Vanity had once seen a bent Worker hiding in a thorn park, her eyes all glazed with dust, her hands drawing an invisible screen around her as if to cut herself off from the crowds she found so repellent.

Feed your head, Vanity ordered herself. She ran pictures through her mind, only to whimper when they broke up like old reels of film. Her father and Loper kept appearing in the cracks. What would happen to Loper when he got too old for space? Loper would never get old.

Feed your head. She constructed a fant of herself and Hump rolling in cool white sand while behind them glistened the blunt nose of her ship, its hieroglyph blazing red in the morning sun. Hump's kitchen vanished as the fant became reality in Vanity's mind. She stared blankly at the wall, seeing a long beach, green waves, black cliffs thick with giant twisted trees.

When she glanced at the purple sky, four or five of the planet's blue winged bird people swooped down to sing one of their ancient hypnotic epics. The oldest race in the universe, their sharp beaks jerked up and down excitedly as they described a time when great crystal boats sailed between and even through the stars, dipping through the burning hydrogen of a million suns.

Vanity shook her head, annoyed at the way the fant was turning. Why did she always think of ancient races; it raised historical ghosts from their mass graves two hundred years ago. And then the fant would break away from her, sliding down too far into her head. A metamorph—a snake.

Once started, fants don't stop easily. Held on her sandy world, Vanity heard a roar overwhelm the great beating of purple wings as a golden space ship swooped down to burn the birds in the fire from its crawl tubes. Hump lay paralyzed in fear as the Terror Lord, a tall heavy man in a black stone mask, leaped to the ground. His hands were carrakin claws, his legs and arms were laced with wires. He removed the mask, and Vanity stared at Loper's flat brutal face.

Vanity stamped her foot on the kitchen floor. Hazily the

walls reappeared, the counters, the dirty dishes. She rubbed her
eyes. Thank the stars she wasn't working a ship, she thought.
Loper would have had to execute another shrieker. And what
could Jaak offer him with Vanity dead? She remembered the
great ship, her namesake, remembered the time Loper used to
ferry her and Jaak from world to world. And one time in
particular, when Jaak stayed home.

"Filth," she shouted, and spit on the floor like a god-haunted
Arbol herder. Angry at herself, Vanity left the kitchen to go see
what she could find on the teev.

Upstairs, his shower finished, Hump dressed slowly, thinking
about his incredible lodger. Despite what she'd told him he still
knew nothing about her; there was too much to know. He
glanced at himself in the mirror. What a choice for the man to
make the first cultural contact with the aliens.

He wandered into the spare bedroom. A mess, blankets and
pillows on the floor, curtains half drawn, books everywhere. He
grunted. Vanity had thrown a sheet over the closet door. A door.
A door in a dream, she'd said. A dream that for a moment Hump
had shared, when his mind had stared through Vanity's eyes.

A door in a dream.

obsession, he often thought obsessively. Look at Jaak in his playroom, pretending he could banish the galaxy. Or the mask parlors, where psychi-helmets projected you into some ridiculous market world. Or the mind zoos, where a similar contraption inserted your mind into some filthy animal. Burst, he thought, without fants you couldn't even amuse yourself. If you refused to give your mind over to illusions you closed yourself to any entertainment more sophisticated than a whorehouse. And a slave whorehouse at that.

When he returned his attention to the room he only irritated himself further. The chairs and the walls demonstrated so clearly how all of Center had trapped itself in its own gimmicks. A number of years back, even before AAri had come to Center, the SA and the companies had tried an experiment on one of the market worlds. Rather than merely conceal all evidence of the fant system (and thereby avoid the awkward questions that arose whenever you told market worlders a portion of the truth), they decided to disguise the system in terms of the local culture's value constructs and so, hopefully, intensify control. They chose a world particularly well-suited. In caves all over the planet a certain jellylike creature called "laana" generated powerful psychic fields. The humans saw them as gods and built temples over the caves. At first the SA thought to use the laana as fant aids, but found that the creatures, actually parasites, drained rather than enhanced psychic energy. Besides, you could depend more on machines. So the SA used the laana in another way. They described their ships and Workers as physical creations of the laana, sent to lead the people into a golden age—as work servants of the companies. To aid the cultural deception they designed their ports and centers to resemble laana caves. The chairs originally formed part of an elaborate initiation rite.

All that had happened years ago, with no notable results. Now, however, like a curse bouncing back against its makers, the various gimmicks had become the latest fashion on Center itself. Everywhere you found damp dark rooms, clammy walls, and slime dripping jelly chairs. Even here, an official executive viewing room, some idiot had brought in laana chairs, projected full sense holos of barnacle-like slugs onto the walls, and piped a sweet odor of rot into the air.

Where could you escape it? The whole planet wallowed in it. No, he thought unhappily, he knew one place, the very next place on his schedule, in fact, where fads almost never penetrated. The fant schools themselves. The Nauikkrans who generated and promoted such weak dependence on fantasies would never relax their own controlled environment for the sake of fashion.

Ever since the discovery of Nauikkra, that planet's master manipulators had worked their way, like *boreworms*, deeper and deeper into the structure of Center. AAri knew; he'd researched the history himself, not trusting even his closest assistants to keep his interest secret from the Nauikkrans.

Why couldn't other people see the danger in the Nauikkrans' power? Had they inserted their mental mechanisms into everyone by now? AAri thought of the report that had come to him on the Event the Nauikkrans had staged "to enhance appreciative attitudes among Earth negotiators." A masterwork of Nauikkran creativity; they'd invaded the Earth leaders' minds, brutalized their egos, and the poor market worlders were left *thanking* the SA for the opportunity to talk together.

Details of the Event ran obsessively through AAri's mind. It had actually begun months earlier, with the SA request for "non returnable samples from the local populations." When the SA summoned the Earth leaders they told them that the "samples" had been tested to "demonstrate ways in which Earth might contribute to galactic culture," as if such a thing had ever existed.

One of these supposed contributions was "artistic production." The Nauikkrans had taken the current Center fad of body sculpture and grotesquely altered it. The market worlders saw their people with animal legs replacing arms, with exposed muscles and bones torn or twisted into obscene images, with tentacles growing from holes in their chests and groins.

Another demonstration, called "organ farming," had come from Earth itself. Apparently, if an Earth person's heart or liver failed the doctors took one from someone else to put inside the first person's body. AAri couldn't guess at the origins of such a bizarre custom; he only marveled at the Nauikkran's use of it. The Earth leaders were led into a room stinking of formaldehyde. There they saw Earth people in various stages of dismemberment, their remaining bodies kept alive by automatic machines, their miserable brains kept conscious because it supposedly "slightly lowers maintenance costs." The sickened Earth representatives hadn't even protested. Instead, they'd asked if the SA technology could be applied to extending life on Earth. And of course the SA had hinted that all they had to do was sign their planet over to the companies. Long experience told AAri that it wasn't more than a few months before another humanhome became a complex row of markers on the SA's ownership charts.

Disgustedly he got to his feet.

"Director?" one of the techs said.

"I'm just stretching myself. Go on."

"We're almost done actually."

"With no result."

"Well, not entirely." Seeing his director's angry stare the technician went back to his monitors.

On the three screens AAri watched the gruesome sight of human brains being dismantled. "Memory retrieval," they called it, a nicely sterile name. The problem: find out everything possible about Golden Vanity. Solution? Take everyone expendable (and Jaak had three times overrode AAri's decisions about just which persons that term included) who had ever known Vanity and screen all their memories of Vanity, then do a channel survey and extrapolation. Simple enough, except that access came only through direct probing of the brain, so that afterwards you might as well junk the body because not enough remained of the personality field to make the body worth sewing up again.

And what did they ever learn from it? That just before Vanity broke loose she refused to answer a routine 'mitt call. Or that even before the flight her repressed anger had led her to attack her own body servants. Junk. Idiocy. A waste of good material.

In the middle screen, on a solid air operating table, lay the director pilot of Vanity's convoy, her head neatly sliced open like a melon. What waste. The finest young Worker to come out of the company academy since— He smiled bitterly. Since Loper. Someone else sacrificed to Golden Vanity.

Without a word to the startled techs, AAri strode from the view room and down the corridors to a tunnel station. Angrily he punched the call buttons for an executive car.

Noises. Whispers, hums, even muffled shouts and shrieks, rising and falling in pitch. In the electron tracking car AAri switched on the projector screen in front of him, then switched it off again. He could have voice-cued any of hundreds of dramas, from real-time factory production on Ktaner's Planet to the finals of the orgasm contest held last year on Center itself. The luxuries of a director's car. Except that none of these scenes would have relieved the tension swelling up inside his chest. If anything, the darkness helped a little.

He wished he could shut out the noises that streamed past him like the musical breezes on a cure satellite. In a sense, they weren't even real. Since no sound could penetrate the air tunnel walls that prevented the cars from shattering buildings at the higher speeds, the cars' Litlithian designers had installed selective pickups, making each car a moving antenna.

It wasn't a Litlithian idea. Silence, more exactly, complete isolation, was considered an aberration on Center. It smacked of retro culture, like a desire to study Center's history before it became Center, before the ships arrived and the companies formed, when people lived in the open air, in cities, on farms, on boats cruising the now deserted seas. In short, when people lived as they live on any other humanhome. Now the companies and the SA covered almost a quarter of the planet's land surface with their offices, ship housings, holo centers, regeneration centers, dormitories, detention halls, devotion centers.... And these people who lived completely indoors feared silence almost as much as they feared the outside.

Or rather, they feared it on Center. Those who could afford to vacation offplanet very often chose remote corners of undeveloped worlds. It was as if one could only act uncivilized on uncivilized planets. On Center, silence made you feel someone was plotting against you.

AAri scowled at the black window. From the brain dismantlers to the brain controllers. If nothing else, he hated Vanity for forcing him to visit that wretched Nauikkran fant teacher of hers. He'd known all along he'd have to. No one else could give him any real clues. No one else knew the secrets stored in Vanity's mind. AAri wondered how many secrets the Nauikkrans had collected about *him*.

Precious few, he knew, as long as he refused to take one of her special "director courses." As if he needed to dwell on morbid private fantasies, like some rundown Worker hauling junk cargo round the outer market worlds. AAri knew the real reason Cixxa wanted to "train" him in ego fantasies. With his mind laid out in charts locked away in her tape decks, AAri would no longer remain the only director outside Cixxa's control. If only he could prove what he knew was the truth about her. The one time he'd hinted to Jaak that Cixxa might not be a selfless servant, the chairman had laughed at him.

Well, AAri had stood up to her before and he could do so
again, whatever lies she spread about him. It was just that the
last few weeks he'd felt so weak, so pressured. He leaned back
against the seat. How like Cixxa to secrete herself so far away.
The distance made no difference; all journeys took more or less
the same time due to the tracking cars' displacement programs.
But the teacher had established herself near the outer wall, and if
AAri sometimes liked silence it didn't mean he had to like the
untreated air as well. For a moment he thought of the wide skies
of his parents' city. How could he ever have lived there?

As the car neared the teacher's sector, it automatically slowed
down. AAri could sense the slightest deceleration while the
filtered noises changed from the high-pitched scream to nearly
distinguishable voices and machines. He heard a shriek, possibly
laughter. These were real-time sounds; at this speed the speakers
conveyed direct pickups. Impulsively he reached forward and
de-blacked the viewscreens.

The car was passing through an entertainment district. On
either side of the air tunnel stretched miles of theaters, parks,
arenas, food and liquor centers of all sizes, every pastime
imaginable, from honeycombs of clay rebirth cubicles to giant
festival and pseudo-suicide halls, from drug and electrical
centers to pink and gold entranceways to underwater immersion
parks, from human and robot sports arenas to body alienation
grids, all of it under a ceiling so high that a visitor might have
mistaken it for sky.

It was evening here and in the neighboring sectors, for the
people flashing past AAri's car had forsaken their uniforms for
the flamboyant costumes currently fashionable. AAri made a
face at a group of young people lounging near the air tunnel,
their heads adorned with glowing cultures of S'suseranian color
worms. At sight of the executive car they flung aside the bright
webs the worms had spun across their faces to shout some insult.
Had they recognized him? Cixxa's spies? No, of course not, he
was going too fast. It was just modern respect. Vanity's kind.
AAri remembered his own first arrival on Center, the evenings
spent visiting sector after sector in awed amazement. Or fear?

As the car left the entertainment district AAri noticed a
group of people, drugged on ghost by their faces, floating on
cushionfish in a giant aquarium. Enormously fat in the style
affected by lowerlevel directors, their naked globes of flesh were
decorated with traditional torture scenes from the Click world.
AAri glanced curiously at the tattoos flitting past. The subjects

bored him but he found a certain charm in their history and the knowledge that their peculiar fantasies sprang from the undoctored imagination.

There was something *clean* about these formalized images of cruelty, something aesthetically honest that the fant teachers, with all their probing and stimulating, could never duplicate. Something else about them appealed to AAri. They represented cultural images, something given by an artist's imagination to all society, unlike the strictly personal, and therefore petty, fantasies of the Workers. The traditional scenes, first composed thousands of years ago, reminded AAri of the Grand Spring Festival, held every year on his home world.

The director slumped down in his bubble seat. What a time, he thought, to go slumming in the past. The past few days he'd thought so much about G'GaiRRin, the charms painted over the doorways, the picture tellers, his family to whom he'd never even sent a tape, and especially the days when the first company ships had landed, and AAri, a young apprentice councillor-priest, had watched his parents' society crumble in shock.

Senility, Jaak's chief assistant told himself. The senile mind vomits up the past. Senility, or a crumbling company? *Vanity*, he thought, *burst her slimy selfish—*

He sat up and rubbed the back of his neck. Maybe he should have sent someone else to Vanity's teacher. He'd have to pass on to assistants anything he learned anyway. But who could he trust? Even Zdri or Johu could go over to his enemies at any time. Hadn't they both taken fant courses?

The car stopped with that lack of any real deceleration that AAri always found so unsettling. After he'd cued the car to wait for him, he stepped out onto the grass-covered waiting platform, making a face at the cold pain in his back and legs. He should see his Arbolian nerve doctor, he knew, though he'd avoided her for weeks. On either side of him the corridor widened to allow large trees with fan-shaped red leaves to grow serenely beside rainbow pebbled pools. Wistfully, AAri looked at the seats grafted organically onto the trees before he entered the long hallway that ran spine-like through the teacher's offices and workrooms.

As director of the company's fant program, Vanity's teacher maintained an establishment at once smaller and larger than her underlings. While they processed whole groups of Workers (or on the higher levels, small classes of lower directors) their superior treated only the most special cases, requiring smaller laboratories and workrooms. Like any director, however, she spent much of her time in meetings and a great number of the rooms off the center hall were conference rooms, offices, libraries, each one a miniature communications center. AAri liked the idea of Cixxa (a Centerization of her actual name, which AAri suspected even she couldn't pronounce) belabored with admin work.

Today, nothing could have relieved the anxiety tightening AAri's chest as he walked down the hallway, with its dark blue liquid-walls, and its living carpet that ran like cool fire under his feet. How he hated this place. They could all fall, he knew, ripped by the SA and the other companies, but Cixxa would survive. He hated her.

And he hated her gimmicks. This silent hall; beyond those tumbling liquid walls hummed vast machines developed on Nauikkra to work on the mind of anyone walking along the corridor. Sensors in the floor picked up AAri's brain wave structures, which then activated minute vibrations in the walls and floors, supposedly to awake his lower ego. Similarly, nearly subconscious structured noise (psychologically truer, the Nauikkrans claimed, than culturally biased music), again based on the electric "noise" of AAri's mind, would follow him throughout the complex. The whole process, and especially the fact that he couldn't consciously observe it, frightened AAri. He felt invaded.

Almost against his will AAri remembered the picture tellers' academies on G'GaiRRin, the times he and his father had gone there to hear the Great Stories, the birth of the mountain, the Song of Light, GGaddu's seven labors and seven joys. Some of the academies, particularly in the southern cities, decorated themselves with tapestries, carpets, embroidered couches. But the older, truer academies kept the traditional bare walls and hard floors. The picture tellers adorned themselves, with paints and feathers and elaborate wrappings, each costume personally designed, to demonstrate the dominance of human fantasy over the physical world.

AAri looked first in the conference rooms, then in the test chambers and training rooms, with all their image makers, hypnotic relaxers, wave structure projectors, desire probes. No one; Vanity had suspended business here too.

AAri found Cixxa in her private office at the end of the corridor. As the ancient door, built of some black bone-like substance from Nauikkra, slid shut behind him, some of the tension seeped out of AAri. The manipulative technology that permeated the rest of the sector stopped here. The plain reddish walls (giving off a light supposedly like Cixxa's home sun) broadcast no subtle noise, the webbed floor didn't vibrate, the clonewood desk and chairs made no attempt to massage his lower ego.

Sadly, the feeling of safety didn't last. The moment the teacher looked up from the mass of plastic squares that covered her desk panic tensed AAri's muscles and shortened his breath. *I shouldn't have come*, he thought. *I didn't know it would be this bad.* Was she taping his brainwaves to search them for weaknesses she could exaggerate to his enemies?

"AAri," she said with a wide smile. "Come in, come in. Sit down." She waved airily at a deep bubble chair at the end of her desk. AAri sat down instead in a straight armless chair made of Arbolian white rubber. "I've been expecting you. In fact, if you hadn't arrived soon, I would have sent for you."

"And no doubt if I'd refused to come you would have told Jaak to order me."

She laughed. "Yes, of course. Though I gather Jaak wouldn't listen much to either one of us these days."

"The only person Jaak listens to has sliced herself somewhere across the galaxy." *Careful*, he thought. He had to watch everything he said with her.

Cixxa's deeply lined Nauikkran face, with its small flattish eyes and long sharp chin, looked curiously at him. "Don't judge Vanity too harshly," she said. "Her experience leads her to regard the company somewhat differently than you or I."

"Yes. She's never had to work for it."

There was a pause. "Have you heard any news yet?"

"Nothing." He rushed into the silence formed by her waiting. "We get streams of reports, of course. Faithful searches, interrogations. They can't tell us anything. We need to narrow the search area."

"I agree." She ran a surgically elongated finger down her cheek; subcutaneous makeup, slightly luminous, gave her reddish skin a deep glimmer. As AAri looked at her, Cixxa appeared to move far away, half hidden in a red haze. *She's done something to my eyes*, he thought. Something must have shown in his face, because the teacher abruptly said, "AAri, are you all right?"

He smiled sourly. "Oh, I'm fine."

"Do you know, I sometimes worry about you."

"Please don't bother."

"You feel a lot of anger, don't you? That you can't express anywhere?"

"Everyone feels anger that they can't express. It's a fact of reality."

"Maybe. But a fant course would help. It would at least give you outlets."

"I thought your worries might lead you there."

"You fear us, I know. That alone indicates your need to release your fantasies."

"Aren't you making yourself rather important?"

She ignored him. "You think we want some sort of control, some power over everyone in the company, like a psychic SA. Actually, AAri, we can't spare the time or the energy. Fant teachers do one thing as well as we can. We liberate emotional energy. As you would know if you ever submitted to a course."

"I came here to submit to some information. Is that possible?"

"About Vanity?"

"About her impulses. Where she might have gone. We've got to narrow the range before we can make any real search. Can you tell us anything about where she might have gone, how she might have worked the ship after the override?"

Apparently Cixxa accepted the change of subject. She leaned forward across her desk. "The same idea occured to me. And of course, as Vanity's teacher, I could map her impulses better than anyone."

"Including Jaak?"

"Oh definitely. No father ever knows his daughter; he only knows his personal fantasy of her. But teachers don't rely on our subjects' fantasies. We *know* our subjects. I suppose you might say it's a paradox, that we free ourselves from our fantasies by studying theirs, but after all, we do have their mental topography laid out before us. Look here." She made an attempt to gather the plastic squares scattered over her desk. AAri recognized the wave structure bits, collectively called "head maps;" sweat gathered under his arm. *That's why she wants to train me*, he thought. So she could lay him out across a clonewood desk.

Cixxa went on, "Look at this overlay. And this one. And this one." She moved the squares like a hand artist in one of the swindler shelters. "Look at this verticality. The narrowness, the way it stays rigid and broken all at the same time. Now look at this point motif, how it keeps moving back, even here where you'd never expect to see it at all."

AAri resisted sweeping the plastic squares onto the floor. He told her, "Maybe you can put them on display in the Nauikkran Gallery. Right now the aesthetics don't interest me. Have you got any practical suggestions?"

"Yes, of course." She looked up wistfully. "A shame, though, you can't appreciate something so unique. I've taught now—"

"The suggestions."

She laughed. "AAri, in a way you remind me of Vanity. Head maps scare her too; she'll never look at her own or let me explain them to her. Though I think if I ever could get you started on a course you'd overcome your terrors sooner than you'd think. I think you'd surprise yourself."

"I'm not scared, Cixxa, I'm impatient. Why don't you surprise me with some useful information? Jaak's waiting for me."

"Is he really? Then let me think." She leaned back. "There are four points actually. I could show you them topographically but I'll summarize. First of all, Vanity hates space. A great many people do, but the feeling penetrates much deeper in Vanity. For one thing space took away her mother; for another the incident with Loper occurred in space. But mostly the very vastness of space frightens Vanity, that appalling openness. "AAri nodded He knew that fear very well, he remembered the terror that crept over him once as he sat next to Loper on a long run for Jaak, with Loper as cold and silent as the Great Darkness itself. Did *she* know about his fears? Was she really talking about Vanity, or about AAri himself? He suddenly knew that the tranquilizers released from the neck studs of his collar were giving way. He felt a pressure under his skin as if his veins would burst open.

Cixxa continued, "Vanity lives behind complex walls, like those radiated time-shields on Litlithia. They protect her, from Jaak, from the company, from history. Above all from history. Vanity's psychic balance requires physical walls as symbols of protection. And there are no walls in space. Even the walls of the ship vanish as soon as the Worker connects himself to it."

"All right, space frightens Vanity. She detests it. What does that tell us?"

"In a moment. As much as Vanity hates space, she hates non-space more. *Nothing*, nonexistence, is much more awful than emptiness. Therefore, point one: Vanity would quickly find her ship, without a charted program, without a fixed destination, unbearably frightening. Point two is this: Vanity has never done anything on her own before, certainly never in open defiance of her father. She's impulsive, she's built a strong ego, upper and lower, and that's no illusion, I could show you the maps. But the point is, Vanity cannot maintain an action, not alone. I can understand how she would seize the opportunity to break loose, but after that first step she must have leapt wildly through non-space without any plan or destination, just trying to get away."

"Do you consider that a practical help? You have her leaping everywhere at once."

"You've forgotten point one. Panic or not, she'd still hate the ship, and as soon as the panic abated enough she would have looked for a place to stop. The nearer the better."

"How long would this panic last?"

"That's the key, isn't it? I would guess between five and six tenths, no more. And during that time she would have gone as far as possible."

AAri made a mental calculation based on Vanity's initial leap distance at the break. "All right, that gives us a little help. It definitely helps." If it was true. And not calculated to disgrace him. It did sound like Vanity. As much as he wanted to leave he forced himself to add, "Anything else?"

"Let me ask you something. From your non-topographical knowledge of Vanity's personality, what sort of world do you think she'd choose?"

"My non-topographical mind has thought a lot about that. I would guess one of the more sophisticated. Vanity wouldn't know how to handle herself on any world very primitive. The simple discomfort would repel her."

"True. But remember, we must consider emotional imperatives as well as practical needs. I completely agree that Vanity would never choose a world that would leave her shivering in some rain-soaked shack. But I also know she would reject a world where she might keep encountering the companies. First of all, the exposure would scare her. Secondly she wants to forget Jaak, she wants to forget Center. Vanity, as you know, tries not to think of things she dislikes. No, she must have chosen some world recently opened up, simple but still comfortable, with a minimum technology, say 2.5 on the Rih scale."

"You say 'must' as if you sat next to her. How good are these guesses?"

"They're not guesses. I could show you the maps—"

"Please don't. And forget your propaganda. I want to know if we can really narrow the search."

She shrugged. "You can do as you like. If your fear imperatives insist you reject my information I can't make you accept it. I wouldn't want to."

They sat silently for a moment, staring at each other til AAri looked away, and Cixxa went on, "The last point is money. Vanity will need money, a good deal of it just to function. Remember, Jaak or Jaak's name has always given her everything. Now she's on a market world alone. She must create some security, some walls for herself. Money can get her whatever *things* she likes. She can use them, throw them away, and get more. That represents a very basic need to Vanity."

"Unlike most people."

"With Vanity the real economic needs become exaggerated. Alone, frightened, she'll need money like food."

AAri grunted. "The money boxes." Cixxa raised her eyebrows. AAri explained, "On a lot of worlds, particularly the new ones, the company reps haven't established automatic credit, so we operate a money box, a gimmick to supply our people with local currencies. All the companies share it. I'm sure Vanity's imprinted. Yes, that's right, she traveled with Jaak and me once, I forget where, and Jaak sent her for money." He stopped, absurdly out of breath.

"This box," Cixxa said, "how much money will it give her at one time?"

"Not too much. She'd have to go back."

"And keep going back. Can you put tracers on these boxes?"

"Yes, of course. We'll check all the worlds in range." He stood up. "Is that it?"

"For now."

"Then I'll get started."

She watched him walk awkwardly to the door before she called his name. He turned. "I wish you'd consider a course."

"So you can know me as well as you know Vanity? And Jaak? Don't worry. I won't run off to some market world."

"Don't you see what happens when you can't release your fantasies as fantasies? You start to live them. Your lower ego snakes on you. I don't want to control or persecute you. I want to help."

"Like you helped Vanity?" He closed the door softly. Instantly, cramps nearly doubled him over. Fixing his mind on the car, on safety, on anything but the noise and the moving walls and floors, he hurtled down the spine of Cixxa's empire. A group of techs, all Nauikkrans by their reddish faces, moved aside to let him pass. He tried to ignore their smiles and whispers.

Finally, he reached the end of the hallway. Oblivious to the bent trees and still pools, he nearly ran to the tunnel and his waiting car.

Except the car was gone. AAri stared, horrified. Someone must have overrode his cue; unless Cixxa had managed to send it away. He spun around but no one had followed him. His fingers pushed the call button again and again. Burst Vanity, he thought. He wanted suddenly to beat her, to slash her grinning face. He discovered himself crying.

Deep in space a pulse point picked up a message sent between universes and relayed it to a ship moving in a long slow orbit around the flickering point. Inside the ship a large man looked impassively at his flashing transmitter; he pushed the switch that would open the channel.

A nervous face filled the screen. "Something's happened," the transmitter said. "They've drastically narrowed the investigation."

"Narrowed it how?"

"Cut down the ring. Also the kind of worlds."

"Why?"

"I don't know. I think they've gotten some fresh information, but AAri's keeping it to himself."

Loper scratched his neck with a long thumbnail. "What are the chances they've already found her or know where she is?"

The stoop shook his head. "No, no, I told you I'll know when it happens. And you'll know. Don't worry about that. But they are more optimistic. Much more than a few days ago."

Loper's face stayed blank. "Let me know as soon as anything happens." He switched off the transmitter and sat back in his seat. Outside, the intermittent beam of light from the pulsepoint bounced violently off the golden hieroglyph on the ship's side. Inside, Loper stared through his wide window at the great blackness. He waited.

Chapter Seven

"Look at that," Vanity whispered hoarsely. "look at how they stand. Burst, did you ever see such crude—Want to buy some slimy lick-lick, mister?" She tried to push out her hip like one of the prostitutes lined up along the buildings. Instead, she stumbled against Hump who shoved her angrily away to fall against a wall. One of the women laughed. Someone honked a horn.

Vanity was drunk. It had taken Hump two days of experiments to find the right drink for her. Wines made her sick, beer she disliked, whiskey made her sneeze. Finally, nearly out cold himself, Hump had mixed together a viscious brew of three parts ouzo, and one part lime, with a dash of gin. Instead of killing her, the mixture had lit her like an exploding comet. "Not as good as—" She'd pronounced some word, presumably an alien liquor. "But drinkable." She drank three in a row and kept on for the next two days. Hump soon wished he'd never bothered. Vanity drunk became even more obnoxious, conceited, arrogant, self-centered, secretive, and selfish than Vanity sober.

Their tourist idyll had lasted a week and a half, and by now Hump was sick of it. They'd ridden cable cars up and down the bridges, they'd climbed to the top of the Statue of Liberty and bounced down the air chute, they'd sampled all the night spots:

liqueur bars featuring avant garde double sonic music, amateur night at a sex theater, a disastrous attempt at a Broadway show (bored, Vanity had torn up her program and spit it at the people in front of her until the ushers asked her and Hump to leave), soya steak houses with topless folk dancing, s and m bookstores, the Necrophile Art Gallery, and the Times Square Explosion Emporium, where for five dollars you could blow up a replica of the White House, or the Empire State Building, or the Kremlin, or—of course—the spaceport. Vanity had bought a watch from Jimmy Wu's Great Interstellar Floating Riot Sale, a back-of-a-truck operation that claimed to sell loot picked up from the great spaceport riots of the previous year (the watch declared itself made in Manila). They'd watched a Satanist parade and attended a sermon by Cardinal Michael Sullivan, the prelate of St. Patrick's Cathedral, who was nearly excommunicated for ordaining robots as priests and calling the bread and wine "food of the stars," a title also claimed by Vita Flakes. When their money had run out they'd simply gone back to Grand Central for another thousand dollars.

For a while Hump had enjoyed it, particularly Vanity's reaction, but more and more he grew nervous, irritable, certain something terrible would happen, but not sure what or when—or if he could do anything about it. Vanity had also gotten touchy, easily angered or scornful, laughing at Earth's attempts to adjust to its greater horizons.

They'd get along better, he knew, if only she trusted him. A few times she'd almost opened up; warmness flowed between them at odd moments, while wandering through the Museum of Natural History, or throwing mudpies at police effigies in Central Park, or even just sitting in Hump's devastated living room after the party Vanity had thrown for the local drunks. A look would come over Vanity's face, pensive, worried, and she'd start to speak.

Before Hump could learn anything, however, she always closed up again, as if she sensed some alien censor shaking his head over her shoulder.

There was one time in particular, the afternoon they'd spent in the World Trade Center's Earth Museum. At first Vanity had loved the showy attempt to restore Earth chauvinism; she'd howled at the Voodoo ceremonies and even tried to dance along until the guard threatened to throw them out. She'd clapped her hands at the animations of Islamic Desert Warriors, and laughed at the film loop of astronauts playing golf on the moon.

And for once Hump didn't get angry or resentful, but only laughed along, perhaps because of the way Vanity kept hugging him or curling against him when he put his arm around her shoulders.

Then the Greek exhibit had done something strange to Vanity. And to Hump as well. A replica of the Delphic oracle where any question received a cryptic answer from a robot sybil. The fake cave allowed two people to enter at once, but Vanity had insisted on going in alone.

While Hump had slouched outside, it happened. As suddenly as the time on the stairs, he was somewhere else, looking out through someone else's eyes, Vanity's eyes. The vision lasted only a moment, just long enough for his mind to register a swaying mechanical snake and a raspy recorded voice. Then, like a released spring, his mind rejoined his sagging body before it fell against a table. He stood there shaking his head, ready to mumble "Petit mal" to any curious guards, until a few seconds later when Vanity hurtled through the cheap mist blowing across the cave entrance. She stopped, her eyes fixed wildly on his face, and Hump knew this time he couldn't fake ignorance. He stood stupidly and waited.

Vanity had pressed against him, her arms tight around his back, her face against his shoulders as Hump awkwardly stroked her trembling back. They stood hugging for a long half minute until Hump clumsily broke her hold and suggested they go on to the next exhibit, Jahweh giving Moses the Ten Commandments.

Vanity had said no. She wanted—hesitation—she wanted to talk to Hump. About? About "something." Instantly excitement had replaced Hump's fear as he guided her to the high-domed coffee lounge where they sat on the fake whaleskin cushions set on the synt-ivory floor. Behind them an Eskimo totem pole glared at the ceiling which was a replica of a mosque in Isfahan. This is it, Hump thought, Vanity lets loose, spaceships, Daddy, galactic culture, the whole scoop.

And instead his starborn visitor had prattled some nonsense about fantasies. Daydreams. Ego games. *Fantasies*, for god's sake.

Of course, Hump had gotten furious. And of course, Vanity had gotten twice as furious. That ended it. She'd tried to tell him something important—she said—and Hump had bulled her aside.

It always went like that. Any time he thought she might trust

him, something, some little quirk or arrogance or chauvinism or
fear, had clicked in her alien brain, and clang, down came the
gates.

And now the drunken space lady—who, as far as Hump
could tell, knew less about sex than a tadpole—had decided to
ridicule Earth's quaint ladies of the street.

"Let's go home, huh?" Hump pleaded, grabbing her wrist.

"No." She yanked her hand away. "I want to watch the night
women."

"Fuck off, snig," a woman yelled through a frozen smile.

They were sitting on Second Avenue south of 13th Street,
Meat Street as the local people called it, where shifts of whores
worked day and night to satisfy the downtown market. All along
the street noisy diners and bars served the buyers and sellers who
wanted a break. (The women conducted all business on the
street; they insisted on it.) Behind Hump and Vanity the
Salvation Army Jazz Band blasted screeches and squawks from
the doorway of the "God is Love Community Center." Despite
his pained ears Hump looked wistfully at the center's big front
room with its dim lights and couches full of sleeping whores and
pimps. He could use a nap. Supposedly the center operated a
slave market behind the chapel stage; Hump wondered if he
could get a good price for Vanity.

"Just look at them," she went on. "Look at the way they
stand. Crude. Shoddy. Too stupid to get what they're worth.
Stupid, stupid, like the idiot borksons in their idiot cars." She
giggled wildly.

Several of the women marched down the street to a dark cafe.
A bad night to bother them, Hump knew. The Palestine Terrors
world champion soccer team had come to town, promising hard
work and high wages. *Shit*, Hump thought, *any night's a bad
night*. A moment later the women came back with a short skinny
man in velvet trousers, a purple silk shirt, and an old police
jacket. One of the women said something, pointing at Vanity
and they all laughed. Hump rolled his eyes.

The man marched up to Vanity. "Street officer," he said.
"Sisters knocked you down for business obstruction and
disturbing the peace." Two of the women snickered. "You break
orbit or I crack you."

"Sure," Hump said quickly. "She didn't mean any harm.
She's just stupid. Come on," he ordered Vanity.

She only laughed. "Break orbit?" she slurred.

"Will you move?" Hump shouted. The "officer" ran his finger up and down inside his jacket as if caressing a gun or a knife.

"No," Vanity said, "I want to give them some advice."

"You stupid bitch," Hump grated. "He'll carve us up for souvenir bonuses to the customers." Half the street had gathered around to laugh. Even the band had stopped and now lounged in the doorway.

Shaking her head Vanity began to cry. "Don't you see, they've got to learn to market it. Burst, it's all so filthy crude. So *helpless*. All of you. If I can— Jaak'll carve you up, can't you see that? The whole bursting planet—"

Hump slammed his hand against her mouth. While the officer watched him warily he began to drag Vanity down the street, jabbering, "Sorry everyone. She's sick. Brain drain. Her mother died last week. Malpractice. I'll keep her home. I promise. Sorry." At a nod from the officer the crowd parted, but Hump didn't release Vanity for a whole block, not until the crowd had returned to business.

For two blocks neither of them said anything. Then Hump stopped by the locked gate of a small square at one time cleared by the community and planted with trees and grass. Most of the trees had died, garbage covered the grass. Scrunching his nose at the smell, Hump said, "Listen, you've got to leave. I can't take this anymore."

Vanity pouted. "I just wanted to help."

"Help? Oh mother."

"Yeah." She looked down sullenly. "I wanted—"

"How dare you?" he whispered. "How dare you come here and *hide out* and act so goddamn superior. Maybe back home everyone's so pure no one even thinks of prostitutes—"

"Oh, you bursting slime! Pure! Don't you listen to anything I tell you? Anything? It's a market galaxy, Hump. Money. No purity, no idiot salvations, just screed. Money. A thousand different kinds of it. Buy, sell, buy, sell. Prostitution's the only kind of sex we have, Hump. No romance and love, just sell the product. Only we don't line ourselves up and down the road like insects. We market that filthy product for every filthy screed we can pull for it."

Lamely he said, "I don't understand."

"Of course not. You've fixed your little mind on one little loop and you won't change the tape. The superior race. Star beings. Whoosh. Oh, stop looking up and down the street like a hungry welperr. No one's listening. Your sweet vision's got one thing wrong with it, Hump. You want to make us superior according to *you*. Pure. Whatever the slime that means."

"It doesn't mean anything, all right? It's another stupid Earth term. Oh hell, I just don't care anymore."

"You've got to care." She started to cry, spitting out words between gulps. "All of you. If I care— Hump, it's your planet. You don't know what Jaak'll do to you. You don't know. You don't *know*." The sobs took over.

For a moment anger held Hump back. It's not fair, he thought. She does something, and now I've got to apologize? Let her cry. She can stay here all night. He looked up and down the street. They were already by drunkland; scattered men and women lay curled in doorways. Hell, he thought, and put his arms around Vanity. She leaned into him. "It's all right," he said. "Come on."

"You won't make me leave?"

"How could I? You're my curse. The world would never forgive me if I unleashed you." He dug in his pocket for his dirty handkerchief.

"Ugh." She laughed through her sniffs. "I'm sorry I acted that way."

"Sonofabitch. You apologized."

"I mean it."

"I know."

"That show upset me earlier. You know it did."

Hump nodded. That afternoon he'd taken her to a simulation theater, where real scale holograms and syntasound gave the appearance of a live performance. At the start the play had looked and sounded exactly like real actors performing a domestic comedy. Suddenly, with no warning and no change of dialogue and action, the actors' faces began to disintegrate, until at the end humans with monstrous lizard faces sat drinking coffee and discussing politics. Hump had thought it a pleasant novelty until he'd seen Vanity's rigid body and frightened eyes.

He said, "Look, suppose we go home."

She nodded. Like kids, they held hands down the block.

At first they didn't hear the hoarse whisper. "Hump, Vicky." When they stopped to look around, it took a second before they could locate the voice coming from the alleyway. "Over here. Hurry." Vanity led Hump into the alleyway.

Garibaldi stood behind a pair of garbage cans, rubbing his arms. "Jesus," he said, "I thought you'd never come. I thought sure I'd missed you, or you'd come the other way. I couldn't figure what to do."

"Take it easy," Hump told his resident drunk. "What's wrong, Gari?" But he already knew.

"Men. Two of them. They came to the house asking questions."

With a gasp Vanity fell against a wall. Hump said, "Oh my lord. My god."

"I was sitting on the step, you know," Gari said. "Keeping things straight."

"Slice it," Vanity said. "What happened?"

Gari jerked his head up and down. "Yeah. Sure, well. Those two guys came up to me."

Vanity cut in, "Was one of them really big, heavy shouldered, lots of thick hair, grinning, or maybe just blank faced like a statue?"

"No. No, they were both kind of skinny guys. Short hair."

Vanity sighed, pushed her hair off her face. Hump asked, "Jaak?" She shook her head. To Gari Hump said, "What did they want? Did they identify themselves?"

"No, they just asked questions. First they rang the bell, you know, then they asked questions. Like, who lived in the house. I said Hump, and they asked if a girl lived there too, and I kind of laughed, you know, like a joke, and said yeah, sure, whenever you could find someone. So they asked how about now, and I said I didn't know."

"What else? What else did they ask?"

"When you'd come back. I pretended I didn't know nothing."

"Good. Good. I love you. What'd they do?"

"They hung around a bit, looked around the house, you know, then they left."

"Did they come back?"

"I don't know." He rubbed his arm across his forehead. "See, what I did, I figured I better warn you before you reached the house. So I pretended like I was going off to get a bottle for the night, you know, and kind of slowly—" he did a little pantomime shuffle—"made it down here where I pretended like I kind of fell asleep. Cause, you know Vicky said you was gonna walk past Meat Street."

"She did, huh? Did you get a bottle?"

"Well, yeah."

"Good. Get another one. Get a whole bunch." He gave the drunk a handful of bills. Gari squinted at them a second, as if confused, then shoved them into a pocket. He looked at Vanity. "What did they want? Who are they?"

She shook her head, then asked, "What did their skin look like?"

"Their skin?" He screwed up his face in concentration. "I don't—"

"Did it look like mine? Like Hump's? Or some other color?"

"Oh. Oh yeah. I guess like yours. Kind of—Oriental, you know."

"Jaak's men," Vanity said. Hump covered his face.

"Who's Jaak?" Gari asked.

"Hump," Vanity said, "we've got to get away." Hump only stared at the open garbage can, as if his enemy would leap out at him. "Burst you, you can't leave me." She grabbed his shoulders and shook him wildly until his head banged against the wall and he shoved her away.

"Why the hell do you think I know what to do? I'm the hick, remember? The dumb savage. You brought them here."

"Hump, please. Help me."

Gari whispered, "Who are they?"

"Satan," Hump said. "And God."

Vanity turned to Gari. "Did they follow you here?"

"I don't think so. I waited a good while."

"Maybe they didn't come from Jaak," Hump said. "Maybe a couple of SA cops just spotted us on the street. Like that other time."

"You want to take that chance?" she asked.

"No."

"We can't stand here and talk. We've got to get away." Her voice pleaded with itself, as if it begged her not to give up, not to panic.

"What about your ship?"

"Leave the planet. Yes, yes, of course, you're right."

Gari stumbled back into the darkness. "Leave—" he gulped.

"Is it safe?" Hump asked.

"I don't know, I don't know. It depends on the tracking—no, of course it's not safe. They'll be looking."

"Get a hold of yourself." Hump tried to toughen his voice; it came out as a whine. He said, "So we've got to hide somewhere on Earth."

"On Earth," Gari whimpered.

"You're not leaving me?" Vanity begged.

"Leave you? How the hell can I leave you? I let you suck me in this far, either I stick it out or I turn you in."

"You wouldn't—" She looked around for a weapon.

"I said I wouldn't, didn't I? Don't tempt me. Jesus, we better start trusting each other. It's a good time to start. I'm babbling. Look, you know the enemy, I know the territory. Together maybe we've got a chance." Yeah, sure, he thought.

Vanity turned to Gari. "Can you get a taxi?" He only shook his head and stammered something.

"They wouldn't stop for him anyway," Hump said. He forced himself to step out of the alleyway. Vanity watched him move his arm a couple of times—an hour passed, she thought, fifty tenths—before a cab slid up against the curb. While Hump got in and held the door Vanity whispered to Gari, "Thank you. Long live the king of Italy." Gari cringed back. Vanity dashed for the car.

Minutes passed before Garibaldi dared leave the alleyway. In the half light he took out the money Hump had given him and counted it over and over while tears soaked his face. After he'd put away all but one bill he wiped his face on his sleeve and then walked slowly, pain stiffening his body, down to the all-night liquor store.

Though the lights dazed him, he stayed in the store until the owner threatened to throw him out. At last he bought a bottle and returned to the street. Got to go somewhere, he thought. Get away. Make plans. But he only walked, very slowly, back to Hump's house.

Alan Jacobi was depressed. Cold, tired, disgusted, and depressed. Over twelve hours he'd stayed in a cold dirty cramped doorway, while the thought grew stronger and stronger—you slopped it, Jacobi. You really slopped it. God knows how many weeks he'd spent living like a goddamn bum, just so he could watch McCloskey waltz around town with his goddamn female alien. If only he'd never seen them that day at the delicatessen. If only his hotshot agent's mind hadn't hit on the creamy idea of playing drunk—some game—so he could spy on them and

maybe find out why an alien would hang out—hide out more
likely—with a waste like McCloskey. You're a whizzer, Jacobi.
A real whizzer. Oh, go home and go to bed, he told himself. The
case finally breaks, and where's Jacobi? Sitting in a doorway.
Mother humping luck.

Twice that day aliens had come to the target house. Both
times they'd questioned the old drunk hanging around the
stoop, once in the afternoon, the second time hours later, after
the drunk had come home with a bottle—and where did he get
that bottle, Jacobi? Where did he get the money? Why can't you
learn to think?—and sloshed himself to sleep. The second time
they'd even taken the drunk away with them. Both times whizzer
Jacobi had quizzed himself, do I follow them, do I try to find
their base? And both times he'd decided no, wait for the female.
She's the key, right? So wait until she gets back, then zip, make
your move.

Only the female didn't come back. Surprise. And now the
two alien agents—and if anyone ever looked like agents those
two certainly did—had taken away the only other clue, the bum.
Luck, huh? Try stupidity.

Another hour passed and Jacobi imagined he could see the
sky lighten, though he knew it couldn't be later than three or
four o'clock. Suddenly the drunk returned, shuffling up the
street, hugging himself. The old man climbed wearily onto
McCloskey's stoop where he collapsed against the door. He
stared at the night, all expression stunned from his face. What
now, Jacobi thought. Interrogate the bum, or wait for someone
else to show? He decided if the bum left he'd follow him this
time. The hell with it.

Less than half an hour had passed when a car, modern, a
rental job maybe, pulled up to the curb. A heavy man with a
great mane of hair got out and walked lightly up the stoop.
Alien, Jacobi was sure of it. He recognized the flashy loose
clothes, but more, he saw a cold brutality that his innocence or
intuition, associated with space. And now, of course, he
recognized the car, one of those robot jobs the aliens used. For
the first time in his short career Jacobi wished to hell he carried a
gun.

"Hello, market friend. Rousing time," the alien said,
prodding the human. The bum's eyes blinked open; he shrunk
back. "I've come to make friends with you. You can use a new
friend, can't you? All you have to do is do me a favor." The

drunk jabbered something. "See that door? That's your target, work servant. Get them to open it and you've made yourself a new friend."

"You're—you're the one. The one she said—"

The alien made a noise, crouched down. "That's an interesting word, that 'she'. Just what she do you mean?"

"You—Vanity said—I mean Vicky—Vicky—"

Jacobi bit his lip at the single burst of alien laughter. "Vanity. Perfect translation." He laughed again, while one great hand held the bum's shoulder. "Didn't I tell you we'd be friends? You've already helped me. Now all you've got to do is get them to open that door and then you can crawl away to some safe warm smokehole where no one will ever bother you."

The bum shook his head. "Not home. They're not home. They've gone away."

The alien ran his fingernail up the drunk's neck. His deep voice said, "Do I trust you, filth? You wouldn't wreck our friendship, would you?"

"They're gone. Please, please. It's true. It's true."

"When did they go?"

"Tonight." The old man was crying.

"Alone? Or did someone take them? Don't lie."

"Alone. Alone."

"Where?"

"I don't know."

The alien slapped the drunk's face. "Where?"

"I don't know, I don't know, I don't know."

Like someone throwing away an empty box the alien shoved the old man against the sidewalk. The grizzled head hit the pavement; blood ran into the gutter. "Holy mother Jesus," Jacobi whispered.

Unhurriedly the alien took some sort of thin handgun from inside his shirt. Laser probably, because he used it to cut a hole in the door, though Jacobi didn't see any beam of light. The alien reached his hand inside as if to open the lock, but a moment later withdrew it. Try again mister, Jacobi thought, you'll never get a New York lock open that way. The alien ran his gun up and down the door, just inside the locks. Jacobi heard a hiss and then the door swung open.

The alien spent less than two minutes inside before he walked slowly to his car. Something in the careful graceful movements scared Jacobi more than the earlier explosion of force. As he watched the car head east, maybe toward the spaceport, he thought, *get out of here. Cops'll come along. Get out.* His eyes refused to leave the drunk lying in the gutter. Cliché, he thought, drunks, gutters. Oily street water mingled with the blood. Jacobi imagined he could taste it. Sick, he thought. Gonna be sick. Get away. His legs moved, he reached the corner, ran north on Second Avenue. The garbage city air sliced into his lungs but he kept on running. "Bastards!" he panted. "Goddamn mother cracking *bastards*!"

Part Two

Chapter Eight

The Worker called the Gardener hunched up his thick shoulders as if they could cover his face. He hated walking through the grimy corridors of a Worker's Refuge, the combination dormitory-recreation center set up in every port for landside Workers. He hated all of them and Luritti was the worst. That vile red dust poured through the air filters (the best available, they *said*; they kept the air clean enough for the execs, he guessed), cutting your chest open with every breath. On Luritti even the Refuge made you feel covered in oily mud.

On either side of the narrow corridor the metal doors leaked solitary noises from the cubicles. Most of the Workers spent their planet hours dancing Ghost, a practice the Gardener detested. When he could he spent his time in woods or at least parks, even places like the blue moss caves on Hrrhrrhrrhrru, anywhere growing. On so many of the worlds, however, the companies had sliced every tree and scrub fern within a hundred dots of port, so where else could you go but the Refuge?

Like most Workers the Gardener never mixed with the local population (mostly outworlders in the port itself, but you could go out and see the market people unless the companies had altered or erased them). You didn't become a Worker unless you liked solitude, and then the work nurtured that preference into a compulsion. When the companies first built the Refuges they

supplied them with every kind of recreation they could possibly
think of, from party girls and boys (from age nine, and if you
wanted younger they'd get that as well) to sport simulation
chambers. The Workers had huddled in the corners, glaring
suspiciously at each other. So they took out the green halls and
put in cubicles, small and dirty but private. Each Refuge
contained a kind of café; usually Workers went there only to buy
angelshit, sell angelshit, or fight.

The Gardener hated it all. When he couldn't find a green spot
he simply lay on the cot in the cubicle, thinking of Arbol. Arbol,
where the World Tree filled the sky and its roots ran down to the
center of the globe. As he stepped outside and the dusty, oily air
slammed against the scarf mask covering his head, he clutched
the single amber leaf in his pocket, the only memento he carried
from his single visit to the World of Joy and the lower levels of
the Tree.

The acceleration scramblers lowered the *g* effect as the crawl
engines lifted the Gardener into orbit. Behind the live space,
Luritti ore filled the cargo hold. The Gardener didn't go look at
it even once while he arranged his pitiful few plants on the green
floor, on the corners of his jelly bed, and on top of the solid air
table. His Gxggn red prickly spine plant waved its thick spores in
anger at the artificial light and flat recycled air. "I know," the
Gardener murmured. "Just a few more years and then we retire.
I'll take you to the Tree then. You know I promised." Very
carefully he laid the amber leaf on a small black realwood shelf
above the 'mitt. With a sigh he hooked the fant wires to his head,
ready for the first jump series on the way to Ktaner's Planet.

No matter how much a Worker enjoys his fants he still must
rest between series. Despite his head world—the fantasies he
weaves around him—the Grey Nothing presses on him, never
quite blocked out by even the strongest mental creations. So the
Gardener rested for two ship standard days, tending his plants,
running his holotapes of Arbolian ceremonies. Cracks in the
tapes opened gaps in the projected scenes, like the ultimate
reality of non-space breaking into the illusion of the material
universe. The Gardener shifted in his seat. A great many
Workers secretly believed the universe only another fantasy;
most of them kept the idea secret.

At last the brain monitor (mandatory in each ship but not

used by many Workers) judged his wave structures strong enough, with only a few jagged lines and "understructures," for a new jump series. He put on his wire helmet and watched the needle register a connection of his lower ego wave levels with the alter engines. Soon another mission done, written up towards retirement. His eyes glazed over, the ship dissolved into a sun flooded live space high in the top levels of the Tree. Dimly the Worker felt the ship kick into its first jump.

Terror shattered the Gardener's fant world like a shell fired at a wall. Outside the ship—no, inside, in his face, in his skin—the Grey Nothing, empty for all eternity, blazed with fire. Flat, stretched out on all sides in the dimensionless non-reality, flames beat against the ship.

Out, the Gardener thought. Get out, get out, anywhere. He slammed the jump override, hit an outpost—

And the terror followed. Fleshing out to a tentacled fireball in the four dimensional world it hung there, vast, angry, while the ship scrambled wildly to get away from it. But only for a moment.

A wave of energy smashed against the thin cocoon of metal. Inside, the Gardener grasped for his Arbolian leaf; it sprang away from him.

And then the shrieker, hungry from its exile, swallowed him.

Chapter Nine

Gloria McCloskey—"Glory" people used to call her, years ago, before her figure filled out—lifted the coffee urn, then set it down again. She frowned at the clock. Seven thirty. Why did she get up so early? Such a useless habit. Before the kids had gone off to college—certainly didn't stay long, after all the work she and Mac had done to get them there—before Mac had died, she used to get up at six o'clock just so she could drink a quiet cup before the house erupted. Now she couldn't sleep past seven. She looked again at the coffee and sighed. She got so jittery from it. Maybe she should try that syn stuff again.

She looked outside at the lawn covered in dew. Billy hadn't raked up all the leaves before he'd run off to his football game. Charged enough, didn't he? She supposed she'd have to speak to him.

She thought—for what, the hundredth time?—that maybe she really should dump the house. About twice a week she came that close to putting the suburban development house on the market. It was just so big, three bedrooms, a den as well as a living room, a finished playroom in the basement (filled with cartons of her children's books, clothes, and junk, but a new owner could clean it up), and a good-sized lawn that got harder and harder to keep up. She remembered all the summers she used to slavedrive the kids, Mac, herself—get up the weeds, put down the grass, plant the trees, spray the tomatoes—Gloria chuckled. She remembered when the rest of the family had organized into a union and drawn up a list of demands, beginning with "Half day—twelve hours—on Sunday."

Too big, she thought. She'd sell it, she really would, except, well, where else could she go? Apartments had gotten so scarce, even in a small city like Beacon, seventy miles north of New York. People had just stopped building everywhere. She couldn't blame them—with those aliens sitting in New York like that, what kind of plans could anyone make?—but it sure made things rough for people who wanted to move.

Sometimes she thought her sister Marilyn had the right idea. Maybe she should join her. She giggled. *Her* in the underground.

But of course Marilyn didn't exactly fit the general picture of a radical either. Middle-aged, a little plump, always so tired looking. Gloria shuddered, remembering the questions asked by all those government agents. She'd amazed herself then; not only had she convinced them she knew nothing of Marilyn's whereabouts but she thought she'd even gotten them to doubt the seriousness of Marilyn's involvement. "I don't care what your spies say. It's just silly. I know all about the feminism, but this is different. No, I haven't seen her, didn't I tell you that, but I certainly know my own sister." Gloria sat down at the formica breakfast bar. She grimaced as she gave in and poured herself another cup of coffee. Now what could she do to get through another boring day?

She jumped when the doorbell rang. Who— Old fears leaped up to clog her throat as she crossed the carpet and opened the door.

A young man and woman stood huddled in the small entranceway. It took her a second before she recognized the hunched over man as her nephew. "Humphrey!" she said and breathed again, suddenly conscious of her pounding heart. "What a surprise. Come in."

The two of them shuffled inside, looking very cold and very tired. Something about the girl struck Gloria as odd. Her skin was a peculiar color, Asian maybe, but it wasn't that. Something she couldn't pinpoint. The girl stared openly at the house, as if she'd never seen anything so strange. "Gloria," Humphrey said, "this is Vicky." He waved feebly at her.

"Hello," Vicky said. She sounded *so* tired. "I'm sorry to

bother you." Her voice might have been pleasant, with a little sleep.

"No, no. I'm just surprised. Humphrey, you know I always like visitors." She laughed, feeling foolish.

"We should have called," said her nephew, actually her second cousin on Mac's side. He looked so much like his mother, God knows whatever happened to her, running off to Arizona for a three way marriage— "We decided to leave the city so suddenly," he went on, "we would have had to call during the night, so we figured—"

"Humphrey, it's okay. Really. I'm delighted." Awkward silence. She realized suddenly they hadn't brought any luggage. "There's fresh coffee," she said.

"Great," Humphrey said. The girl had already crossed to the bookcase Mac had built years ago. The way she examined the books reminded Gloria of Marilyn. "Vicky," Gloria asked, "how about a cup of coffee?"

The girl smiled. "Hey okay," she said and turned back to the books. Something about her, maybe that funny smirk as she looked around, made Gloria uncomfortable. But she liked the girl.

"Come in the dinette, kids," she called. The two of them sat at the breakfast bar, like refugees or people rescued from a fire, huddled over, green. "I'd better make some eggs," Gloria said nervously.

"Don't bother," Humphrey said. "We can get it."

"Don't be silly. It's a pleasure cooking for someone besides myself." She threw some bread in the toaster.

"How are Helen and John?"

"You tell me," she laughed.

"Don't they write?"

"Are you kidding? Too much trouble."

"That's really crummy." He sounded so distant, trying to be nice. Light years away, as they said on television. "Where are they? Or don't they even tell you that?"

"Helen's still in Colorado."

"Working?"

"Hopefully. Or begging. As long as she's not walking the streets."

"And John?"

"He sent me an air letter two months ago from Guatemala, complaining that the Indians were racist because they wouldn't

let him join their religion or something." She and Humphrey
laughed; the girl only stared at the table. Smirking.

"How are things in the city?"

"Rotten."

"Are you from New York too, Vicky?"

The girl shook her head. "No. My father and I moved around
a lot, but I've never been to New York before."

"Gloria," Humphrey broke in, "can we stay here for a couple
of days?"

She stared, amazed, at the pleading in his face. "Yes, of
course. You can stay in the children's rooms upstairs."

"Thanks." The two of them drooped back in their chairs.

Gloria wanted to ask what was wrong, wanted them to
confide in her as her children did—years ago. She didn't dare.
They'd built some barrier around themselves. Like her children.
Like all children, she supposed.

"Here's the eggs," she said cheerfully, dishing out a couple of
plates. She smeared butter on the toast and set it on the plates.
"Served with a smile."

"Thanks, Gloria," Humphrey said. The girl was already
gulping down the food. Nothing strange about her appetite.

"How did you get here, by the way?"

"Hitchhiked."

"At night? Isn't that dangerous?"

"We got a ride in a truck almost the whole way."

"Why didn't you wait until morning?"

Vicky looked up. "My fault. I couldn't stand New York any
longer, too many strange things crawling around. Then Hump
told me what a nice house you had, and I wouldn't let him sleep."

Gloria couldn't decide whether to trust that smirk or get
insulted. "I'll go make the beds. Don't argue, just sit and relax."
She walked hurriedly through the living room to the stairs.
Better make up both bedrooms, she thought, let them decide
whether to sleep apart or together.

For some reason she whistled when she came down, as if
they'd want a warning. They were sitting silently, holding their
coffee cups. "Let me know if it's too cold up there and I'll turn up
the heat." They stood up.

Humphrey said, "Listen, Gloria—"

"Now please. Don't worry about putting me out or anything
like that. I'm thrilled to have company. At any hour. So don't get
churned, all right?" She smiled at using the kids' slang.

"It isn't that, really." He paused. "There's a very outside

chance that someone might come here, and, uh, ask about us."

"Oh. Oh, I see." She swallowed, managed a smile. "And you want me to pretend I haven't seen you for months and haven't the faintest idea how to find you."

"Yeah, I mean, you can give them my address in the city."

"You don't have to give me instructions. I've got experience, you know. More than you."

"I'm sorry."

"Don't be. I just wanted you to know." She sighed. "You two go to sleep. We can talk about it when you wake up. All right?"

"Thanks, Gloria," Humphrey said. "Thanks a lot."

Vicky looked up, hugging herself as if she still stood in the road, waiting for a ride. "Thank you," she said. "Thank you very much." The smirk had vanished.

After a moment's silence Vicky turned abruptly and marched upstairs. As Hump dragged himself after her, Gloria thought how she'd seen that kind of sunken look before, in the mirror when she'd discovered herself caught in things beyond her knowledge and meager powers. She walked slowly back to the kitchen and the dishes.

Filling the eaves of the small house, the two upstairs bedrooms were decorated traditionally, a boy room and a girl room. The one on the left was all pink and fluffy with dolls lying on a quilted bedspread, the one on the right done in browns with seashells and rock collections mounted over a rolltop desk. Vanity didn't look at either before she chose the one on the right.

Hump grabbed her arm. "Hold it," he said. "We've got to settle something first."

"For burst's sake, let go of me."

"I could still dump you, you know. I could turn you in."

"Good. As long as I get some sleep."

"You goddamn— Listen, I've involved my family now, it's not just me. If you don't start showing some—"

"What do you want me to do?"

"For a start, tell me about that guy you described to Gari. The big one with the hair. Was that Jaak?" She shook her head. "Then who?"

"A man named Loper."

"Where does he come in?"

Vanity inclined her head towards the bedroom. "Let's go in there."

As they sat down in two wooden chairs near the window,

Hump noticed that Gloria had closed the curtains. Vanity stared at the thin green carpet. "Loper used to work for Jaak. He was once the company's chief pilot, taking Jaak around and doing the jobs that didn't get channeled down for SA inspection."

"What happened to him?"

She looked up with that infuriating blank expression. "He tried to rape me."

"Did he succeed?"

"Yes, of course he succeeded. Idiot. We were all alone in a spaceship. How could I stop him?"

She was baiting him, Hump knew; start an argument and you can avoid telling the truth. He said, "That still doesn't tell me why you're more scared of him than Daddy."

"Oh, all right. Anything so I can go to sleep." Beneath the bravado her voice wavered. "Jaak—Jaak wants me because he owns me. It's that simple. I've stolen something that belongs to him, myself, so he's angry. I understand Jaak. I know his power and how he uses it. But Loper—Hump, no one knows anything about Loper, what he wants, why he does things, what he can or can't do, anything. I know he can do things with a spaceship that no one else even thinks is possible. But *why* he does anything— A fant teacher once got Loper to sit down for a head map."

"What's that?"

"Oh, it's just a mapping of the wave structures of someone's brain. They use it to train people."

"Oh." Train them for what, he wondered.

"The point is, she couldn't understand Loper's map at all, it made no sense to her. There's something perfect about Loper, horribly perfect. He's so precise and so filthy empty."

"He got passionate enough to go after you."

"That's just it. The whole time he was raping me I had no idea why. It wasn't for the sex, I'm sure of that. He didn't even come until the very end, and only then as some kind of extra insult, like *I* expected it. He made it seem like he was paying me by filling me up with his blood filthy slime."

"You sound like it went on for awhile."

"Yes, it went on. Days I think. He made it clear he could keep it going as long as he wanted. Months if he felt like it."

"Months?"

"It wasn't just in and out, Hump. It was—he did things to me, first my head, my fantasies. He'd gotten ahold of this machine which could trap you in a snake, that's a kind of waking nightmare, and just keep you locked inside it until you start screaming and begging him to stop. He did it all in non-space so—"

"Wait a second. What's non-space?"

She hesitated only a moment. "It's what a ship jumps through to get from one place to another. It's horrible. The Workers call it the Grey Nothing. You can't imagine it. Even with all the walls opaqued it presses on you like some huge animal. Except it's completely flat. And you could never call it alive. Loper probably loves it there. His true home. He's even found some way to stay there as long as he wants. Most people just want to get out."

"Could someone have gone in and got you? I mean if he had tried to keep you there."

"You don't understand. On the outside no time passes at all. But you can't tell that in the Nothing. It can seem hours or days, except Loper's found some way to make that weeks. Anyway, you're getting me off the story. The best part's coming, so pay attention."

"I just want to know what's going on."

"Shut up. I told you to pay attention. When he'd worked on my head for awhile he finally decided to move on to my body. He had a way of stroking me—oh *burst*."

"You don't have to—"

"*Shut up*. He made me swallow things, burning things, things that knotted me up or exploded me inside, things that gave off a smell like a dead bork. He put things inside me, Hump. Filth things. And my skin—" Vanity's face took on a cloudy look, her voice dull and monotonous while her mind, so used to fantasies, took her back to Loper's spaceship. "There's these little things—the Company's biologists developed them, I think for the security people—they're like insects, very small, and you can put them under the skin, with an incision. And then they crawl around inside."

"Oh Jesus," Hump said. He wanted to run.

"And all the time, all the time I never could figure out *why* he was doing it."

"And he still wants you."

Vanity didn't hear him. She shook her head wildly back and forth as if the memories could fly out of her ears. Then she made her hands hard, like flat wooden boards, and slapped them against her thighs. A ritual gesture, Hump guessed, and wondered if she'd invented it or if someone had taught it to her for god knows what reason. Either way he hoped it worked.

"Anyway," she said, "Loper's really responsible for bringing us together. So I guess we should thank him. We could send him a talking postcard."

"What? How did he do that?"

"Well, not directly. Something happened in space, a breakdown that could have gotten Jaak and the whole company in a whole lot of trouble. They needed someone who could get rid of the problem—they call it a shrieker—before the SA found out about it. And for that they needed Loper. AAri contacted him and apparently—they didn't tell me but I can guess—Loper demanded a prize."

"You."

"Jackpot. That's how I got away. When Loper came to pick up the ship—"

"What ship?"

She grinned, and Hump thought he'd never seen a more beautiful face. "The *Golden Vanity*, of course."

"What?"

"Jaak's two favorite possessions bear the same name. The ship came first. Jaak and Loper designed it together years ago, a special one-man smuggler, courier, and all-around emergency ship. The *Golden Vanity* can do anything, especially with Loper working the controls. When he left he tried to take it, but Jaak put it under a barrier as soon as I told him Loper had attacked me. I don't think Loper expected me to do that, tell Jaak. He had to leave in the first ship he could jerk from a docking ramp. Anyway, as part of the deal for killing Jaak's shrieker, Loper demanded the *Golden Vanity*. They couldn't really refuse since no other ship has such elaborate equipment."

"Did he succeed?"

"How do I know? I suppose so. Anyway, Jaak decided he would trick poor stupid Loper. Whatever he promised he meanwhile planned to spirit me away to some nothing planet on the edge."

"Except you escaped."

"Yeah. I skipped off on my own. Right to you."

"How wonderful. It's enough to make me religious. Why did you think it was Loper when Gari told us about the men?"

"I didn't. I was scared it might be. You don't know him, Hump."

"Thank god. Do you really think he can find you all by himself?"

"I told you, no one knows what Loper can do."

Hump rubbed his eyes. "I wish I could say I felt reassured by all these revelations. I asked for it, though. Thanks, I guess. Do you want to sleep in here?"

She shrugged. "Sure."

"See you later." Gloomily he walked to the other room. Vanity closed the door.

"She looks like a lovely girl," Gloria said. "How long have you been seeing her? Or shouldn't I pry? My children would probably say I'll never learn." Busily she put away the extra food she'd brought (going to a shopping center miles from her usual stores) while Humphrey sat there, gloomily staring at the floor, saying almost nothing. Vicky was still asleep. "You know, I used to think what a terrible person I must be the way my children talked about me. The worst part was when I visited them at school. I could just imagine their friends thinking—"

"Gloria," Humphrey cut her off. She froze, squatting in front of the cabinet. "I want to see Marilyn."

Using her hand on the counter Gloria heaved herself to her feet. She walked over to the dinette and sat down. "I thought so," she said. "I wish you wouldn't, Humphrey. Really I do."

He shook his head.

"Believe me, Gloria. So do I. You can take my word for it."

"Then why—" She stopped, cast her eyes toward the ceiling. "All right, I won't try to stop you. I just hope you're making your own choice, that no one's forcing you. Because Humphrey, once you get involved you can't stop. You do realize that, don't you?"

He shrugged. "I'm sorry. I said I wouldn't pry. But there's one thing more I must ask you. Look at me. If I help you, will I some day regret it? Bitterly? I love you, Humphrey, but I love my sister more. If I help you, will I be hurting her?"

"Believe me, Gloria, the last thing in the world I want is to hurt Marilyn. Or you."

She sighed. "All right then. I suppose I have no right to ask anything more than that."

"You do know how to find her, don't you? I never believed the official line."

Gloria made a face. "Do I know how to find my own sister? What a strange time. Do you think they realize what they've done to our lives? Do they have any idea?"

He shook his head.

"God," she said. "I hate them. Sitting in their great big starships. Sometimes I really hate them." Humphrey looked at her blankly, an annoying trick that she'd never seen before. She sighed. "Will you stay here for a few days?"

"I wish we could, Gloria. But I think— Well, maybe a couple of days."

"Good. Then let's forget about everything and pretend it's a family holiday."

He managed to smile. "Sure," he said miserably.

Vanity took delightedly to the family holiday, dancing (totally off the beat) while Gloria pounded the old piano in the basement, playing Scrabble and Space War, looking at Gloria's endless family scrapbooks. At first Hump worried that someone might realize Gloria had guests. Somehow, though, without a word spoken, the two women never raised their voices, never left on too many lights, never even sat too close to the curtained windows. At one point Gloria walked over to Hump curled on the couch and patted his head. "My sister once stayed here for five days—sick—and not even the druggist guessed a thing."

"Well, I guess so," Hump said. Later he watched sourly while Gloria and Vanity giggled over pictures of Hump as a fat wobbly baby.

Hump lay awake on the big soft bed, looking at the moonlight pierce a bare patch of window above the pink ruffled curtains. Tomorrow, he thought. Tomorrow night we get out of here. He wished he could get up and read, but he didn't dare turn on a light.

A noise. Frightened whimpers. Hump sat up. The noises ended, replaced by sharp sobs. He grunted. Vanity crying? How disgustingly human. How earthy. The sound pulled at him, like the jerk of a wire. The hell with her, he thought, and turned over. The cries stopped. Good, he thought, let me go to sleep. But a moment later, when they started up again, Hump sat up in bed. "Goddamn it," he muttered. He got up, grabbed his pants, threw them down again, and marched across the tiny hallway in his underwear.

Vanity turned her head as he entered the room, then turned it back again to stare rigidly ahead. She was sitting up in bed, naked, the nightgown Gloria had given her thrown on the floor. Her chest heaved despite her attempt to stop crying, and Hump grinned as he saw how furious it made her that she couldn't control herself. He sat down on the bed.

His own breath shortened as he watched Vanity's breasts (she made no effort to cover them) bob with each gulp of air. Though he forced himself to raise his eyes he couldn't make his voice anything but resentful as he asked, "Is something wrong?"

"Go away," she said. Sniff.

He looked about, saw a box of tissues on the desk. He gave her one. "Glad to," he told her as she blew her nose.

He was at the door when her voice stopped him. "Hump. Please don't go."

He sighed. "Why? So you can distract yourself by ridiculing me?"

She laughed between sniffs. "Sure. What's wrong with that?"

"Everything." But he sat down and put his arms around her. To his amazement she leaned into him. He said, "You've really wigged yourself, haven't you?" His arm grew heavy as her breasts pushed against his chest.

"I had a dream," she said.

"You shouldn't take those things so seriously."

"I feel so wierd. Like nothing's real."

"You dreamt about the red door again."

"How did— Oh, I told you, didn't I?"

"Just that it had a red door. You want to tell me the rest?" While he waited for her to pull away with some sarcastic comment, he let his hands slide down her back and along her waist.

"It starts differently each time," she said, "but it always ends the same."

"How did it start this time?"

"I was back on my ship, jumping, running away, I mean, and I kept trying to go faster and faster because something was chasing me, just outside the walls. Some kind of animal."

"In space?"

"Yeah. And I was naked, I remember. But something, little creatures inside the ship, kept biting me." She stopped for breath.

"It's all right," Hump muttered. "You're awake now."

"Then I landed, but when I jumped out of the ship I found myself in the tunnel again. That's when the real dream started. It always starts in the tunnel. It's got stone walls, except they're perfectly smooth and straight. The ceiling and floor too. And down at the end I can see the door, a red door that takes up the whole wall."

"Red. The color of blood?"

"Huh? Oh. I never thought of that." She shivered.

"Go on."

"I never want to walk but I can't help it, it gets so cold whenever I stop. So I start walking." Hump held her tighter, thinking what a rat he was as he stroked her back. "And while I walk, this horrible yellow slime oozes along the cracks between the floor and the walls and the ceiling. It keeps coming closer to my feet but it never really touches them. But as it gets closer I start to run, so fast I can't even breathe. And then the noise starts."

"Noise?" He stroked her hair.

"Just loud noises, voices but more like animals than people, banging, screams, explosions, things being ripped apart, laughter, I think, but horrible, and just a *roaring* all the time. All of it mixed up together. I put my hands on my ears but that only makes it worse until I start to scream myself. And I can't even hear myself. Then there's a great boom and the door breaks open, but I always wake up before I can really see."

"No wonder that closet door scared you. But you're awake now, you know."

"I don't know." She shook her head against him.

He placed his hand on her chest. "See. Solid. Like rock."

"In my dream I touched myself and my hand went right through, like a cold holo."

He stroked her thigh. "Solid."

One more sob came out as she fell against him. "Hump, what can we do?"

"It's all right," he told her. "Brave Sir Humphrey has arranged everything. Tomorrow we get to someplace safe."

"Safe? Some dumb little gang trying to throw out the companies and their own government with homemade bombs and pamphlets? How can you call that safe?"

For the first time Hump didn't get angry; she was right, of course, but mostly he only half listened, distracted by her soft clear skin. "Their dumbness works for us, though you better not tell Marilyn that."

"What do you mean?"

He kissed her shoulder before he answered, "Well, it's the kind of place your father would never think to look for you." He let his lips move down to the top of her right breast while his hands moved around her hips to the tops of her thighs. Silently he commanded her, "Melt, space lady, melt."

She sighed as he kissed her nipple and then she lifted his head to kiss him on the lips, a long open kiss, and Hump thought, "Bingo." He fumbled off his shorts with one hand, then swung his legs into the bed and scrambled under the covers. Vanity was sliding her hands down his back and Hump feared he'd go off before the proper moment. Like a spaceship taking off without a passenger. He kissed her neck and then his body shook as she held him tightly against her. *It's for real*, Hump thought.

She kissed his lips and then his neck; a queasiness settled on him. *She's too damn cold-blooded*, he thought, and tried to pull back but Vanity only held tighter. When she wrapped a leg around him, his half erection dwindled to nothing.

"Is this galactic position number one?" he murmured.

"Shh."

Moving his hips back so she wouldn't notice his weakness Hump kissed her breasts, then her side, her belly— "Uhh!" He drew back so suddenly he hit his head against the sloped ceiling and didn't even notice. Her belly—hair—*hair* covered her belly. *Alien*, his mind screamed. *Animal*.

"Hump, what's wrong?" He shook his head. "Why did you—Oh. Oh, of course." She laughed. "You people don't have any hair there."

"Animal," he snarled at her.

"Don't be a borkson idiot. Belly hair doesn't make anyone less human."

"On this world it does."

"The people on Gthnu have no hair at all, the ones on—" she made a whistling noise "—are covered with hair, Terropians grow hair on their feet and legs and nowhere else. They've also got seven toes. So what?"

"So what? How can you make love to someone with seven toes?"

"Easy. We're used to it." She grabbed his hand. "Come on. Touch." He let her move his hand up and down her belly. "See? Nice and soft. Now kiss." Hump swallowed, then brought his lips down to graze her skin; the hair tickled. Suddenly he bit her.

"Ow!" Vanity hollered. "You burst of slime." The two of

Chapter Ten

Early the next morning Gloria drove them to the river's edge, two blocks from the train station, kissed them goodbye, with an extra hug for Vanity, and then drove home again before any of the neighbors would wake up for work. Silently Hump and Vanity watched the polluted Hudson, its dead fish and chips of wood floating on oil slicks, until they judged the station had been open for more than an hour. Shivering (Gloria had given them old woolen jackets her children had left behind, but the thin plaid didn't keep out the autumn chill) they walked to the station and bought tickets for Yonkers, just north of New York. A few minutes later they took a southbound New York train that required they change at Harmon, where they left the platform and bought a ticket north for Albany, the state capital. In Albany they walked from the train station to the bus station, where they bought a ticket for Boston. They got off at Springfield.

Tired, they trudged through the small city, impatiently snapping at each other until at last they found the address Gloria had given them, a small apartment building in a shopping area. In front of the house sat a parked car two or three years old. With a set of keys Gloria had given them Hump and Vanity drove the car out of town to a rundown motel called The Springfield Rest. It was early evening.

The clerk, a middle-aged paunchy man with baggy eyes, pudgy hands and a face dotted with pimples took their registration as Mr. And Mrs. Joe Lang so smoothly that Hump was sure they'd made a mistake and gone to the wrong motel. Neither of them relaxed until an hour later when Hump looked out the window to find that someone had driven away the car.

It would have been curious to watch Vanity confront the room if not for their fears and exhaustions. With its two saggy beds, its red synthetic cloth chairs with broken springs, its color teev almost as bad as Hump's, its faded brown walls and yellowed curtains, its thin red carpet and stiff sheets, the miserable room stood about as far from Golden Vanity's experience as her spaceship compared to a moped. Who knows, Hump thought, maybe motels fill the universe. He imagined a billboard on an asteroid, "Spacehop at the Galactic Rest."

Without a word Vanity sunk into the supposed easy chair and closed her eyes. Hump took a shower and shaved; when he came out Vanity lay asleep on one of the beds. After a moment's doubt Hump crawled into the other one.

Sometime during the night, Vanity slipped into Hump's bed, her body hot, her face cold. Before Hump could even kiss her she fell back asleep.

Vanity was in the shower the next morning when Hump awoke with a headache and a greasy face from the old-fashioned radiators. He staggered out of the bed to part the curtains enough for a look at the sunlight on the gravel parking lot. What do we do now, he wondered, certain Gloria had sent them on a fantasy ride. He yanked open the night table drawer. There lay the Bible, the same one the Gideons had sent to the aliens. He could spend the time converting Vanity if he believed in anything himself.

The doorbell rang. Hump jumped like a shocked cat. Fumbling on a bathrobe from the small suitcase Gloria had given them, he hollered, "Get dressed," then ran to the door. Scowling at his own terror he yanked it open.

A tall heavy woman stood there, not as round as Gloria, but thicker, big-breasted, wide-hipped. She was wearing little makeup on her surprisingly youngish skin, her light brown hair was cut short and simple; she wore a shapeless red coat open over a man's white shirt and dark green cuffed trousers, an old brown shoulder bag, scuffed boots. Hump stared at her extraordinary ordinariness.

She stared back at him. "Hump. What the hell?" Before he could answer she shoved him inside to storm into the room and slam the door. "What are you doing here?"

"Gloria sent me."

"Oh wonderful. Perfect. I tell my sister a system worked out for emergencies and she uses it for family reunions."

"For God's sake, Marilyn, I need help."

"Do you? Well, I'm afraid I'm not running a social service system. I don't know what the hell is wrong with Gloria."

"It's my fault. I didn't give her a chance. Please don't—"

"Oh, scram the apologies."

"Will you just listen?"

"No. I've got to decide what to do with you, and then I've got to get out of here. I've got no time to listen to your troubles. Look, Hump, I like you, you know that, but so what? I can't—" She stopped. Vanity was standing in the bathroom doorway. A smile twitched on Marilyn's face; she cut it off. "Has my sister sent me a whole touring company?"

Hump said, "Marilyn, this is Vicky."

"Vicky what?"

"Uh, Vicky Katz."

"All right, Vicky Katz, what are you doing here?"

As Vanity's face took on that blank look of hers, Hump prayed she wouldn't drive Marilyn right out the door with some sarcastic remark. She said instead, "We want to join you."

"Join me in what?"

"In getting rid of the aliens."

Marilyn nodded. "And how will you do that? Push them all in their ships and tell them to go home?"

"We'll let you decide how to do it. We just want to help."

Hump broke in, "We're in trouble, Marilyn."

"Shut up," she told him, her eyes on Vanity. "What will you do if I send you away?"

Vanity shrugged. "Try to do something ourselves."

"And suppose you get caught. What do you tell them about me?"

"Since we don't know anything, nothing."

"You know this place." She turned to Hump. "How did you get here? Your route." He described their zigzag journey. "All right," she nodded. Hump thought, it's all over, she'll never take us. To his surprise she said, "Let me think." After a moment she sighed. "I've got no choice, I suppose. Either I take you two along or change the whole system. Get your stuff together."

Hump threw on clothes while Vanity stuffed their suitcase. Outside, Marilyn led them to an old station wagon where another woman, younger, about thirty five, sat at the steering wheel. When they'd all climbed inside, Marilyn said, "Ann, meet Hump, a cousin of mine."

Ann's eyes widened. "A cousin?"

"And this is Vicky Katz." Ann stared briefly at Vanity. "Let's get going," Marilyn said.

They drove slowly along the old winding highway, past bare trees and damp mossy rocks until they reached a picnic rest stop, where Ann pulled over beside a table covered in wet leaves. "Blindfold time," she said and turned around with two heavy gray sashes.

Vanity jerked back. "What does she mean?" she asked Hump.

"They don't want us to know where we're going. It's all right."

Vanity shook her head. "No, I don't want that thing on my eyes." Her face took on that frightened look of nightmare, of unsought visions. Her reaction had nothing to do with secrecy, Hump realized, or trust; the blindfold itself scared her. "I won't look," she promised. "I wouldn't even remember anything."

"You take the blindfold or you leave," Marilyn said.

"Let me talk to her," Hump said. "Vicky, nothing bad'll happen. I'll go first so you can watch. Okay?" Vanity said nothing; suddenly she made a noise and snatched the cloth. After she'd tied it around her eyes and Ann had reached over to make sure it was tight, Vanity sat back heavily and folded her arms, her hands in fists. Hump turned sideways for Ann to tie his blindfold.

The trip took somewhere between twenty minutes and an hour. By their slower speed and constant curves Hump guessed they'd left the highway for most of the trip. He thought also they were climbing into the Berkshire Hills, but he couldn't really tell. They passed other cars, going either way, only twice.

For the last few minutes the car turned onto a rough dirt road. When they stopped and Ann took the blindfolds off, Hump and Vanity discovered themselves by a large wooden house surrounded by dense trees. Behind them the road sloped down through the woods, and the steepness, plus a sharp drop in temperature told Hump they must have climbed quite high into the mountains; the trees made it impossible to really tell. As they all walked to the house, Vanity looked around with that eager curiousity that arose in the oddest moments to swamp her fears.

Inside, the house showed the elegant casualness of a rich man's country retreat: giant living room with a picture window showing the trees, paneled walls, fireplace, big cushiony wooden furniture in yellows and greens, a large well-equipped kitchen, a bare wooden staircase leading to the upstairs bedrooms. But the servants had gone, and the good china dishes lay scattered about the living room and kitchen while dirty clothes filled a chair and a bright blanket with two pillows lay before the ash-filled fireplace.

While Ann made them all tea Marilyn removed the message recorder from the telephone and took it into one of the back rooms. Hump and Vanity stared gloomily out the window at the dead grass lit by the sunlight.

"Come in the kitchen," Ann called. They brought in the dirty dishes with them, and Hump set them on the dishwasher while Ann put out cups. "Thanks," she laughed. "We do so much of the good work here we never get to clean up."

"How long have you known Marilyn?" Hump asked.

"A couple of years." Ann had a round pleasant face with pursed lips that made her look slightly doll-like. She wore wide white trousers and a heavy brown sweater. She looked a little like a big lumpy quilt.

"Do you like doing the good work?" Hump said.

She grinned. "It's all right. It's exciting when it's not scary or discouraging. Though a lot of times I just get tired. Basically, you know, it's a lot of garbage work, good old routine drudgery." There was a moment's silence as Hump decided not to ask about what the drudgery led to, the "choreographed" riots in Washington, the bombs hidden in food shipments to the spaceports. Maybe, he thought, Marilyn just dealt with the propaganda side.

"Anyway," Ann said, "it gets us this place for the winter."

"Wouldn't it be a lot nicer in the summer?"

"That's for sure. But the kind family who lets us use it like to come here themselves in the summer. Besides, there's neighbors around in the summer." She filled the teapot with hot water. "Grab the cups and we'll go inside."

"How do you get out when the snows come?"

"Fold-down helicar in the basement." She grinned. "But

don't expect any joy rides. It's all locked up. Marilyn wears the keys around her neck with a little device that gives off a nasty shock if anyone but her touches it."

Vanity was fidgeting, crossing and uncrossing her legs, staring around the room. Now she jerked her head up to ask, "This helicar thing. Could we use it to get out if someone comes after us?"

"I suppose we could all squeeze in. Are you expecting someone?"

Hump said, "She worries a lot."

"We all do." Her face kept its pleasant softness as she stared at Vanity. "No one's found our winter refuge yet. Why should anyone now?"

"Maybe they haven't known how to look."

"Then what would suddenly inspire them?" The soft voice prodded like a gently pushing hand.

Marilyn's voice came from the doorway. "Maybe the aliens will teach them." As Marilyn sat down by the window, Ann quietly poured the tea. "What do you think, Vicky, will the aliens start looking for us?"

Hump broke in, "How should we know what the aliens will do?"

"Be quiet, Hump."

"Sugar?" Ann called. Hump nodded; Vanity paid no attention.

Marilyn took the cup handed out to her. "All right, Vicky, you want to join the Earth Resistance Movement. What can you do for us?"

"Whatever you ask."

"Not good enough. Why should we do your thinking for you?"

"How can I say what I'll do until I know what you do?"

"Don't you read newspapers? Haven't you read any articles or pamphlets from our surface division?"

"I'm illiterate."

"Also arrogant. Well if you don't know about us how did you know you wanted to join us?"

"I didn't. Hump decided that."

"And he decided by family loyalty, no doubt. Do you believe in family loyalty, Vicky?"

"No. People in families eat each other."

"How vivid." Marilyn leaned back against the chair and

closed her eyes. Nearly half a minute passed before she jerked her head forward again. She said slowly, "Suppose I said I planned to return you to your father. What would you offer me, Golden Vanity?"

"Goddamn it," Hump said. Hot tea spilled on his leg. "Shit!" He threw the cup against the fireplace. Ann was staring at her toes.

"How did you find out?" Vanity said. "What do you know about me?"

"That doesn't matter."

"You filthy market beast. That's all that does matter."

Hump muttered, "Vanity, scram your goddamn mouth. We're stuck here."

"Thanks to you."

Marilyn laughed. "Don't worry, Hump. Bad manners don't disturb me."

Ann looked up. "She's right, Mar. We owe her the information. Especially if we want to use her." She turned to Vanity. "The reports'll hit the newspapers in a few weeks or so anyway. The Earth governments have received a communiqué from Company One. The chairman's daughter is supposedly being held hostage somewhere on the planet and the company, backed by the SA, is demanding her return."

"Jaak would never ask the SA to back him on anything."

"I'm just telling you what the communiqué says. At any rate, Earth got lucky for once. It appears that some weeks ago a security agent on leave from one of the services, God knows which one, noticed a very strange sight, an alien woman living with an Earthman in a slum. According to the neighborhood drunks she called herself Golden Vanity. Curious, the agent decided to watch the house. He was watching it when alien agents came looking for the woman. Apparently the agents killed an old bum who was sleeping on the stoop."

"Gari," Vanity whispered. She started to cry; Hump's head dropped into his hands.

"At any rate, when the communiqué from the company came in, some bureaucrat developed a hunch that could almost justify his existence. He ran a computer check on outstanding reports of alien movements. And discovered you."

"And me," Hump added.

"Undoubtedly, though our contact didn't get your name.

And hopefully *they* won't find your connection to us."

Marilyn cut in, "When I saw the two of you in that hotel and remembered your house, Hump, with its resident drunk, I realized who she had to be."

Vanity said coldly, "What happens now?"

"You answer my questions," Marilyn said. "Then maybe you can stay."

"What do you want that I can give you?"

"Information. Knowledge of the companies. Knowledge of their plans for Earth. Knowledge of the SA, knowledge of the people who run things. Technologies, laws, economic systems." She leaned forward. "Don't you see—what do you call yourself?"

"Vanity."

"Don't you see, Vanity, we've never gotten a break like this before. If we play you right, if we offer you up for grabs, we can finally apply some real political pressure. *You've* got to make it worthwhile for us to help you instead."

While Vanity stared at the floor Hump thought he'd never seen anyone look so miserable. *Try a mirror*, he thought. Vanity mumbled, "I don't—I don't really know what I can do."

Hump said, "Does she get time to decide before you cut off her head and mail it to Washington?"

"Of course," Marilyn said. "I'm much too tired to bother her tonight, anyway." She closed her eyes then opened them again immediately. "It's not really so bad here, Vanity. The house is comfortable, the grounds are lovely. And for the moment no one is turning you in."

Vanity said, "Right. Hump told me we could count on you." Marilyn smiled and closed her eyes again.

Ann beckoned them to follow her. She led them into one of the back rooms, a library with hundreds of books and chairs so large you could live in them. Closing the door Ann whispered, "Please try to understand. She doesn't want to harm you. She's desperate."

"What about us?" Hump demanded, but Vanity cut him off.

"Desperate for what?" she asked.

"For the planet to come to its senses. For people to wake up and see we're letting our whole world collapse just because we've discovered there are other ones. I don't know how much you know about Earth, Vanity, but we can't go on like this. No crops, factories shut down, people starving. In the last six months five separate epidemics have broken out, diseases we once thought we'd completely eradicated. Don't you see, we've got to break loose."

"But how could I possibly help you?"

"You could give us some kind of information, just anything we could use for a bargaining edge. We're so powerless. We've got contacts in most of the major cities but we're still such a small group."

"And if I don't, you use me."

"If you force us, yes."

The three of them stood awkwardly for a moment before Ann turned and left the room. "I didn't realize," Hump said lamely.

Vanity growled, "Forget it," and marched past him to the living room where she shook Marilyn by the shoulder. "Hey you," she said, as Marilyn's eyes blinked open. "If I try to help you, will you do something for me?"

"We're already hiding you."

"Not enough. I want to learn something."

"What?"

"Earth. I want to learn all about it. History, money lines, everything. Will you teach me?"

Slowly, Marilyn nodded.

That night, Hump woke up alone in the bedroom he shared with Vanity. A faint noise sounded in the room below him. Barefoot, he walked downstairs to the library where he looked in at Vanity sitting on a chair, wrapped in a large blue robe of Ann's. A thick book lay open before her, and as she stared at the page she sobbed, her body heaving like a child's after a nightmare. Softly, Hump said, "What's wrong?"

Her face jerked up, twisted in fury, and her hands grabbed the book to slam it shut. Leaping forward, Hump stuck his wrist inside the book. Vanity fought him, kicking and biting, for just a few seconds before she shoved him on the floor and ran from the room.

Hump stared at the book. Chronioun's *Political History of the World*. Takes her course work seriously, he thought. He opened it to where his hand still held the place.

A squeamishness gripped his groin, spreading upwards to his

stomach. He skimmed the passage, read it, read it again. It told the story of Cortez, how he and his conquistadores stole all of Montezuma's treasures, and then, their greed satiated, Cortez and his adventurers slaughtered the Golden Emperor and all his court.

Chapter Eleven ─────────────────────

Alone in his bare office, hunched over in his Arbolian womb chair, AAri held the report, a plastic sheet of graphic symbols, loosely in his hands. He didn't look at it. Instead, he thought, for the first time in years, about his father. He couldn't even remember the man's face, but he remembered how his father used to mangle every book he read. Bent covers, torn spines. AAri hadn't seen a real book in years, just flash walls and rescrambled plastic sheets.

Angrily he rose and pushed open the door. Ignoring the people lined up to see him, he marched through his outer office and down the hallway towards Jaak's magnificent private rooms. "Enough nonsense," he muttered to himself. He could play with his childhood memories after the crisis; now he had to prod a half-crazy chairman back into some useful action.

For just a moment the Voice, that alien creature that had filled his mind the past weeks with thoughts that didn't belong to him, whispered in his ear, "He's waiting for you. He just wants you to expose yourself, then he can take you to the old places beneath the building, where no one will ever find you. The torture places. He and Vanity arranged it all. Cixxa told them how. Cixxa ordered them." AAri dug his nails into his palms, shook his head. He forced himself to keep going.

The watch-guard door, a device imported from Hgzy the privacy world, scanned AAri's body print, found him one of the four people automatically admitted to the chairman's outer rooms, and opened the door. He entered a room filled with shouting people dancing or striding around, and through, the furniture. As soon as Jaak saw AAri he pressed a button and the people, most of them Vanity, all of them projections, vanished. AAri shook off the momentary aftereffects as he marched across the arena-like office, past the tapestries, the bells, the paintings and statues, the ancient weapons, the stuffed beasts, all the curios of more than thirty worlds.

"Any news?" Jaak said. He sounded tired.

"If you mean about Vanity, no, I haven't heard anything at all. But I've definitely got news. A lot of it."

"Keep it to yourself. I've told you, AAri, I don't want any channel about anything but Vanity. You're trying to annoy me and I don't like it." Like an anxious child with candy he watched the projection button. "When I find a use for you I'll call you. For now, go away."

"Not until you listen." AAri fought back the fear rising in him that Jaak would grab one of the knives off the wall and cut him open. "Have you seen this?"

The chairman sunk down into the high collar of his Arbol general's field coat. "AAri," he said slowly, "I'll tell you once more. I'll listen to news about my daughter. Information on where to find her. Plans on how to get her back. Actions against the animals who've hid her from me. I want no other reports, ideas, problems, or anything else. Do you understand, work-servant?"

AAri jerked back. *Work-servant.* There was no deeper insult, no sharper slap Jaak could have given him. He swayed, empty. Work-servant. Jaak was looking at him with hooded eyes, a slight smirk twisting his mouth. AAri's mind careened back and forth between the long years he'd worked with Jaak and that time long ago when the companies first came to his parents' great city of stone towers and brilliant lights shining on fabulous tiled streets. They'd called his people, priests, craftsmen, beggars, governors, farmers, even the picture tellers, "work-servants."

"The worst kind," they laughed, "poetic morons," and they asked for "any thickheads who could think and work." AAri could think, and he worked years to get past that term. Later he learned to use it himself, to describe the lowest form of life, like the genetically altered slaves digging ore on Luritti.

Work-servant. AAri wanted to run; paralyzed, he dropped his eyes to the report. "This deals with the shrieker, the one Loper claimed he'd killed."

"I've seen it."

"Good. I presume that means you've also read it and possibly even remember what it says." *How could he stay?* What else could he do? So many years. "Which means you know the prediction of what the SA will do to us when it discovers we let a shrieker grow beyond the point where we, or maybe even they, can handle it." Jaak waved a hand. "We've got two weeks," AAri pushed on, hearing his own voice like a meaningless noise, "That's all. We wouldn't even have that if the time in non-space hadn't weakened it. Two weeks. What the burst do you propose to do about it?" He didn't care. He argued from habit, not purpose.

The chairman leaned forward. "You want my proposals for action. All right, that's a reasonable request. I propose nothing, AAri. Nothing at all." He smiled at AAri's sickly face. "Except to find my daughter. Do that and I'll deal with your shrieker and whatever other slime you find so bursting important." He pushed the button, and AAri left the room chased by the shouts and stamps of twenty nonexistent people.

Halfway back to his office a sudden stabbing in his stomach doubled AAri over in pain. "Belly fear," he muttered in his father's language. Only, his father would have chosen one of sixteen words to describe exactly the pain he felt for exactly AAri's combination of panic, shame, and impotent fury. Bent over, he made it to a guest room, where he locked the door then fell into a wide feather couch.

For a long time he lay there, moving only to override the lights. Wildly he stared at the darkness where images more vivid than Jaak's holograms danced across the room, strange beasts, journeys across the sky riding on the back of the sun, stars falling from the giant crust of a pie eaten by an infant god, a woman who became a silver fish served on her children's plates, the summer wind pictured as an old man too tired to roar, all the ludicrous luminous stories forgotten since his childhood on a bankrupt world, stories tossed aside at first sight of those great glimmery beasts, the starships.

Towards morning AAri pushed himself up from the couch

and shambled through the busy corridors to his own rooms. He waved aside the one or two early petitioners who might have waited all night for him. While he washed he wondered—odd thought—what the day looked like outside the vast network of connected buildings known as company center. He wondered also what a picture teller would have made of the company buildings that dotted the planet like crusted sores.

What had happened to his fears, all the plots and plans to kill him? It all sounded so, so unoriginal. The flood of True Images, as the picture tellers described the archetypal stories, had washed him clean.

Conscious only of a vague annoyance at the dullness of his clothes, AAri rode a tracking car down the building's central spine to a set of rooms near the eastern edge. There he stood in a doorway and watched the woman instruct a class of future fant teachers until the woman's robot receptionist informed her that Jaak's assistant wanted to see her. She dismissed the class. "I want a course," AAri said immediately. "A short one."

She nodded. "We can start right away," she said, while her eyes examined his face, and her mind calculated brain waves, structures, reaction mechanisms—

"Something else." He waved at the machines, the head chips, the hypnagenetic gadgets. "I don't want any of this. I want the course done someplace else." He frowned. "Someplace clean."

"Yes, of course." She hesitated. "We can go outside." The wildness was catching; her skin broke out in a rage of sudden excitement. "The desert goes down to the sea not far from this edge of the building. Have you ever been to the sea in winter? We'll go there." For the first time in years she thought she might learn something teaching a novice. "We'll go right now." With his face lit like the red beak of a firebird from the legends of his childhood, AAri followed her through the machine-filled rooms to a small door set in the shell of the labyrinth.

Chapter Twelve

As the days passed Vanity and Marilyn developed a truce, then a
friendship. Each evening they sat in the library with a table full
of books and Marilyn excitedly lectured Vanity on the radical
version of history, wildly moving from book to book, country to
country, hammering into Vanity all the different class systems:
birth, race, sex. Whatever other responsibilites Marilyn had at
the moment she had apparently put them aside. Vanity was her
assignment now, and she pursued it with a joy that surprised her
as much as anyone.

Once or twice Hump had tried to join in, but he'd never cared
much for politics and he gave up when he couldn't decide if
Vanity really wanted to learn or only played a game on the Earth
woman's enthusiasm. He noticed that Vanity parried most of
Marilyn's efforts to make comparisons with Center of the
companies. Whether Marilyn prodded, cajoled, or threatened,
Vanity gave out nothing but the most general information.

Often the two women walked in the woods while Hump
brooded or told Ann stories about Marilyn's relatives, a subject
Marilyn had dismissed to Ann as trivial. Sometimes Vanity and
Marilyn returned bright and laughing, at other times they
plodded wearily into the house to eat silently whatever Hump
and Ann had cooked for them.

Vanity refused to tell Hump what they talked about on their

walks. "Why don't you ask your cousin?" she'd say. "I'm sure she'll tell you. Family loyalty, you know."

One evening not quite two weeks after Hump and Vanity's arrival, Marilyn received a phone call which she took in her bedroom upstairs. When she returned, an hour later, she looked frightened, shrunken. She sprawled in a chair and looked down at Vanity sitting by the fire. "They want action," she said.

"Who are they?" Hump asked.

Ann said, "The movement. Or at least the five or so people who run it."

Vanity said nothing, only watched her fingers play with a tuft of rug. Suddenly Marilyn jerked forward and shouted, "You alien idiot! Don't you understand? You've got to give me something. Anything. Just some scrap I can use to justify your damn existence."

"Why bother?" Vanity said. "Why not just throw me away in the snow? The filth from space."

"You are the most obnoxious creature I have ever seen. I can't possibly imagine why your father wants you back."

Ann broke in, "Did they give us an ultimatum?"

"No. Not yet. But they're angry. Piet accused me of betraying the movement."

"Rhetoric. What did you say?"

"What I've said all along. That I discovered her and I would decide what to do with her. Piet then called me an élitist." She laughed.

"That won't hold them long."

"I know." She turned again to Vanity. "Listen, I don't want to turn you over to your father. Believe me, from what you've told me of him, I wouldn't turn a borkson over to the bastard. But the others couldn't care less about that. Last week, the Paris pigs busted one of our oldest links. Yesterday, the American president announced that as long as he remained in office he wouldn't negotiate with the ERM on any subject at any time. We're desperate, Vanity. All we've got is you, something the aliens want so bad they've broken their monolithic silence to actually threaten Earth if it doesn't turn you over."

"Not all the aliens," Vanity pointed out. "Jaak."

"Apparently the SA is willing to let him speak for them."

Hump asked, "Threaten Earth? What kind of threat?"

Marilyn smiled. "They've threatened to withdraw. Leave Earth for good."

"You don't believe that?" Vanity asked.

"Of course not. The point is, if the ERM announces that we've got you, Earth will bargain with us so they can then bargain with Jaak and the SA. The movement heads are obsessed with this idea. They imagine all the wonderful deals they can make by selling you to Daddy. I can't hold them off much longer."

"Why bother then? Maybe you could chop me up in little pieces and give me away to everybody."

"Oh shut up. Can't you accept that someone wants to help you? Vanity, I'll tell you once more. Either you give us some information we can use as a bargaining point or we sell you to the government."

Vanity sat up. "What precious bits of information do you think I keep stuffed inside myself? What do you think I know, for burst's sake?"

"For your sake, you better know something."

"Well I don't. Believe me, no information could possibly make the companies slice this planet. They never let go. Never."

Marilyn stared at her. "I thought you understood. We're not aiming that high. We don't really care what the aliens do. We just care about Earth."

Vanity shook her head. "*You* don't understand. Not anything."

"I understand that a weak little group can't chase away the entire SA. But maybe we can make our own puny terrestial governments bring their priorities back home, not up in heaven. Maybe we can make them forget about the companies long enough to patch up their own planet."

"No. No, no, *no*. The companies'll tear you apart, Marilyn. They'll rip the whole planet into bite-sized chunks. That's what you've got to think about. That's the only thing that matters. You're all so slimy weak. Listen to me. Jaak's company once bought the rights to a planet named hcKou."

"The whole planet?" Ann asked.

"Uh huh. The entire land, all the sea, the air, and all the creatures. They all became his property. It's an SA custom. A planet below a certain level of technology goes up for auction."

Hump said, "Does Earth come below the line?"

"I'm not sure. Let me go on. If Jaak wanted he could have burned the entire planet. Instead he stripped it for minerals. Wherever he found what he wanted he first killed all the plant life. That not only made it easier to mine, it made sure the people wouldn't refuse the powder food he offered them, especially after all the animals had starved to death. They didn't clean up the rotting bodies, by the way. They simply mixed immunizers into the food, and left the people to cope with the smell. Of course, without the plants, they had to doctor the air for oxygen, but that didn't require much to make it livable. Not pleasant, just livable. Naturally, Jaak worked the seas as well as the land. AAri once told me the dead fish floated up for years. Along the way, the company analysts decided that hcKou didn't need so many people. So they got rid of some, half, two thirds. Don't ask me how. No one ever told me. Maybe they gave them as food to their workers someplace else."

Hump moaned. He thought of Cortez and the Aztecs.

Vanity went on, "But then another study indicated they weren't getting full efficiency from the workers left over. Not because of any resistance, just because of human limitations. So they brought in genetic engineers. A few changes over a couple of generations—they were quick breeding them, by the way, speeding up pregnancy and then rushing the infants to adulthood by growth hormones and injection learning—"

Ann, who had turned her face to the window and the shadowed trees, suddenly said, "Vanity, stop. Please, just stop it." They sat in silence a moment, a half smirk twisting Vanity's mouth. When Ann turned, Hump flinched at the sight of her face. She ignored him and went to Marilyn, who stared stonily at the fire. "Well?" Ann demanded.

"Well what?"

"You've pulled some information out of her. Is it good enough?"

"I don't know. At least we've finally got proof of malevolence." She looked at Vanity. "Will you go public with us? Can we quote you on all these things to the government and even the press if we have to? In fact, can we make up a pamphlet and put your name on it?"

"We could go even further," Ann suggested. "Suppose we announce that Vanity has joined us? An alien who hates the alien exploitation. We could mount a big surface campaign."

Marilyn told her, "You're as bad as any of them."

Ann clenched her fists. "Didn't you hear her just now?" She turned back to Vanity. "Will you do it? It's the only way we can save you. Maybe you can even save us."

"I don't know—Oh all right. All right." She ran from the room.

Marilyn stared at the doorway. "Let's just hope it's good enough."

They came late one night, dropping down in their helicars like wild hungry birds. Three men and two women, all ages, all colors. They greeted Ann, looked curiously at Hump and Vanity, then silently followed Marilyn upstairs. All night the meeting lasted; occasionally the three downstairs could hear a shout or a stamp, and twice someone came down for coffee, saying nothing, staring at the stove. Towards morning Hump and Vanity fell asleep by the fire, leaving Ann alone, huddled in a chair. She didn't move when the five leaders marched silently past her to the door.

As the dark birds rose into the air Marilyn stood by the door, silent, her shoulders shaking with exhaustion. Silently Ann took Marilyn in her arms; Marilyn cried against her shoulder.

The four of them held their own conference in the kitchen. "In a way," Marilyn told Vanity, "your testimony tipped the balance against you. It hardened them, made them say that nothing mattered now except the Earth."

Ann said, "Couldn't we protect it better with Vanity on our side than if we dump her in one short bargain?"

"Maybe, but they've got that covered. They're going to announce publicly that the chairman's daughter has joined the ERM—they can get some actress—while privately they bargain with Jaak and hand her over."

Vanity asked, "How much time do I have?"

"A week, two. It'll take them a while to set it up."

"Then you'd better guard yourselves. Because I'm not staying here. I won't go back to Jaak."

Bleakly Ann said, "Even if you kill us you won't get past the fence."

"I'll find a way."

"For what I'm worth," Hump said, "she's got me on her side."

"Will you three scram the melodrama?" Marilyn demanded. "Of course you're getting out. Do you think I'd let them sell you back to slimeface?"

Hump smiled for the first time in days. "Hallelujah," he muttered. Vanity said something in some alien language.

"Where can they go?" Ann asked.

"I thought maybe the Daniks."

Vanity asked, "Who are they?"

Marilyn grinned. "A religious group. Some interesting ideas. Half-baked really but they live out in the desert, and they take in strangers, no questions asked."

Ann pointed out, "Aren't they far away?"

"Yeah. Vanity, if we take you to your spaceship, can you fly it down the continent? First of all, do you think Jaak's found it by now?"

Vanity looked at her suspiciously. "I doubt it. I hid it from sight pretty well, and it's got an ego field around it to block any instrument checks. Only I can approach it."

"Will they catch you if you take off in it?"

"Not if I don't leave the planet."

"Then we'll go tonight. Where did you put it?" Vanity froze. "Listen," Marilyn said. "I'm not trying to trick you. If this sounds like an elaborate gimmick to get your ship, I'm sorry. You'll just have to trust me."

"Let me think. I left it on an island, inside the superstructure of something like an unfinished arena. The island's right next to New York. I remember a bridge there, and a ferryboat. I took the boat into the city."

Hump laughed, doubled over. "Staten Island!" he roared. "She parked her spaceship on Staten Island."

"You can't tell me that toy carries you through outer space?"

"Sure it does. Wait'll you hear it beep." They walked across the open dirt of Cuomo Stadium, one of the half-finished projects canceled when the aliens came. Before them, stashed under a balcony in an area possibly intended for locker rooms or souvenir stands, lay a brilliantly white delta-winged plane no bigger than some corporation's private jet. From the transparent snub-nosed cone—Hump's stomach leaped when he saw the two seats—the hull swept back in a narrow line until about ten feet before the end, where it suddenly opened into a fan-like wall of metal, or maybe plastic; it looked incredibly thin.

Hump pointed at it. "Doesn't that mess up your wind drag?"

She shrugged. "I don't know. Ask an engineer. The crawl engine's in there."

"The what?"

"Later. I want to get out of here." Fresh fear washed Hump as he saw Vanity look quickly at the night sky. He imagined a whole fleet of saffron-faced goons in aluminum foil clothes swooping down on Staten Island.

Vanity pressed her palm against some sort of hieroglyphics on the ship's side towards the front. Silently a section of wall slid away to reveal a small chamber bare of furniture yet elaborately painted with mandala-like designs in bright colors. Hump's legs wouldn't move. It's just a funny airplane, he told himself, but his mind tossed pictures at him, steam baths on Venus, ice follies on Pluto, big ugly creatures swimming in the blackness. Why did Ann and Marilyn leave him here? He shook his head. They had their own hiding to do; the ERM would not take calmly the loss of their prize.

"Will you hurry up?" Vanity pleaded. Hump stumbled into the ship. As soon as the outer door had closed again, a second door opened into the front cabin.

"Was that an air lock?" he said.

She turned to pat his cheek. "Aren't you smart?"

Hump wanted to kick her, but he let her direct him to the seat on the left. Incredibly comfortable, the seat molded to his body without relinquishing any firmness. "Isn't there a safety belt or something?"

"Not necessary," Vanity mumbled. "Just lean back and the seat will hold you." He tried it and discovered that the seat curved slightly over his arms and legs. It released him when he lifted first one leg and then the other.

It wasn't till then that Hump noticed the odd contrast with the air lock. Here, no mandalas covered the pale yellow walls. About the size of a lounge on a small luxury airplane, the cabin was decorated with extreme severity. Against each side wall lay a low couch or bed made of the same soft green substance as the chairs. The floor also came from the same material; as Hump remembered its springiness he wondered unpleasantly if the green stuff was alive ("Earthman eaten by chair in alien spaceship"). Next to one couch stood a cylindrical booth of milky plastic, possibly a shower or some sort of body treatment, and next to that a smaller booth, probably a toilet. Did they recycle the body waste or dump it on the universe?

By the other wall stood a yellow box, metal or plastic, about as long as a man's height and wider. Three feet high, it was divided into two parts, each with a small door in the center. Washer-dryer, Hump thought, but then he considered that

maybe one side gave out food and the other gobbled up the
scraps and dishes. Several other, much smaller machines lined
the walls, but except for some sort of projector and small stock
of cassettes (home movies for the long nights in space?) Hump
couldn't imagine their purposes. The cabin contained only one
item he might have called a luxury, a low square table in the
center of the room. Made of some stone that constantly shifted
color and texture, the table held in the center a black
glimmery—something—not a jewel, he saw, for it moved, slowly
changing shape as he looked at it. It made him queasy to watch
it, and he turned away. Other than the table, the instruments,
and the bare requirements of life, the cabin contained nothing at
all, not even a small chest of clothes or a book. "This makes no
sense," he said. "The air lock looks like a museum, and the
cabin's a monastery. Don't you have that a little backward?"

Vanity looked up from the row of instruments. "It's an old
custom. You wouldn't understand."

"Thanks. For someone as rich as you I'd still expect a little
more opulence."

Vanity grinned. "See that pile there?" She pointed to the
cassettes. Hump nodded. "Take the top one and stick it in the
slot next to the pile. Go ahead." Hump got up to gingerly pluck
the tape and drop it in the machine. Instantly, a rug appeared on
the floor, woven tapestries and lavish jeweled plates appeared on
the wall, fireballs hung in the air, and people, fully-fleshed and
dressed in outlandish glittery costumes walked about the room
or lay on the floor, or lounged across the instrument panels,
chattering in a strange fluid language.

Hump yelped, then jerked the tape out with a thumb and one
finger and let it drop to the floor like something on fire.
"Goddamn you," he said.

"I'm sorry," Vanity mumbled. "I didn't—I should have
warned you."

Hump, recovered, raised his eyebrows. "What do you know?
A show of sympathy for the hick."

"You'd better lie back," Vanity said when they'd got back in
position. "We'll bounce a little until we get in the air."

"Why? Haven't you got your license yet?"

"Usually we land and take off on ramps. The ship's not made
for dirt. When I landed I must have torn open half the bottom."

"What?" He struggled clumsily against the seat.

Vanity pushed him back. "Will you sit down?"

"How can you fly without a bottom?"

She rolled her eyes. "The ship repairs itself. Each ship carries a blueprint of itself in case anything goes wrong. In fact, they even build themselves. The robots start it and then the blueprint takes over."

"Then the ships don't need people at all," he said. He leaned back, sweating despite the cool air flowing through the ship.

They flew low, going out to sea and keeping well below the radar level. Surprisingly smooth, like a flying easy chair, the ship flew at what seemed incredible speed for such a low altitude. Vanity refused to talk, and after a while Hump grew bored with both the waves and thoughts of his mind-boggling precedent. He fell asleep.

Chapter Thirteen ————————————

Vanity shook him awake. "Hey, I need you." Hump rubbed his eyes, then suddenly jerked awake like an electric whip. Vanity giggled. "Calm down," she said. "Nobody's chasing us."

"What do you need me for? I can't do anything."

"I figured that out a long time ago. But you can locate this sanctuary of ours." The sky had brightened and Hump saw, through that horribly exposed transparent nose, that they were heading towards land. "We're almost at the area you and Marilyn worked out on the map. But we still have to find the people."

Hump thought about the Daniks. "Oh, of course," he said, "we'll see the lines."

"What lines?"

He grinned. "You just crisscross the area, Sister Vanity. Brother Hump'll tell you where to land."

"But how do I know—?"

He patted her knee. "Fly high so they don't see us."

Vanity punched a few buttons and leaned back. The ship jerked up its nose and took off; in seconds they could see the earth's curvature.

"I'll kill you," Hump tried to say; only a croak came out.

Quickly Vanity ran her fingers over the instruments and the plane went into a soft descend. "Hump, I'm sorry," she said.

."Really. I keep forgetting. I'm sorry." The ship leveled off at cruising height for a small jet. "Don't you see," she pleaded, "I've ridden in these things all my life." Hump let out his breath. Though secretly he was pleased at her sudden concern, he certainly didn't plan to show it. Vanity asked, "Are you angry?"

"Angry? You stupid bitch. I'm terrified."

Vanity laughed. "Oh good, you've recovered. We've gotten a little off course," she went on, "but we're almost back. You'll tell me where to find them?"

Hump growled, "Yeah."

Vanity guided the ship in a wide arcing circle over the barren hills. From so high up the Great Defoliation Desert looked like a lumpy brown patch on the green earth. Once, this area looked like all the land around it, sparse, scrubby, but alive. That was before a left wing Mexican government decided to expel all American interests during a right wing administration in America. As a news magazine put it, "The US gave Mexico twenty-four hours to clear out of town." Actually, they allowed two weeks for Mexico to evacuate an area the size of Rhode Island. Then came the chemical bombs. Hump looked down at the empty hills and thought of Jaak doing *that* to the entire planet.

"Fly lower," Hump directed. "I can't make anything out."

"Brace yourself." They descended in a graceful curve. Now he could see a wavy streak that might have been a yellow river, tiny tracks— "There," he said. "Do you see?"

Vanity squinted down. "What the burst are those lines doing there?"

Hump laughed. Five bright blue lines ran like marching columns across the hills and valleys. "Wait'll you see the pictures." The ship followed the lines to two purple stick figures, their heads on a hilltop, their feet in a dried out river bed. A triangle "skirt" on one of them indicated a woman. Vanity said, "What comes next? A giant bowl of Vita-flakes?"

"Maybe a yellow borkson. Fly around and look for an arrow."

"Who drew those things?"

"The Daniks. It's their trademark."

"Why?"

"You're ready for this? They did it so the aliens will know where to land."

Vanity laughed. "Got your golden spacesuit ready, Commander Hump?"

"Aye aye, Rocky Vanity."

"Hey, is that it?" Vanity pointed to a bright red arrow laid across a hilltop like a ribbon on a mound of dirt.

"Right. It points the way to the settlement." As soon as they could see the first prefabricated house, Vanity turned back to search for a place to land. They chose a narrow place between two hills several miles away. "Can you remember where we are?" Hump asked as they got out.

"I can always find my ship unless there's a damper on it." When he looked puzzled, she added, "Tracer ghosts. Oh, never mind."

The heat soon baked away any chill left over from their night ride. Slowly they trudged across the hard caked ground as pools of sweat gathered under their arms. The packs Ann had given them ("You don't want them to know you fell from the sky") cut into their shoulders, but they quickly appreciated the canteens hooked onto their belts.

"Tell me about the Daniks," Vanity said.

"Delighted. The Daniks take their name after a man named Erik Daniky or something like that a number of years ago, before the companies arrived. He claimed that aliens visited Earth thousands of years ago and gave rise to the gods pictured in the various religions. Space gods, he called them."

"So now the gods have come back?"

"You got it." Vanity snorted. Hump said, "My sentiments exactly."

"What are they doing out here? Do they think the gods like bathing in sweat?"

"No, they come here to punish themselves."

"Why? For what?"

"Unworthiness. They think the aliens haven't handed out any spaceships because of Earth's sinfulness. They think of the aliens as pure ethereal types, come to spread wonders and wisdom."

"If they want to suffer let them wait until the aliens really come."

After a moment Hump said, "That reminds me of something I've wanted to ask you."

"Fire when ready, Griddle."

"That's Gridley. Anyway, how did humans get on all these different worlds? From what you say the companies have found humans on every habitable world. They couldn't have all evolved."

Vanity hesitated, and Hump guessed he'd hit one of those

touchy areas, something the local folks weren't supposed to know. Vanity took a breath before she said, "The Ur-humans put them there, of course."

"Who?"

"It's obvious. Originally, humans must have lived on one world. These people, the best translation I can think of is Ur-humans, somehow spread out around the galaxy, leaving little versions of themselves at every stop."

"But that's exactly what the Daniks believe."

"Then they must be right."

"Only they think the companies are the same people."

"Oh, it happened a long time before the companies."

"Do you people know this for a fact?"

"How could we know a fact that happened millions of years ago?"

"Has anyone ever found the original planet?"

"Not that we know. Maybe Earth's the original."

Hump thought, *there's a lot more she doesn't want to say*. "Let's take a rest," he said. Grunting, they took off their packs and set them down as pillows. Vanity closed her eyes and opened her shirt for the small breeze to cool her chest. For a moment Hump stared at her breasts before he leaned back against the pack. "Tell me this," he said a moment later. "If the Earthies believe the aliens are angels what do the angels believe?"

Vanity turned her head. Her face bland, her voice cold, she said, "Nothing. Absolutely nothing."

"No religion? No philosophy?"

"I told you. Nothing." She stood up. "Let's get going."

A Danik spotted them as soon as they came in sight of the ten or so large white buildings. "Hey," called a girl's voice. "Hi. Hello. Over here." They turned and saw a woman about Vanity's age or a little older in a dirty white dress, thin sandals, and a burnoose to keep off the sun. She ran over to them. "Hi," she said. "Welcome to the Universal Church. I'm Judy."

Vanity said, "I'm Edie. That's Harry." Hump suppressed a dirty look. It had been hard enough getting used to "Vicky."

"Great," Judy went on. "Come on, I'll initiate you." She giggled. "That sounds fancy, but it just means show you around." As they walked towards the buildings Hump noticed several people in meditative positions scattered along the hillside. He wished they'd parked the ship farther back. "What's your sign?" Judy asked. "I'm Gemini."

Hump said, "I'm Aquarius. She's Cancer."

"Oh man, a couple of real water babies. You two must have had a rough time crossing the desert."

"Not too bad. We got good directions and a ride straight to the edge. We took it slowly."

"It's not too bad, I suppose. I'm really sick of it. It gives me the creeps. Everything's dead, you never even see any insects, just a few birds and they almost never land. They just steal something and fly away. And it's *hot*. But most of all, I guess, it just gets horribly boring."

Vanity said, "Why don't you leave?"

Judy laughed. "I want to be here when the ships come down."

"Do you really think the aliens will bring their ships here?"

"It's possible, isn't it? The fact that they've come back after so many thousands of years means they're checking us out, so if we show them that we really want to change and be deserving, maybe they'll come here first. Anyway, that's what I keep telling myself."

There was a long silence. Finally Judy said, "You guys American?"

"Yeah," Hump said.

"I thought so. Most of the people we get are American. Do you think America's the spiritual forefront or something?"

"Either that," Hump said, "or we've got the most to atone for."

"Yeah, I thought of that too. I don't know."

Hump asked, "What sort of routine do you follow? Do you hold services or something?"

"No, not really. We have a kind of morning service in the chapel, but it's really a meditation gathering. No prayers or any of that stuff. Well, sometimes we chant. But mostly we just try to synch our minds together. Putting all our heads in one basket someone called it. It's nice when it works. A couple of times we actually made contact. It was beautiful."

"Contact?"

"Yeah. On the astral plane. Man, you should have been there."

"What about when it doesn't work?" Vanity asked.

"Then it just gets boring."

"What else happens?" Hump said.

"Let's see, there's discussions about once a week. Did you bring your own texts, by the way?" Hump shook his head.

"That's okay, we've got plenty in the library. Anyway, the discussions just happen whenever someone's got something to say. What else? The work details, the food, cleanup, but that's not much. Otherwise, you just do whatever you want. Oh, except the festivals. A real big one's coming soon. You're just in time."

"What's that?"

"The Festival of Return. It celebrates the alies coming back to us. We put on a pageant and everything. You can help us make the costumes."

Vanity asked, "But how do we purify ourselves?"

"Don't worry, the hills'll take care of that. Seriously, just try to contemplate the alies and kind of move towards them in your head. I know it sounds pretty silly, but you'll see."

The white barracks-like buildings, scattered in no particular pattern, covered an area of several thousand square meters. Aside from a dome-like chapel, where, according to Judy, the "circular vibrations" helped the meditation, the buildings were all rectangular, of different sizes, with small high windows. Judy pointed out the eating hall ("but you'll probably want to fast first anyway"), several dormitories that looked big enough for around twenty or thirty beds each, a water recycling plant, and the library, the smallest building.

"How did you get all this set up?" Hump asked. "Pass around the beggar bowl?"

"Didn't have to. One of the pseuds hit us with it."

"Pseud?"

"Someone who calls themselves a Danik but won't cut themselves off from materialism."

Vanity said, "But how can they move their heads to the aliens if they won't give up their money and sinfulness?"

"Exactly," Judy said without irony.

Hump jerked Vanity's arm to hold her back so he could whisper, "Listen creep, you keep your sinful mouth shut or I'll move your whole body to the aliens."

"I think there's room in here," Judy said, pointing to a dorm. They entered a large bare room with twenty cots topped by thin mattresses. A small green chest of drawers perched beside each cot. Some of the cots had sheets and pillowcases, others lacked even pillows.

"Doesn't look very comfortable," Hump muttered.

"Can't pamper yourself with material comforts," Vanity

admonished him. She glanced at two pairs of beds tied together with ropes. "You don't separate people?"

"Of course not. Didn't the alies tell us to multiply their seed upon the wind?"

"Oh yeah. When was that again?"

Judy raised her eyebrows. "In the Babylonian Manuscript, of course."

"Can we take these beds here?" Hump cut in.

"Sure. Just make sure the drawers are empty."

Outside, Hump looked around at the few people leaning against white walls or sitting on the hard ground. "Where is everybody?"

Judy shrugged. "Don't know. Unless—" She walked between two buildings to the largest of the rectangles. Inside they could hear shouting and arguing. "This is the eating hall, the Food Palace, but we also use it for a teev room. Maybe something's come on the news." They hurried inside to where a couple of hundred people swarmed over the tables surrounding a large flat wall television, blank now. "Judy!" Someone called over the din, "Have you heard the news?"

"What news?"

"The gov's kidnapped an alien, that's what news."

"What?" Excitement, the thrill of monstrous acts, sent her pressing forward. "How did it happen? Was it on the teev?"

"Oh sure. Their version of it."

"What did they say?"

"Get this. The gov claims that an alien woman has run away from the encampment, *and*—are you ready?—she wants political asylum on Earth."

Judy rolled up her eyes. "Oh! Those bas— What do the alies say?"

A woman told her, "How do we know? According to the news the alies hold us all responsible for not turning the woman over to them. But who knows what they really said."

"The idiots," someone wailed. "They'll strand us for another fifty thousand years. We'll never get off the physical plane." In the corner someone softly beat his chest as he rocked back and forth on the floor.

Hump pushed forward. "What else did they say about the woman? Did they describe her or say who was with her?"

One of the men glanced at Judy who said, "They're new. Just arrived."

The man told Hump, "Naturally they said as little as possible. They've got to pretend they don't know much so it's not so obvious they've kidnapped her."

"What about the Ermies?" Judy asked.

"Oh yes, the good old Earth Regression Movement has also slithered into the act. Wait'll you hear this one. According to the ERM, the alien has joined their organization. Can you believe that? And get ready, she's even writing a pamphlet exposing the 'truth' about the aliens."

"Blasphemy," Judy whispered.

Someone leaped on a table. "Listen everyone. Attention." The noise quieted. "We've got to decide what to do." Everyone started to shout. "Hold it. One at a time. Now I think we should issue a statement, no, two statements, one right away, and then a longer one when we can really work on it. We can say the Daniks denounce the whole plot and beg the alies' forgiveness."

As everyone started to argue all at once Hump grabbed Vanity's arm and dragged her outside. A few Daniks were still filing into the big hall but the area away from the camp's center had already emptied, with space for them to talk alone. Before them stretched the desert, more fearful, more alien, now that they'd found the human settlement. Other than the muffled shouts behind them the only noise came from the thin wind moving between the buildings. They could taste the air, dry, chalky. "Welcome to your church, angel face," Hump said.

Vanity hugged herself. "I don't like this place."

"How odd. Creepy, huh?" A couple of birds glided overhead, looking for scraps.

"Where can we go, do you think?"

"Go? Why should we go anywhere?"

"But Hump, now that they know about the runaway alien—"

Hump's laugh sounded more like a bark. "You didn't run away. You were kidnapped. Listen Vanity, you couldn't find a safer place than this. They've got their own version of the story and they couldn't care less about the facts. The teev could show a picture of you and they wouldn't even recognize it."

"But if they concentrate so much on aliens won't they recognize me? My skin alone should tell them."

Hump suspected she just wanted an excuse to leave. "You don't fit. You're too degenerate. If you told them you're an alien they'd bring you up on blasphemy charges." He tried to pat her cheek but she twisted away.

"I just don't like it here," she said. "It's too much—"

"Too much what?" The anger in his voice surprised him.

"Forget it."

"No, I want the truth."

Vanity turned to go but Hump grabbed her wrist. "Come back here."

In one movement Vanity ducked under Hump's arm and came up to slap him backhanded across the face. Stunned, Hump slapped her cheek as hard as he could. He would have knocked her down if she hadn't danced back so that only the fingers caught her. Quickly she hit his mouth then leaped away again.

Hump tackled her around the waist. They rolled over, trying to claw, punch, or strangle each other until Hump caught a glimpse of Vanity's bared teeth coated in dust. He started to giggle; Vanity fell on top of him, laughing.

Hump hugged her, delighted at the pressure of her filthy body. "We'd better resurrect ourselves," he said. "Their holinesses should emerge soon."

"Hump, do we really have to stay here?"

"We're about as safe here as anywhere else. Anyway, I don't think I could handle another flight."

"But I don't like it here."

"I don't like it anywhere. What have you got against this place?"

She made a face. "You wouldn't understand."

"Yeah? Well screw you, Edie."

"Burst you, Harry."

"Another great intergalactic cultural exchange."

Chapter Fourteen

Krishna, Jesus, Buddha,
Gliding from above,
Flying down to save us,
Astronauts of love.

Vanity's voice, as off key as ever, sounded through the chapel. She loved the Danik songs; she'd even tried getting everyone to sing them in the dorm before they all went to bed, until Hump threatened to tear out her larynx.

The song ended, and they rose from the bare almost cool floor to walk outside into the brutal sun. "I wish I could sing like you," Judy said.

Mario, a young Italian who'd run away from his family while they toured Mexico, said, "You give the words such deep meaning."

Vanity waved a hand. "It's easy. Just push the love vibrations through your throat."

Judy laughed. "I think they get stuck somewhere in my esophagus. You guys coming to discussion?"

Hump squinted against the bright light. "What's the subject?"

"'The True Legend of Prometheus.' Marc wants to talk

about the zodiacal symbolism." She giggled. "Sounds impressive, huh? I don't know, sometimes I think it's all just nonsense, we're all kidding ourselves."

Vanity said, "Hey, I just thought of something. Really, more like some power put the idea in my mind."

"Wow," Judy said, "tell us."

"Well, suppose the alies chart their ships according to the zodiac. Then the reason they didn't return for so long was they had to wait for the Great Wheel to turn the way it was so they could find us again."

"Fantastic," Mario breathed.

Judy said, "I wish a power would put things in my head. Come on, let's go tell everyone."

Vanity looked blandly at Hump. "You coming, Harry?"

Hump shook his head. "No, now that I've heard the idea I think I'd like to go meditate on it in private." He watched the three go off laughing at some joke. Someday, he thought, the Daniks will realize the joke's on them. He headed back to the dorm.

It amazed Hump and frightened him a little the way Vanity had blended into the community. They'd let her lead the "mutual blessing" the other night at dinner, and in fact, she'd even joined the committee writing a full statement to the world press on the "sacrilegious kidnapping." Her style, however, turned out to be too purple even for the Daniks. "Vibrate with love. Keep hate in the wrong end of the telescope."

Danik sayings filled Vanity's speech. Earthpeople became "lokies," the local inhabitants. She called the aliens "alies" or more reverently, "the new gods."

In the dorm Hump lay down on his bed and stared at the white metal ceiling. He sighed; he didn't like being alone. At first they'd stayed together all the time, lurching through the desert days, fighting off dysentery, crying in the night. "The two piglets," Hump called themselves with all their squealing. They'd early wired their beds together. To Hump's surprise the lack of privacy didn't bother Vanity at all sexually. When she saw Hump's discomfort she took to bouncing noisily under the covers, and even calling out various slogans learned on television until the other communards told her to shut up and let them sleep.

After a while the gags began to wear thin. Hump couldn't help it; he knew Vanity's antics substituted for calmness, but he had his own hysteria to battle. "I wish you wouldn't ridicule the

Daniks so much," he grumbled one day on the edge of the settlement, Earth City.

"Why not?" Vanity said. "They're ridiculous."

"I don't care. They're not your people."

Vanity opened wide her eyes. "But Harry, *The Flaming Garuda* teaches us we all belong to the same godhead. Holding hands across the universe. Nebulas of love."

"Oh scram it."

Vanity laughed.

But it wasn't the jokes that finally banged their heads together. The Daniks were planning a festival for the Day of Return, the anniversary of the first alien ships' appearance in orbit, and they expected Hump and Vanity to help prepare. They needed noisemakers, banners, costumes, mock-up spaceships, and huge paper-mâché masks, by which the lucky Daniks chosen to play the alie gods would transform themselves into the glorious visitors from heaven.

Vanity refused to work on anything. "I just don't want to," she told Hump on top of a hill outside the city. "All right?"

"No. Of course it's not all right. You damn—" He looked over his shoulder as if to catch eavesdroppers crawling across the ground from Earth City like giant worms. "Listen, Vanity—"

"Edie."

"Edie then. Listen, I don't care if you jump in a dune and drown yourself. But these people stand between us and eighty two million cops. Not to mention Daddy and Loper. We've got to play with them."

"I play the game a lot more than you. You don't even talk in discussions. You just stare at the floor and make little animal noises."

"That's just the point. If you hadn't built up such a reputation as a saint it wouldn't matter what you did now."

"Hump—" Vanity stared at him and his heart stopped. The eternal smirk had vanished in a great gulp of fear. He'd seen that look before, with the red door and later, at the Earth Museum. And the memory of those moments, with their sudden telepathy that even Vanity didn't understand, made him nervous with a new kind of fear. He backed away, as if that could keep him out of Vanity's mind. This time, however, they stayed apart.

He said, he hoped with sympathy, "Vanity, why does it scare you so much?"

"The whole thing—"

"What about it?"

"It's too much like my dreams."

He rolled his eyes. "Why are dreams so important to you? Look, I once met a man who dreamed that his mother tied him to the bed and threw an axe at him. But that didn't stop him from chopping wood."

"How resilient you Earth people are."

"Can't you just do *something* in their precious festival? Maybe you could help build a spaceship."

"No. Absolutely not. I will not work on your filthy lokie pageant."

"Why?"

"Why has nothing to do with you. Nothing. The whole thing just reminds me of something I don't want to remember." She hesitated. "Something from my people's past."

Hump's curiousity leaped up. "Your people? What about their past?"

"Well, it's— You know what I mean. The companies. What they really do a planet. The Daniks' ideas are so wrong they're monstrous."

Bullshit, Hump thought. Whatever the companies had planned for Earth hadn't stopped her singing hymns or chattering about "zodiacal navigation" or "holy stellar vibrators." Whatever disturbed her about the pageant struck a lot deeper than her newfound sympathies for Earth. What the hell, he thought, what difference does it make? He squinted over his shoulder at the intolerably bright sun. "Look," he said, "I'll tell you what. Don't work on the pageant. We can tell them you want to meditate on your first days here." He pointed a finger at her. "But you're coming to the festival." He walked away before she could argue.

That night he moved their beds apart.

"It's going to be fabulous. Aren't the ships beautiful?" Judy stared rapturously down the hill at the pointynosed cardboard and wood tubes painted in gold, blue, and red, "the colors of the Deep," according to a Danik text. Beyond them the shadowed hills loomed over the makeshift stage like a troop of ghosts. Judy said, "I can't wait to see the costumes at night. You know, a lot of times I feel like this whole thing is really dumb. Like we're kidding ourselves if we think the alies'll come to us instead of the governments. But tonight I just don't care, I never thought these ugly hills could look so beautiful."

"How long does it last?" Hump asked. He looked nervously at Vanity, sitting with her back to him, her shoulders squared angrily.

"Hours, I hope."

They sat on thin pillows, wrapped in blankets against the chill breeze. Hump wished they'd gone farther down towards the stage area, away from the wind. The Daniks had set up their "holy reenactment" at the bottom of a small natural amphitheater formed by two hills near Earth City. The "enactors" who would play the aliens waited in their three spaceships, as patient as the Greeks waiting in their gift horse. A few yards away stood another slapped together structure of wood, cardboard, and canvas, a shapeless hut meant to symbolize man's early squalor. Loudspeakers stood guard on either side of the stage.

Floodlights lit the buildings and the hard ground. The people didn't need them, the full moon gave enough light, but the videos did. The Daniks always recorded their adorations in case the aliens wanted to check; or else for rental fees when the rest of Earth woke up to the truth.

Hump looked at Vanity. She sat like stone, like blind fury. The day had gone all right. Vanity had joined in the parades, the singing, the noise celebration (a monstrous clatter that supposedly symbolized the alien rockets landing on Earth) with an antic wildness that made Hump want to kiss her or slap her. But as night approached and Hump insisted she attend the enactment, Vanity had gotten more and more sullen, not talking or even snarling the whole way out to the amphitheater. Now Hump wished he'd let her stay back. If she did something, if she broke up the festival— *I'll break her neck*, he thought. And yet, Hump felt sorry for her as well. Whatever the reason, the silly pageant really wigged her. If only she would tell him why, just trust him.

Hump shivered, not from the cold, and wrapped himself tighter. Even the air tasted dead here.

A bell clanged, and Judy whispered, "It's starting." She squeezed Hump's hand. A woman in a long red dress and wooden sandals stepped clumsily from the grey hut. Cardboard and plastic models of ancient tools and modern inventions filled her arms. She'd painted her face and dyed her close cropped hair a bright orange, reminding Hump of a candy skull he'd once eaten at a Halloween party.

"That's Janian," Judy told him. "She plays the Spirit of Progress."

The Spirit dumped her cargo on the ground. "Look, O Earth," she cried. "Look upon the gifts the lords have given us. We were ashes, we were dust, before our lords dropped from the sky to breathe fire on our cold dark land." She bowed her head as the spotlight left her.

Hump's stomach uncoiled a little. Leave it to the Daniks to make their pageant so ridiculous it couldn't scare a stuffed poodle. Unfortunately, when he glanced at Vanity she sat as cold and motionless as before.

The pageant continued with "cave dwellers" swinging their arms as they wailed about human misery ("Even the baboons make fun of us") and the Prophetess, a woman who pranced around naked and shook herself in an agony of revelation somewhere between gangrene and an orgasm. "They come, they come!" she shrieked. "The Firelords!" Finally she fell down on the ground as the cave dwellers shuffled off stage. "Is it over?" Hump whispered.

"Don't be silly," Judy said. "The aliens haven't even landed yet." She looked at Vanity. The gold red hair had blown in tangled knots across the rigid saffron face. "Edie?" Judy asked. "Are you okay?" She tried to brush the hair off Vanity's face; Vanity swatted her hand away. "Hey," Judy said.

"She'll be all right," Hump said, "she always gets like this at festivals."

"I guess so. I thought Edie would really like this, you know. I mean, she really gets going in the incantations and stuff. Much more than I ever do."

"She's just overexcited. Don't worry about it."

While the lights stayed down, the loudspeakers boomed the jumbled squawks and screeches of Margot Eiffer's piercing composition, "The Coming of the Aliens." Hump thought, just what we need, schiz music. Lights began to rise, and the cave dwellers looked up like dogs under a dinner table. Abruptly the music stopped, replaced by the recorded sound of a giant jet. The lights vanished as the roar got louder and louder, and Hump jammed hands against his ears.

The noise stopped. Looking up, Hump saw seven figures in wooden stilt shoes. In the darkness they looked naked, their skin discolored, though Hump knew they wore brightly painted body stockings. Large masks covered their heads and shoulders.

Vanity shook herself; her blanket fell from her shoulders. Nervously Hump looked from her to the stage.

A blaze of light splashed over the bodies. "We are the Firelords!" boomed the loudspeakers. "We are the Death and the Life. We are the Firelords!"

And suddenly Hump's mind left his body to invade the rigid female form sitting ten feet away from him. For a long moment he stared through strange eyes, everything the same yet totally different, at the glowing masks, the wild gestures. He could feel the pain racing through her body, he could *feel* her remember—remember— And then his mind flew back to his own body, sprawled like a dropped doll on the cold dirt.

Vanity screamed.

A disgusted voice yelled, "Stop! Stop the video, damn it. For God's sake." Hump paid no attention as he scrambled over to reach out to the weeping Vanity.

She shoved him away and got to her feet. Someone hollered, "What's going on?" and Judy called, "Edie, what's the matter? What's wrong?" She looked at Hump. "Harry, what's happened to you guys?"

"She prefers musicals," Hump muttered. He made another grab at her, but she jumped to her feet and started to run over the hill, away from the stage, away from the people and the buildings. *She's heading for the ship*, Hump thought. Before he could follow her Judy grabbed his arm. "What is it, Harry?" she asked. "What's wrong?"

"Let go of me," he pleaded and realized he was weeping. He pulled loose. "Everything's okay," he shouted to the staring Daniks. "Go on with the show."

He sprinted up the hill.

He caught Vanity less than a quarter mile away, an extraordinary piece of running he attributed to sheer panic. Vanity may have been schiz scared, but Hump was cold terrified. If Vanity took off in her ship, the Daniks would certainly grab Hump—accuse him of sacrilege or something—and if Hump caught up to her too close to the ship, someone might have decided to chase them in the community Jeep, in which case they'd see the ship and grab both of them. So he pumped his legs and flailed his arms, and somewhere on another hillside he knocked Vanity to the ground.

They rolled halfway to the bottom before either of them could get a hold on the bare hard earth. Immediately Vanity tried to run again, but Hump grabbed her ankle and pulled her down on top of him.

"Get away from me!" she shrieked. "You stupid slimy bursting piece—"

"Me?" he yelled back. "Me? Me?" like a parody of an opera singer. "You raving maniac. You'll get us both chopped up in little pieces."

"I don't care. I don't care about any of it."

"You've got to care. You got me into this mess. You're responsible for me."

"I'm not. I'm not responsible."

"That's it. That's the goddamm Golden Vanity credo. Well learn, you stupid space bitch, *learn*." He was screaming, his fist shook as he raised it above her head. She only stared at him, abruptly calm, cold. "Oh hell," he said, and fell down on his back, still holding her wrist.

Vanity sat up. "Let go of me."

"No."

"Hump, I admit I was scared. I admit I acted stupidly by running like that. I admit I put you in danger. Is that enough?"

"Enough? You've got to be kidding. Listen Vanity, you're going to unlock that treasure chest head of yours and let me have some facts. Do you understand?"

"What makes you think I know so much?"

He ignored her. "For a start, you can tell me what's been happening to us."

"What do you mean?"

"Oh scram it. You know what I mean. The mind reading act. The esp. Whatever you want to call it."

"I have no idea what you're talking about."

"How can I punch through that thick skull of yours?" He realized he was shouting again and took a breath. "Okay. So you won't take any questions on telepathy. Subject closed. How about this; why did the play bother you? That's a simple little question."

"Look." Vanity waved her arm at the cold hills. "Look at what you people did to this place. What used to live here, trees, animals, rivers?"

"Rivers don't live."

"Shut up. You killed them all. To show off, you said. And then you all come back here and wait for god to fly down in a spaceship and save you."

"So what? Since when does Golden Vanity care about the moral standing of lokies?"

"It bothers me."

"Why?"

"Leave me alone."

"I'm about to." He took his hand away and sat up.

"What do you mean?"

"You know all those times I said I'd leave you? Well, this time I mean it. I'm through, Vanity. I've risked my crummy little life for you, and my family, and the ERM, and the Daniks, and Gari's even dead, and maybe even the whole mother planet, and I get nothing for it. Absolutely nothing, beginning to end." He was taking a chance, he knew. If she panicked again she might just take off before he could get clear of the desert and the Daniks. He didn't think she would. He almost didn't care; he just wanted to dump her.

Her eyes searched his face. "What will you do?"

"Go back to Earth City, wait for morning, then pack some food and slice. If you fly off in your firecracker please wait till I'm gone. That's the only thing I'm asking."

Vanity's arrogance vanished like water in the desert sun. "Please, Hump, don't go. You're not really going, are you?"

"You got it."

"But I need you."

"Well, I sure as hell don't need you."

She leaned forward on her hands and knees. "I'll do what you say. Everything. I should have followed you all along. I realize that now. I'm sorry, Hump. You tell me what to do." She took his hand.

He yanked it away. "I don't know what to do any more than you do."

"Then we should stay together."

"Will you tell me the truth?"

"Everything. Cross my heart and hope to fly."

"That's die, stupid. Boy, isn't it. Tell me about this telepathy stuff. What's going on?"

"I—I don't know."

"What? If you don't know, why does it bother you so much?"

"*Because* I don't know. It bothers you too, doesn't it?"

"Yeah, I'm afraid I might get stuck in there with you." He looked at her staring at the ground. "There's more, isn't there?"

"Why should there be more?"

"Because there is. You're not as good at hiding things as you used to be."

"Well, telepathy like that, no one's ever done that before."

"So what?"

"It's not possible."

"Of course it's possible. We're doing it."

"But if we're doing something that's not supposed to happen then the whole system—" She broke off.

"What about the whole system?" Vanity looked away. "Come on, honey. Over the top. You can do it." She said nothing. Hump got to his feet. "So much for honesty." He started down the hill. "See you later, alligator. You can add that to your lokie repertoire."

"I hate you," Vanity called after him. "I hate all of you, the whole planet, you make me sick. I hope Jaak packs you all in ice and dumps you on Luritti." She stared wildly at the desert. "Hundreds of planets and I had to come here. Billions of people and I had to find you. Hump the truth seeker. If only I'd let those rat fems rip you." When she turned around Hump was out of sight. "Hump?" she called, then louder, "Harry? Harry!"

She sat down and rubbed her hand over her face, unable to decide whether to cry or snicker. Alone. Well, that's what she wanted in the first place, wasn't it? She'd never gotten free until now. She'd only gone from Jaak to this lokie loudmouth who couldn't stop spouting about truth and honesty and trust. Imagine telling that to Jaak.

Cold, she stood up and pumped her legs up and down. Burst, what an awful place. "God's mucous," Hump called it one day. She smiled. Funny, she actually enjoyed listening to his idiotic conversation. She recited to herself a maxim one of market world development. "Human beings can get used to anything."

She climbed to the top of the hill, thinking maybe the height would lift her from the misery of this death-ridden world. But the chill moonlight changed the hills into rows of corpses, frozen and grey. Vanity shuddered. She imagined the whole planet like this, mounds of bodies, burnt and shriveled trees, oceans and rivers nothing but baked dust. Jaak's revenge.

Maybe she could bargain with Jaak. He'd get her anyway, maybe she could make a deal to go back if he'd spare Earth. But why did she care? The companies had ruined better worlds than this one.

Why did he have to leave her here? Anywhere else, the city,

Marilyn's house; could she get back to Marilyn? No, better stay on her own. For all she knew, Marilyn was dead. Anyway, that's why she broke loose, to get on her own. Why should she run to lokies? She should enjoy her solitude. (She remembered Cixxa, her teacher, saying, "Forget 'should.' 'Should' is the great enemy of fantasies.")

She could leave right now, take the ship, go hide. Somewhere. Anywhere. Without Hump to get picky over the place and the people, she could really explore.

She took only a few steps vaguely towards the ship, then stopped. Not at night. She might get lost and anyway, she'd promised Hump. Well, she hadn't really promised, he'd arrogantly assumed she'd obey him. He did help her, though.

She began to walk aimlessly, across the hills and flats, half consciously keeping a long orbit around Earth City. At one point she tumbled down a hill and nearly crashed against a Danik woman who sat on the ground meditating in that slimy simper they all cultivated.

Did they actually like it here? Hump had once told her that Earth people liked to suffer intentionally because they knew they'd suffer anyway, and this way they could consider themselves in charge. Did Hump like it here? No, but it didn't bother him so much either. Not like her. Yet his people had created this horror; willfully they'd killed everything that lived here, even the dirt and water. How could it not bother him? No ghosts. Hump and the other lokies didn't carry any ghosts.

Hers never left, always pecking at her, lying down beside her, the dead faces she'd never seen except in holos, dead years and years before her birth. She clenched her fists. For all their horrors Hump's people had never done what hers had done.

And of course they never could. No one could repeat her people's crime. Like they said on Rocky Jones, it was a one-shot. Over and done for the rest of history.

And the lokies wanted spaceships.

And the Daniks wanted the gods to come out of the sky.

And Hump wanted the truth. Despite the ache in her legs and the dry cold wind that slapped her chest and face she strode angrily ahead as she thought of Hump's demands for truth. He expected it as a show of personal devotion, like a tame cru. A show of selfishness from Hump himself was more like it. Couldn't he understand that she hated the truth? His selfish shallow mind broadcast truth-trust, space-glory, alies-purity, and all the other cherished equations of his bork mentality. Burst, she hated him. She hated his smug arrogance.

A fant, infantile, stupid, sprung alive in her mind. Hump surrounded by Jaak's blank-faced beamers, herself swooping down to rescue him. Pathetic. She'd done better than that when she was eight. Anyway, they could cut him into Vita Flakes for all she cared. For a moment she wondered what Jaak would do to him, but the thought raised a wild panic, and she drove it away before she might run back to rescue him. As if she could help either of them.

Feed your head, she told herself. She remembered Cixxa telling her to break a bad pattern with a new direction. All right, get a starting point. A forest. No, too dark. Make it open air, but green land, water, flowers, long droopy leaves, a stone house, a world all her own, clean. Clean. In her mind, she was running naked through the grass, dew kicking up behind her, while a great blue *keri* loped alongside her. Loneliness yanked at her, but she slapped it away, while she and the *keri* talked in growls and whispers. The beast told her of a cave he'd discovered, filled with drawings of creatures from a million years ago.

No. No caves. And no million years. None of that. She'd almost found herself back in the tunnel.

She clung to her imagined world, the warm air, the keri, the birds that glided over their heads as if to guard them from the sky. Guard? The sky darkened, the birds changed to leatherwinged deelos; she and the keri ran to the house, threw themselves at the door. Inside sat a man, naked, his skin dark red, his shoulders heavy, his hands enormous, scarred, his face hidden by a bleached mask—

Vanity shouted and struck the ground with both fists. She got up, cold, frightened. She couldn't stay the night here. Too many ghosts. She could sleep in the ship and leave the next day. She hesitated, staring at the glow of light that marked Earth City. She sobbed, dry, without tears. How did it all go so wrong? She didn't want anything like this. Was it because of Jaak chasing her? She'd wanted adventure, exploration, but all of it alone, alone, *alone*.

"I don't want him!" she shouted. "I don't need him. I don't need anything he can give me, and I don't want him." She sat down with a thud.

Hump lay on his hard lumpy cot, his hands behind his head, his legs crossed, and made faces at some imaginary picture of

Vanity on the ceiling. He wished he could turn on the lights and read . . . even a Danik pamphlet. But he didn't dare wake anyone up. The slimy—the idiots would just ask more stupid questions. He'd had enough trouble making them believe that the truth of the pageant had overwhelmed Edie's religious soul and she'd wanted to meditate the night away.

He kept thinking he should leave right now, sneak down to the kitchen for some food and get away. But he'd only get lost; he might as well wait for first light. The Daniks never got up early. What for?

Or should he wait for midday and make some proper announcement so nobody got worried and decided to search for him? "Goodbye, folks, I've found God here, but now I'm going home. Preach to the masses." He'd sure hate to stagger through the desert three or four days only to find several thousand police waiting for him.

Damn Vanity. He should have punched her. Just once, right in that smug selfish face of hers. Goddamn bitch.

For a moment he wondered what would happen to her. Despite himself, he hoped she'd escape. Her father sounded bad enough, but the other guy, Loper she called him— What would they do to her? Some vivid possibilities came to mind; he pushed them away.

Angrily he turned on his side. Why should he worry about her? She certainly didn't care about him. Anyway, she'd probably escape more easily than him. He didn't own a spaceship.

He looked up prayerfully at the ceiling, as if God hid behind the lampshade. *Just let me get home*, he thought. *Please. I don't care about anything else. Please. I just want to get home.*

The door creaked open. Hump sat up. Vanity stood there like a little girl who'd gotten caught in the rain, her hair tangled and filthy, her shoulders slumped, her face droopy and stained. Hump had never seen her look so beaten. He bared his teeth, then lay down again, his face to the wall.

Vanity kneeled by his cot. "Please Hump," she said. "Can I talk to you?"

"No," he whispered. "Go visit Jupiter."

"Just let me talk to you."

"Will you shut up? You'll wake the whole zoo."

She smirked. "I'll scream if you don't let me talk to you."

"Oh, for Christ's sake." He got out of bed, grabbed her wrist, and dragged her outside. He wanted to slam her against the wall.

The smirk vanished and Vanity stared at the ground, working her lips. "Come on, what is it?" Hump snapped. But he knew he was faking. He wanted to grab her and press her miserable face against his chest.

"Hump—" she started, then sputtered out like a cold engine.

"Well?" Her eyes pleaded with him as if he could say it for her. "What the hell do you want?"

Her fist in her mouth, Vanity shook her head.

"Goodbye," Hump said. He'd taken a step before Vanity grabbed his arm.

"Hump," she whispered. "Would you like to learn to work a spaceship?"

Chapter Fifteen ───────────────

He lay on a vast feather couch in a long gleaming room, light shining from the hundreds of diamonds worked into the golden walls (pile on the clichés, he thought; how about some harem slaves? The hell with that, Vanity says aesthetics don't count, and if he got off on Sabu opulence let it ride.) Cool breezes poured in through the ebony window. Outside, a cool forest, a shimmering lake.

(Except that the sun bore down on the dirty white cloth covering his face. Try to forget it, he ordered himself.)

Where was he? Diamond room, cool forest. The room, fix the room. He imagined it again, the ebony windows and gold floor. Was the floor gold? Well, it was now. (Like the sun. Scram the sun.) He looked outside the window, but now the forest changed into hills, rolling green hills. (No, no hills. Too much like reality.) Should he keep the lake?

Too many details. He shook his head. Keep it simple, Vanity had said. Hold on to it. Once you let it start changing, you've lost it. As if he ever had it.

"Damn," he said, sitting up. The cloth fell off his head and he shook himself, blinking. "I'm sorry, Vanity," he told his teacher. "I just can't hold on to it. The images just don't come in strong enough."

They were sitting on top of a hill about a mile from Earth

City. It was early morning, before the sun could force them back
to the settlement. Twice a day they came here, sunrise and
sunset, for extended sessions, with Hump supposedly practicing
the techniques privately the whole day. A crash course in
fantasies, the first and most vital step in preparing to work a
spaceship. Working the controls was easy, Vanity insisted; he
could absorb it all through the ship's deep-learning mechanisms
in just a few days. Working yourself was much harder.

"Let's try again," Vanity said. "I'll guide you."

"It's too hot," Hump protested. "And anyway, I don't think
I'll ever learn." Hell, he *knew* he would never learn.

"We've got nearly an hour yet. And you're doing great. Lie
down again." Hump obeyed, draping the grimy sun shield over
his eyes. "Now relax," she told him, her voice still filled with
tension. "Just slice everything from your head. The sun, the
ground, everything."

It's no use, he knew. It was all just a game to keep them
occupied till Daddy came. He sighed and tried to clear his mind.

They'd begun simply, the very next day after the Danik
festival. Hump had to learn to visualize, Vanity said, and she
began with simple geometric forms, scratching a triangle or a
square in the hard dirt. Hump had to first stare at it, then try to
see it with his eyes closed.

It amazed him how hard it was. She would draw a triangle
with a circle in the center; he would fix it in his mind, but as soon
as he closed his eyes, the walls would shift, become a square or a
wavy rectangle, and if he tried to just accept the new shape it
shifted again, a spiky circle or the original triangle, but upside
down. Discouraged, he'd wondered why these visualizations
were so important. He knew how to daydream; it never seemed
to require much talent or training. Of course, Vanity, had
explained, anyone can make a fant. But you had to learn to
stabilize it, to develop it step by step. "Look," she told him, "the
ship needs wave structures. Stable, solid structures from your
head. The ship doesn't care about the contents of your fantasies,
that's your problem, all the ship wants is stability. Complete-
ness."

So Hump practised again and again, until he could keep an
image fixed in his mind for minutes at a time, and even recall it
hours later in the anonymity of a Danik breast-beating
repentance session. He began to get excited, to fantasize himself

as Earth's spaceman, until Vanity jumped him a level. "We haven't got much time," she'd said airily, as if they could possibly accomplish anything real in the time they did have, and set him to making simple fantasies. Nothing would stay fixed. The setting changed, the story changed. Worst of all, he could not stop criticizing. His conscious mind (the "upper ego" Vanity called it, as opposed to the "lower ego," what he called the imagination, though she assured him the term was pitifully vague and misguided) would constantly judge, comment, ridicule, or simply interfere, with thoughts of lunch, home, Jaak and Loper, friends from years ago, the Daniks. "It's hopeless," Hump would moan. "Try again," his teacher would order.

Now, nearly two weeks after he'd started the crash course, he was doing just that, lying on a baked hillside and imagining a cool room (always cool) with a soft gold rug and plush couches beside mosaic walls. (Okay, what next? Maybe a little hero self-worship.) His fant body, graceful, skin all gleaming, rose cat-like from a couch, slipped on a green diamond trimmed robe (funny to discover he liked wealth. Opulence on other people had always looked so ostentatious to him. Maybe this fantasy stuff could teach you something about yourself, if nothing else. He remembered once seeing the Platinum Ensemble and thinking they should spend more time learning expression and less time polishing their instruments. And that made him think how awful the Danik music was. *Shit*, he thought. How could the mind derail itself so quickly?)

Vanity must have heard him sigh, because she intoned, in her teacher's voice, slow and soothing, completely unlike her, "If your mind wanders, bring it back to the fantasy. Learn to stay there."

All right, so where was he? The room, the green robe; make that a Mongolian robe (he remembered a teev show he'd once seen about Mongolian shepherd dancers) embroidered with pictures of hero Hump making his great stand against the aliens (oh, come on). He looked out the ebony window at the green crystal lake ringed with graceful trees drooping their leaves over the mirror like water. Rocks ringed the water's edge, painted upright stones like a troop of guards.

(He remembered the summers spent with his parents and their neo-Irish Renaissance friends at a lake they'd renamed Innisfree, though sometimes they called it Baile's Strand. Hold it. Back to work.)

There was a boat on the lake, a sailboat, deep blue sails furled against the masts. A tall woman stood on the deck, streams of blond hair lifting out behind her, cloak flapping in the wind. (What wind? The water was calm, wasn't it?)

He waved his hand. As the walls of his house opened, he heard music rising from the colored stones, each one like an unearthly instrument. Images came to him, musicians, blind men and women, naked under a full moon, living only in their music that they played through a night lasting a thousand years until at last the Earth Mother changed them into the stones that now ringed the lakes outside Hump's house. (Where did *that* come from? Despite the heat, a chill swept over him.) Now the woman came out of the lake, she was the lake, water taking form, a shimmering woman shaking in the wind.

(Suddenly uncomfortable, Hump didn't like the lyricism that had emerged from under his usual blanket of cynicism. It reminded him too much of that "land of faery" bullshit his parents used to force on him.)

He sat up and rubbed his eyes.

"What's wrong?" Vanity asked.

"The usual thing," Hump lied. "I just keep distracting myself."

She made a noise. "If only I had some equipment."

"You keep saying that but you don't, so what's the point?"

"Cixxa had a thing that could monitor the wave patterns and as soon as you slipped back into the upper ego it gave you a little jolt, sometimes even before you yourself would notice."

"Terrific. Nothing like aversion therapy." He stood up. "Let's get out of the sun."

"There's still time."

"Not for me. Will you come on?"

While they trudged back, their heads down, their eyes squinted against the glare coming off the sand, Vanity said, "I know we could do it if we just—"

"Had some equipment," Hump finished. He suddenly wanted to strike out against her. "We've got one little trick we could use."

"What do you mean?"

"You could slip inside my head. Like I did with you the night of the pageant."

"No!"

"Then when I started to wander you could pull me right back again."

"Stop it. I don't want to hear it."

Yeah, he thought, there's a lot of things you don't want to hear.

The next day, Hump lay on his hot hilltop, itching, sweating, and trying to lose himself in a fantasy of wealth and safety, when abruptly he saw, in his "lower ego's eye" as he called it, a woman, dressed in an old-fashioned silk gown, smile at him and open a door. Inside he saw a small room with red velvet walls, a window with iron bars, an ornate white wooden writing desk, and behind the desk a man in an eighteenth century wig, bent over and scratching obscene drawings with a quill pen on parchment. A chain ran from a ring around his ankle to the desk leg. For nearly two seconds the image held, as vivid as the baked earth, but only when it faded did Hump realize that the man was himself. He jerked upright so fast he almost knocked his teacher over.

"What happened?" she said.

"I saw something. A picture of myself. I thought these were supposed to be controlled fantasies? Nice things. Daydreams."

"Did what you see scare you?"

"Yeah. Well, it felt scarier than it looked. Like it was implying something. It came through so damn strong."

Vanity scowled. "A snake. I suppose it means you're making progress."

"What do you mean?"

"A snake is a fant that twists on you. The lower ego kind of jumps out of control and shows you things that don't belong in the fant. Things you don't want to see. In a ship it's dangerous, but in training it indicates the fant centers are getting stronger. You've just got to learn to keep control."

"But maybe these snake things have some value. Maybe I needed to see that picture."

"Snakes are garbage," Vanity said. Hump stared at her vehemence. "You've got to learn to get rid of them before they take off. Believe me. Otherwise you've got trouble."

"But maybe if you face them you could learn something about yourself."

"You're not doing it to learn something about yourself."

Hump shrugged. "You're the guru."

When they first began, Hump thought of the training as a lot like the meditation exercises they used to give everyone in high school until the schiz scandals stopped the programs. He soon learned the basic difference. Instead of stopping the conscious flow of images, the fant techniques activated them.

But when he tried to compare it to gestalt fantasizing, where you confronted yourself by allowing the subconscious (lower ego) to throw images at you, Vanity again stopped him cold. You didn't want to confront yourself; you wanted to work a spaceship. And for that you needed safe stable fantasies, deliberately cleansed of any elements that might break down the structured ego.

So you drove out anything you didn't like; which resulted, as Hump saw in Vanity, in terror. Terror of nightmares, plays, absurd Danik pageants, anything at all that suggested, even by accident, those blocked out images.

It's all wrong, he thought again and again. But Vanity was the teacher.

For the next few days they went back to basic exercises with Vanity showing her pupil how to break the fant when it got away from him, as if, Hump thought, he would ever get that far.

Three weeks after Vanity's offer to teach him, a discouraged Hump, wishing he could go home, was working on yet another basic exercise: "a gateway into your head" as Vanity called it. You were supposed to visualize a kind of anteroom in your skull, a storage chamber of all your dreams and wishes. Then, once you chose a starting point to get your fantasy going, you went out the other side, like going through an air lock. Which was why the air lock on Vanity's ship was more decorated than the cabin itself. "An old custom," she'd said back on Staten Island.

What's the use, he thought, and then, *At least it'll kill time until Daddy comes. Or Loper. Then it won't be time that gets killed.*

The gateway took shape in his mind, a black oval doorway into a gleaming white building. (He remembered the time in college when he thought it set him off to wear nothing but white and black. Why did all his fantasies revert to adolescence?) Inside he imagined a wall full of doors or windows. (Get it straight. Which is it? Make it doors. He imagined the chained artist hidden behind one of the doors and changed it to windows. Without bars.)

Now a detail, something to get him started. How about that old favorite, a bathtub? (He remembered slipping once in the bath at Gloria's house and hurting his coccyx. How was Gloria, anyway? Had the government gotten on to her?) He pictured himself going up to one of the windows (like placing a bet at the track. What would Vanity think of a horse race? Would she prefer the live ones or the robots?). Annoyed, he reconstructed the room and the window and looked through to an ivory bathtub with platinum fixtures (wealth again. Maybe he should sell Vanity after all. Make a hell of an auction.) Make that a marble tub, he didn't want to hurt any elephants. Okay, a huge cool tub in a room, or maybe on an open patio, surrounded by giant tropical plants.

No. He could think it but he couldn't see it. He imagined some machine measuring his fant output and the operator shaking his head in pity or disgust. Anyway, too many bathtubs and lakes and pools. It just made him feel worse about not getting anything but seven and a half minutes in the lukewarm dribble the Daniks called a shower.

Back to the room full of windows (which seemed less real to him every time he used it).

How about a story line, action instead of objects? From his memory storehouse Errol Flynn swung past on a vine. (Vanity's influence. Her impeccable taste had selected cracked prints of Errol Flynn movies as her favorite entertainment after Rocky Jones.) Robin Hood? How about a modern version? Galactic Hump, Earth hero, robbing from the aliens. (What would the ERM think of that one?)

He remembered Jimmy Wu, with his Great Interstellar Floating Riot Sale, and imagined the two of them trundling up in Jimmy's old truck. He could even feel the bouncing and suddenly noticed his body moving against the ground. Embarrassed, he lay still again. The fant continued (good sign) and he saw himself leaping out close to the ground, running. Neatly he scaled the wall of the spaceport (now he could feel the hard concrete, though he had to dismiss the reality intrusion that spaceport walls weren't made of concrete). Behind him ran his silent herd of thieves, renegade rat fems (them? Sure, why not?) sliding through the shadows.

Suddenly it all just embarrassed him. Clichés, clichés. Vanity might say that aesthetics didn't matter, but couldn't he come up with something better than third-rate Hollywood?

How about a sex fantasy? Maybe a *ménage à trois* with the queen of Holland and a robot taxicab? He sat up.

"Your lesson's not over yet," Vanity said in her governess' voice.

"It is for me. I've had it."

"You'll never learn if you don't practice."

"I'll never learn, period. Earth people don't belong in space."

"You've just got to work at it."

"Come on, Vanity, you know it's a big game. This whole idea is your fantasy, not mine."

"You've *got* to learn."

"What are you getting so worked up about? You don't really think I can learn, do you? Look Vanity, I'll confess something to you. I don't want to learn to work a spaceship. I'm much too scared. You just assumed it because it's what you would want. I just wanted the truth, how things work, what made fantasies and nightmares so important. Now I know, so can't we stop?"

"No. The truth's not worth anything unless you do something with it."

"What do you expect me to do if I do learn? I can't fly us out of this mess any better than you can."

"You dumb kura-lover. I want to give you something. Something valuable. Before it's too late. Maybe if I can teach you, you can teach Marilyn. And then maybe you'll all have some small chance against the companies."

"Wow," Hump said. "You like to think big, don't you?"

"I mean it. Someone's got to find a way."

"It's a dream, Vanity." Suddenly he laughed. "Sonofabitch, the Daniks are right. Prometheus has come to Earth after all."

"What are you talking about?"

"Prometheus. The defector, giving away the secrets of the gods so Daddy Zeus can't wipe away the humans. You."

"Hump, can't you slice the jokes?"

"Look who's talking. Unfortunately, dear Vanity, it's just another fantasy."

She looked about to cry. "We can still try, can't we?"

The next morning Vanity woke Hump even earlier than usual. With hardly more than grunts of information she dragged him unerringly to her spaceship, patiently waiting for her in its little hollow between the hills.

"What the hell's going on?" Hump demanded at the first sight of it sitting there, impossibly clean in the dawn glow. "You're not planning to give me flight lessons, are you?"

"No, no. There's something inside I want to use."

After Vanity had bribed him with a synthetic steak and an air and lotion shower that made him weep with joy, Hump let her sit

him down before the small stone table in the center of the cabin.
"What is this anyway?" he asked. He looked nervously at the
shifting jewel-like bubble in the center.

"It's a fant aid," Vanity said cheerfully. "A hypnagogic image
maker."

"I thought you said you didn't have any aids."

"Yes. Well, I lied."

"What a unique experience. Why?"

"I was duck."

"What?"

"Scared."

"Oh, you mean chicken. Chicken of what?"

"Sometimes it works a little too well."

"That's just great, Vanity. Let's get out of here."

Her hands on his shoulders stopped him from getting up.
"You've got to learn."

"I don't want to learn." He sounded to himself like a little kid
throwing a tantrum.

Vanity said, "I won't just sit here until Jaak or Loper catches
us. Now pay attention. That stuff there in the middle, I don't
know what it is, or even does—"

"That's terrific, Vanity."

"Will you stop it? I just said that so you wouldn't interrupt
with a lot of useless questions. It comes from Nauikkra, where
all the fant teachers come from. And it works. If you look closely
at it, it adapts to your brain patterns or something and you start
to get strong fant images. It's just to get you used to feeding your
head. Once you learn how, you can do it yourself."

"Where does the danger come in?"

"It's not really so dangerous." She fidgeted. "Usually, novices
don't use it. It can flood the mind. But that's only if you look too
long."

"Suppose I don't look at all?"

"We've got no choice. We don't have any time to go slow, and
anyway I'm not that good a teacher."

"That's also reassuring. What the hell do I do?"

"Not much. Just sit comfortably and look at the center."

"That's all?" She nodded. "What do I do if I get flooded?"

"Look away. But if you can't break loose, use the anti-snake
techniques. Shout or hit the floor with the palms of your hands.
Anyway, I'll monitor you and pull you back in time."

"Thanks." Bent forward, Hump stared at the black

mercury-like substance, seeing nothing but flashes of light that hurt his eyes. He turned to Vanity. "It doesn't work for me, teacher."

"Stop playing and look."

Hump shrugged. He remembered his first impressions of the two foot square table. Made of some metal or stone that somehow shifted texture and color—a pebbly gold to a polished blue with a hundred shades in between—the low table, about eight inches high, held *something* in the center: round, black, and almost oily. The liquescent mass moved constantly, changing color with the light. Decorative, Hump had thought. Pretty piece of furniture. He squinted at it suspiciously.

Lightheadedness eased away Hump's anxiety. He laughed when he looked up and saw Vanity's frown. A moment later he forgot her entirely as a delicate heady smell of flowers swirled around him, fields and fields of flowers.

Pictures formed in front of him, faces as real as the ship, then suddenly dissolving; sounds flooded his ears: music, voices, animal noises, a constant roaring somewhere to the left of him. He smelled sweet sugar candy, mounds of it. He stuffed his cheeks, then laughing too hard to swallow, spit it out again, bright glittery knives flashed in front of him, swirls of cloth, of wings, of hands, hundreds of hands, colors, bright blue and green, the sky, the shimmering cool sea.

He turned around to grin at his teacher. For just a moment Vanity looked like an old bent widow, her face twisted by the constant pain of years. When he shook himself he saw the young woman frowning at him. "It's working," he stammered.

"Of course it's working. Maybe you better stop now."

"No, I'm just starting to like it. It's a lot better than lying on a sand dune."

"Are you sure you can handle it?"

"Aren't I your star pupil?"

"Hump—"

"Shh." He looked back at the table. Instantly he lay on his back in a field of trees and flowers, a soft sun warming his face. Suddenly the sun heated up; his skin blistered, cracked. But then the cool night came and everything was fine again.

A room. Long, narrow, a conference room. As Hump walked in, a mixture of faces turned expectantly. Black, white, saffron, yellow, red, saffron, saffron. He'd come to bargain with the alies, the one man they respected and feared. Behind him came his bodyguard, a ratheaded woman dressed in Aztec robes. No. No, he didn't like that one. A swell of panic subsided as Hump waved his hand and the room disappeared.

Cool. Dark. Night. He floated in a pool at night, eyes closed, a roaring noise behind him. No, no noise, he wanted quiet, didn't he make it clear he wanted quiet?

Engines. He opened his eyes and saw, all around his pool, great spaceships blasting the Earth.

Hump knew the stop time had arrived. But how? Make a noise, Vanity said. Hit the floor. With what? His hands had vanished; who the hell had taken his hands?

A horrible smell of rot poured over him. He shook, moaned. Fingers pulled him back and forth, a dim voice—Golden Vanity?—called him, but he pushed her aside and ran ahead, anywhere, away from the smell, until bodies blocked his path, mounds of Aztecs ripped apart by Spanish swords. Hump screamed and slapped the ground.

For a moment he saw Vanity's face in front of him, her hands on his shoulders. And then he saw himself, from Vanity's eyes, a wild-eyed stick of terror. *No*, he thought. *Got to get out. Get out!*

He was running down a long dark street in ratfemland, while girls and boys in filthy rags threw knives, rocks, and broken glass at him.

Suddenly there were two of him. Two Humps, two people running together, their feet flapping in unison. The second Hump took his hand, pulled him along, faster and faster, then changed, melted into a woman, Golden Vanity leading him back to safety, shouting at his pursuers to snake back into their bursting slime. He saw something in the road, white and clean, cool. Vanity's spaceship. She lifted him over her shoulders, he couldn't have weighed more than a couple of pounds, and as the door slid open Hump looked back once more to see flames, and ratfems, and aliens, and the street, all fading into calm.

Chapter Sixteen —————————

Hump blinked, opened his eyes to find himself on the green couch in Vanity's spaceship. His head ached, and when he tried to sit, dizziness slapped him down again. He let out a ragged breath. "Wow," he said. He turned his head. Vanity sat on the floor, her back against the wall, her face stunned. The image maker was gone, either stored away or thrown outside. "You sure were right about looking too long. I'm sorry. Next time I'll listen to you." Vanity didn't answer. "Thanks," Hump said. "For whatever you did, I mean. Hey look, relax, it's all over. I'm fine, just a little schizzed." She still said nothing. "You know what happened? What I fantasized? I thought—"

"You fantasized yourself back in ratfemland, chased by ratfems and alies."

He started to shake. "How do you know that?"

"And then I joined you and pulled you loose. I picked you up and carried you back to my ship."

"That's right. That's exactly it."

"Hump, you were broadcasting."

"What do you mean?"

"Telepathy. No, not even that. I don't know what to call it. Don't you understand? You flung out your mind and pulled me in beside you. Inside your *body*. I was looking at the image maker through your eyes, seeing your fantasies. That can't

169

happen. It just can't. It's all wrong." Hump said nothing. Vanity moaned. "Nothing like this has ever happened before."

With a sigh, Hump said, "Vanity, let's cut out the bullshit. We both know it's happened before. It happened just two weeks ago at the festival. Hell, it happened that first night in my house."

"And it's the one thing you never pushed me on. You're scared of it too."

"Of course I'm scared. I'm scared of everything."

"Hump, you don't understand. No one's ever done or heard of anything like this. Ever."

"So maybe it's something new."

"New?"

"Yeah, maybe we've made a discovery."

Vanity began to cry. "That's not possible."

"What are you talking about? People make discoveries all the time, don't they?"

"You're such a fool, and you don't even know it."

Completely confused, Hump tried to take her in his arms; she pushed him away. "Didn't it ever strike you as just a little strange that my people came up with all this, the ships, the pulse points, the fant system, in just two hundred years?"

My god Hump thought, *she's opening up*. And then he wondered what it was about this ESP thing that could make Golden Vanity let loose her secrets. He said, "Yeah, it struck me as strange. You just made a joke about it."

"Do you know what the pulse points are? The things we use to send messages and to figure out where we are between planets? They're manufactured miniature black holes strung out across the galaxy. Do you know how they send messages? Through another universe. Another *universe*."

"What's the point, Vanity?"

"And yet, it all happened in two hundred years. With time left over to colonize the market worlds. How could you believe me?"

"I didn't. You've told me so many lies I never knew what to believe."

"Oh Hump, we could never have done all this in two hundred years. Or two thousand. Or maybe even two million. Listen. You once asked me who invented the alter engines. And I said I didn't know. Well, nobody knows. We didn't make up the fant mechanisms, Hump. We didn't make up the ships, or the pulse points, or anything at all. We were given them, a complete system for controlling the galaxy. And now you tell me we've discovered something new? It's not possible."

"You were given it? Who the hell gave it to you?"

"Do you remember I told you about the Ur-humans?"

"The original space gods. They invented it all?"

She nodded. "We don't even know how any of it works. You know I told you that robots build the ships? And they repair themselves? They have to. We can't. If the ships died and the robots didn't build any more, the companies would die too."

"This is ludicrous. All these months, Earth's been begging for something the companies and the SA didn't invent in the first place."

"No, it's not ludicrous. Because wherever the ships came from, the companies have them. But they don't have this mind switch of ours. The kurois—that's what we call the Ur-humans—never said a word about it. Oh, they told us about telepathy. It's a sign of breakdown. Ego collapse. But you didn't just broadcast, I went right inside your head. And you haven't collapsed; if anything, I saved you from a breakdown. It doesn't make any sense."

"So what? People still discover new things. What about that image maker? That didn't come from the Ur-humans. The kurois. Or did it?"

"No, no. But that's just a gimmick. It doesn't really change anything. There's nothing really new we can discover that they didn't know about. Nothing."

"Maybe they just didn't tell you about it. Can we ask them? I mean, are they still around somewhere?" She laughed, shaking her head. Suddenly the laughter changed to gulping sobs.

"Vanity," Hump said, "Maybe you better tell me the whole story."

"You won't like it. I guarantee you, you won't like it."

"Try me."

There was a long silence. Then finally Vanity began in a low flat voice. "Two hundred years ago my people, the people of Center, lived on a world a lot like this one. Primitive, simple. Then one day the ships came. Not too many, a few with instruments, a few with robots, and a few with people. I think there weren't more than a hundred of them. Hump, they were beautiful. Old, so old; and graceful, like water. I used to look at holos of them. All day long I'd watch them, over and over. And cry. Just stare and cry. Until my fant teacher told Jaak to take them away from me. Burst, they were beautiful."

"And they gave your people the ships?"

"Some of them. And the robots to make more. And they taught us how to work it all. Do you know how long they said the pulse points have hung there? Four million years. Do you wonder we don't know how it works? For four million years, they said, they'd wandered across the galaxy, maybe beyond it, maybe into another universe. Maybe they came from another universe. Four million years. And you think we can discover something new?" Hump only shook his head. "They seeded the planets, watched them evolve, and finally, they said, they wanted to share the galaxy with their children. They said. There were only a hundred of them because they didn't need any more. They weren't trying to evolve any more. They'd reached the end. They said."

"God, I can see why the Danik pageant shook you. You were the only one who knew how true it was. Except that the space gods' gifts didn't produce any paradise. Just the companies."

"That's not the reason."

"I don't understand."

"You don't understand." She spun around. Tears splashed across her parched skin as her cracked lips spit, "Idiot. Why did you stop? Why don't you ask the next question? Idiot!" Hump squinted at her. "The next question. You want the truth, don't you? The precious bloody filthy truth. Ask the next question."

Hump could hardly stand the thought that there was something else. Terrified, he said, "What next question?"

"Why they stopped with us. Why they didn't go on to the other planets."

"I thought they'd left that to you."

"The idiot lokie solution. After four million—but you're right, Hump. Very right. They definitely left it to us." She slapped his hands away when he reached for her. "Ask me."

"Why didn't the Kurois go on to the other planets?"

"*Because we killed them all.*"

"The Aztecs," Hump said.

"What?" Just outside Earth City Vanity stopped and looked at her pupil. They had walked from Vanity's ship silently, lost in their separate horrors.

"That book at Marilyn's," Hump said.

"Later. I want to get out of the sun."

"But—all right, sure."

Standing in the pathetic shower, Hump wondered what would happen to Vanity. He remembered his spacegirl when he'd first met her, insufferably sarcastic, selfish, arrogant, but also thrilled with Earth, the new sights, with freedom. And now he wondered if she'd get herself back together at all. It wasn't just this new thing of theirs. He could see it was frightening, but certainly no more than having the whole galaxy chasing you. It was more that it forced Vanity to think about the kurois; for Vanity something new was a confrontation with history. He remembered Vanity once saying, "History's the most horrible thing there is." What was it like to grow up with the cultural heritage of a monster?

But when he came out, Vanity was sitting on their double cot, washed, freshly dressed in a sack-like Danik dress, and grinning at him. He wanted to leap on top of her and kiss her. He only said, "What are you staring at?"

"The man who knows the truth. I want to see if you look fulfilled. 'He who knows the truth has drunk from the fountain of the gods.' 'True Legend of Prometheus,' chapter one."

He sat down, looking around nervously for eavesdroppers. "We'll send you as a missionary to the outer planets. Telling the truth doesn't seem to have done much to you. You're still obnoxious."

The smile vanished. She shrugged. "I don't know. I feel lighter, less scared. I still don't know what's happening with us, but, well, I've lived here with you people for months now. And all of you believe such lies. The Daniks aren't the only ones, you all believe it. And I couldn't tell anyone."

"You could have told me."

"You don't know the training we get. I don't even mean directly, just one thing you learn automatically, over and over, if you grow up on Center. You don't tell market people the truth. Not anything. And it's not just that. I don't like to think of these things."

"That I could guess."

"I used to think of them all the time. I couldn't stop. Then my fant teacher made me stop. All my fants were snaking on me, and the only thing to do was just try to put it all out of my mind."

"Maybe you should have tried to work it all through. Follow the snakes and see where they led you."

"I told you, it doesn't work that way. All you get is a

breakdown, a shrieker. Anyway, you wouldn't have liked the truth, either. Not at first, not for a long time. You would have gotten rid of me."

Hump put an arm around her. "I know what you mean. I feel a little like I want to get rid of myself."

They sat silently for a while, then Vanity asked, "What did you ask me before? About Marilyn?"

Hump glanced around nervously, "Maybe we shouldn't talk here."

Vanity laughed. "You always get cautious an hour too late. Don't worry, there're no sneaky stoops under the bed."

"Someone might be sitting outside in the shade."

"What shade? Oh all right, let's go to the chapel. No one'll hear us there."

The chapel stood alone on the edge of the settlement, a circular domed building made of some translucent plastic that allowed enough light in to brighten the chamber without heating it beyond endurance. The building contained no furniture; officially, sitting on the white metal floor aided penitence through suffering; actually the Daniks preferred the slightly cooler floor to chairs or benches. In the center of the room, ten feet high, stood the Daniks' idea of a spaceship, a silver painted, needle nosed plastic rocket ship from 1950's comic books. In place of the inevitable porthole the Daniks had painted a circular Tao symbol. The hull bore the Hindu word OM, while the three curved fins displayed a cross, a crescent, and a Star of David. Hump marveled that they'd left off a Happy Buddha in a spacesuit.

The two sat together facing the single door. The Daniks rarely came here during the day, preferring the illusion of fresh air outside or else the darkened cool of the dining hall and library. "I guess we all look ludicrous to you," Hump said. "Astronauts of love. Though I suppose the kurois did return with love. So the Daniks were right after all, they just got the wrong people."

"Do you think the kurois came with love? The gods bringing gifts?"

"Isn't that what you said?"

"I never said they came with love." She stared at the spaceship. "What were you saying about Marilyn?"

"I was talking about that book, the one you didn't want me to see, about Cortez killing the Aztecs." Vanity nodded. "Well, I thought at the time that you were thinking about us, the Earth I mean, and that the companies would slaughter us. But you were thinking about the kurois, right? They were the Aztecs, the ones who got killed."

"I suppose so." She looked very tired.

"Can I ask how it happened?"

"Simple. The kurois appeared suddenly on a great concrete field outside a city. Don't ask me what the field was for. No one studies Center history before the kurois came. Anyway, they announced themselves and said they wanted to see representatives from the powers. They'd brought gifts, they said. They looked so lovely, so certain. And the others, my people, looked scared, even resentful. And incredibly hungry. You could see them drool as they touched the ships. The kurois announced they wanted to share their secrets. They set up a program, two years to learn everything. The techniques, that is. At first the people wanted to learn the science. Impossible. We could never understand it. It wasn't even science, they said, but—something else. So they settled for what they could get, the ships, the robots to build them, the basic fant techniques, how the pulse points worked."

"Basically what buttons to push."

"Uh huh. And no idea what the buttons do."

"Just like Earth, we say we want the science, but we'll sell our souls for the buttons. No wonder you laugh at us. And the real joke is, you people couldn't tell us the science even if you wanted to. No one can, now that the kurois are dead." He thought about his and Vanity's discovery. With the kurois gone, who could explain it to them?

In the same dry tired voice Vanity continued, "When the training program had finished, the kurois announced they would go on to the other humanhomes and teach them all. They said. That's when our leaders got the idea. Or maybe they decided at the beginning, I don't know, they said to each other, if we get rid of them before they can teach anyone else, we'll be able to dictate to the galaxy. So they invited the kurois to a celebration. I'm not sure the kurois ate food at all, but they agreed to come. And when they were all seated at long tables, the soldiers came in."

"Oh god," Hump said. "It's exactly like the Aztecs. Cortez invited them to a feast."

"No Hump, not exactly. A small difference. The Aztecs

didn't want to be killed." Hump shrunk away. "Doesn't it strike you as odd that we *could* kill them? They'd survived millions of years, and they all get killed by metal bullets?"

"Maybe they didn't realize anyone would do it."

Her laugh made Hump wince. "Poor Hump. You can't give up your lokie idea that somewhere, sometime, there existed somebody pure. Innocent. Sorry. You wanted the truth and now you're stuck with it. Like me. Like the aliens. You've become an alien, Hump. No one on Earth knows what you know."

"What are you getting at?"

"Believe me, the kurois understood violence. They understood everything. After the firing, after it was too late to make any difference, some of us got a guilt seizure. We ran over and begged the few of them left alive to forgive us."

"A little late."

"Yes, but not for the joke. The kurois told us—"

"Why do you keep saying 'us' and 'we'? You weren't there."

"Maybe I feel like I was. But you're missing the truth. Pay attention. The kurois told us they couldn't forgive us, not because of the crime, but because *they* had planned it."

"I don't get it."

"They'd survived millions of years, exactly the same. Evolution had stopped for them, change had stopped, experience had stopped. Planets, space, even the life and death of stars, they'd seen it all, over and over." She stopped for a moment, and they both thought of Vanity's mind in Hump's body. Then Vanity went on, "The rest of their people didn't even exist any more. They'd all 'translated'. That's what they called dying. They believed some complicated thing happened when you died. Or when they died. I don't know if it happened to them or not." She added bitterly, "I hope not. I hope their minds fell apart into nothing, into the Greyness."

"If they wanted to die so much why didn't they just fly into a star or something?"

"Because they were scared. They couldn't know for sure what would happen. The cowards. I *hate* them." She took a breath. "So they figured out a plan. They came to us, the beautiful star creatures bringing gifts. Because they knew what we'd do when they said they were going on to the other planets. They *knew*." She started to cry. "When they came to the feast they wore the most incredible clothes. You can't even call it clothes. Just light. Pure light, like liquid fire all over their bodies. They were so beautiful."

Hump seized her hands. "But Vanity, don't you see? They're the guilty ones. Not you. Your people only pulled the trigger. They set it up."

"What did they set up? What? They gave us everything, then told us they were leaving. That's all."

"But they knew what you'd do."

"Exactly. What does that tell you about us? For millions of years they kept away. Maybe they watched us all, saw how we'd developed, but they knew better than to announce themselves. Because when they did—"

"Listen, Vanity, what does this whole story tell you about them? Have you ever thought about that?"

"What do you mean?"

"We're their children. All of us. And they never helped us, never taught us what really mattered, how to stop killing each other. Why didn't they come back for so long?"

"Maybe they didn't want to die yet."

"Bullshit. You said yourself you couldn't have harmed them if they didn't want it. They didn't come back because they didn't care. They could have helped. If they'd survived so long they must have learned how to stop killing each other. They could have taught us that instead of spaceships. But they never even bothered to say hello until they wanted to use us. And if it crippled our heads, so what? *They've* translated."

"Why do you say 'we'? You weren't there."

"Oh, the hell with that. Don't you see what I'm getting at?"

"Of course, I see. I've thought about them all my life. Of course, I know they tricked us. And maybe they could have changed us instead. So what? We still fired the guns. Don't *you* see, the fact that they tricked us only makes it worse. Not only did we kill them but we didn't even think of it ourselves."

"I still say you can't blame yourself, Vanity. You came along two hundred years later."

"Is that a long time? They came back four million years later."

Hump opened his mouth, closed it. When he put his arm around Vanity, she didn't move away, but didn't move towards him either.

She said, "And now I'm teaching you to work a spaceship. Maybe I want you to kill me."

"You're out of luck. I don't take that kind of contract."

Vanity put her head against his shoulder, and he slipped his other arm around her. They slid onto the floor until they lay side by side at the foot of the plastic spaceship. The light pouring through the white dome bleached their faces.

"Hump," Vanity said softly, "have we really discovered something new?"

"Sure."

"I mean it. Is it possible there's something they didn't get to first?"

"I don't know, Vanity. Anything's possible."

They made love on the chapel floor, silently, sometimes hysterically, for hours, almost until the evening services. Vanity scratched Hump's face, she pinched him, she nearly strangled him. Hump shook her by the shoulders, flinging her head back and forth until it struck the spaceship and nearly knocked it over. Just before the Daniks came to pray, Humphrey Chimpden Earwicker McCloskey and Golden Vanity, the galactic lovers, stumbled back to their thin dormitory beds and fell asleep in each other's sweat-streaked arms.

Two days later, Vanity, walking by herself along the dunes as she tried to comprehend the awful fact that something new had happened, suddenly stopped on top of a hill. For three seconds she allowed herself the luxury of frozen terror as she stared down at the flat. Then she turned and ran to Earth City.

She found Hump in the dormitory, sweeping up. Wild, flecked in foamy sweat, she sputtered, "It's here. I saw it, I saw it."

"Calm down," he told her. He looked nervously around, but no one had followed her. "What did you see?"

"*Golden Vanity* is here."

"Shh. What are you talking about? Of course you're here."

"No! Idiot. Not me, the ship. The ship, *Golden Vanity*. *Loper is here*."

Part Three

Chapter Seventeen ————————————

"Harry? Edie? What are you doing? Hey, wait for me. Come back here!" Judy ran behind the jeep until she bent over, coughing from the dust. A few of the others jumped up to shout or wave their arms; Hump paid no attention as the car bounced out of Earth City. Next to him Vanity sat straight in her seat, one hand held up to protect her eyes against the wind and dust. The ends of the handkerchiefs tied around their noses and mouths flapped out behind them.

Hump grunted as a bump half flung them over the windshield. "How the hell did he find you?" he shouted.

"How am I supposed to know?"

"Well, what about the rest of them? Jaak, the SA. Are we going to find them all lined up on the edge of the desert?"

"I said I don't know. Leave me alone."

"You stupid bitch." The car bashed them against the seats. "You sure can pick a good time to sulk."

"Loper won't bring anyone. All right? That doesn't mean if he's found us the others won't."

Hump stared wildly at the up and down land in front of him. Where could they go? Where could they go? He shook the steering wheel as if he could force the jeep to answer him. The villages? The farms? If they could just get out of the desert.

"Hump! Turn around." Vanity jerked his arm.

He shoved her away. "What the hell are you talking about?"

"We've got to get to my ship."

"Are you crazy? That's the first place he'll look. We've got to get to some jungle or something."

"No, no. I just realized. He can't get into the ship if I don't open it for him."

"Then he'll stand guard outside it."

"He can't take the chance that I won't go there. He'll be looking around searching for us, I know him. As long as we stay in this jeep, he'll find us."

"So we get to the ship. And then he blows it up."

"No." She shook her head wildly. "He hasn't gone to all this trouble just to blow me up. And besides, he wouldn't blow up a ship. No one would."

"Why the hell not?"

"No one knows what'll happen. It could set off a shrieker. Hump, for burst's sake, listen to me."

Hump bent over the wheel, his fingers white, his eyes and forehead caked in dust. "It still won't do any good to hole up inside the ship."

"But maybe we can get away, get off the planet."

Dark terror swamped Hump's mind. Leave the planet, chased by a maniac. "No," he growled and crouched down farther.

"Hump—" Abruptly Vanity gagged as her arm pointed at the roller coaster ground in front of them.

There, splashed across the side of the hill, Hump saw a shadow. It lasted only a moment, before it vanished over the hilltop. A snubnosed, fantailed shadow. Hump slammed the brake so hard the car stalled as it threw them against the dashboard. By the time Hump's palsied fingers could start the engine again, the ship had made two more passes over their heads. He saw it clearly the second time around. Larger than Vanity's ship, the *Golden Vanity* gleamed a brilliant white in the desert sun, all except the transparent nose, nearly invisible in the glare, and the even brighter golden hieroglyph.

Finally Hump got the car started. With Vanity bracing herself beside him, he shot forward—only to hit the brake again when a sudden bolt of *something* tore a jagged trench in front of them. He spun the car around. They'd only gone a few feet diagonally on the hill when another silent bolt followed by an explosion opened the earth. Hump thought he could leap the

gap but at the last moment turned again, speeding downhill,
back towards Earth City. Until the ship cut them off again.

He stopped the car and climbed over the door. "Come on," he
hollered at Vanity. She got out slowly, dazed, staring at the
ground. Once again Hump discovered himself inside her mind;
he saw the baked ground, alien, nightmarish, he cringed before a
maze of memories, he looked, with Vanity, openmouthed at his
own body falling down the hill. Still inside her mind, he shook
her mentally. When his mind snapped back again, Vanity had
come awake and the two of them ran like flapping birds down
the hill and across the flat.

Hump heard an explosion, saw fire in the corner of his eye.
When he looked back the car had burst into flames. A sudden
gust of wind knocked them over as the ship swept down for a
sudden slam landing in the dirt no more than a hundred yards
ahead of them.

"It's no use," Vanity wailed as Hump dragged her to her feet.
"No dispersal shields." But she ran anyway, following Hump's
zigzag pattern. Gasping, Hump looked back over his shoulder
just as a large lion-haired man leaped from the ship to run after
them in a long loose stride that immediately began to close the
space between him and his exhausted targets. His left hand
carried a long narrow tube made of some red metal. *A gun*,
Hump thought, and pushed his legs harder. *Get away from
Vanity. He'll go for her first.* But he ran beside her, stumbling,
getting up, falling again. Vanity helped him, but when he looked
back the gap had narrowed to less than fifty yards. In a frozen
moment he saw the wide face, impassive as a man looking at the
sky, the streamed-back hair, the shiny yellow layered tunic and
balloon-like trousers, the soft soled dark shoes rising and falling
with an easy rhythm. Like a mindless animation of the human
body, the alien moved across the face of the Earth. Until he
stopped and raised the metal tube.

Hump cried out, a guttural release of months of fear as he
threw himself at the ground. No explosion came, no rush of
pain; his senses had, if anything, sharpened. When he tried to
move, however, he discovered his muscles locked.

He'd fallen with his face turned to the side, and now he could
see the tall figure stride towards him; no, past him, for Loper
only stopped briefly to look down at Hump's face wet with tears
and sweat. "Slice your worries," he said in a soft accent. "I didn't
come to pick up souvenirs." He walked beyond Hump's line of

vision to reappear a moment later with Vanity held in his arms like an awkward statue.

Hump groaned. *I can talk*, he realized. His muscles were coming back; already he could feel his stomach tensing and contracting in scared spasms. *Leave it*, he told himself. *Play dumb, he'll let you go*. Hoarsely he called, "What are you going to do with her?"

Hump could hear the smile in the soft voice, "Whatever I want, of course."

"Listen, you better take me with you." Jesus, what was he doing? "She's gotten spoiled here. Thinks she's a space goddess. I'm the only one that can handle her."

Loper laughed. "Are you putting yourself up for sale?"

"Hump," Vanity called. "Forget it. You can't help anything."

"See what I mean?" Hump said. "Uppity." He managed to turn his face as Loper came into view.

"Tell me your terms, work-servant. Maybe I can't afford you." He was grinning, a fake friendly smile with no emotion in it.

"I can't talk in the dirt. Why don't we go to a café?"

After Loper had shifted Vanity to his right shoulder, he hoisted Hump's stiff body onto his left. "You'll have to settle for ****." He pronounced something unintelligible, then added, "Or maybe I should use my salary's adopted market name. Welcome to the *Golden Vanity*." He carried them towards the ship.

Jaak's former flagship was grander than Vanity's personal runabout. The room behind the control seat (the only room Loper used, though the ship contained several others) contained a multicolored tile floor patterned in a complex geometric design, plush couches that looked like giant leaves, vibrating tapestries, three dimensional paintings, and a large yellow-red plant that sang softly as it moved in a private breeze. Somehow all the exoticness appeared out of place, left over from the former owner, like a palace being used for a monastery. A second plant lay withered on the floor, one of the tapestries bore a huge tear down the middle.

Loper dropped the tube gun. With as little ceremony he dropped Hump on the leaf-shaped couch, but he held Vanity against him, smiling—how could a smile look so inhuman, so alien?—at her straining muscles as he walked towards the front. He said something in his liquid language.

"Speak English," Vanity snarled.

"Whatever you like, Golden Vanity." He pressed her into the seat beside the pilot. Behind them ran a row of seats made to look like plants growing out of the floor.

Vanity said, "And put him in a chair too. He's never lifted before."

"Then he'll have to learn all at once. State your terms, work-servant," he called over his shoulder. "Do you want a view seat?"

Only then did the realization strike Hump. *They were leaving Earth.* When he'd demanded Loper take him along, he'd thought only of the cold animal who scared Vanity so much and how he couldn't leave Vanity alone to face Loper. But of course, Loper couldn't stay here with Jaak possibly due at any moment. Loper loved space, Vanity said, the only man she knew who loved space.

"Terms, market man," Loper said. Vanity stood helplessly between them.

Hump stared at the bright lifeless desert through the transparent window and thought how warm and sheltering it looked. "I'll stay on the couch," he said.

Vanity said, "Hump, take the seat. Please."

"No," Hump told her, "I don't want to see."

Vanity cried while Loper forced her down again, arranging her arms and legs for the seat to clamp hold of her. Her sobs cut short when he reached up a long thick finger to wipe her cheek. "Be careful," he said. "You don't want to wipe away the filth of your adopted world."

"Slimemouthed borkson snake!" Vanity screamed. Loper checked his instruments. Vanity nodded towards Hump. "Let him go."

"Impossible. He belongs to me. What would the SA say if I left my personal garbage on a market world?"

"Do you want to be stuck with him? What will you do with him?"

"I'll find something. He can help me devise experiments on what to do with you."

At that moment Hump saw, outside the ship, ten, no, at least twenty and probably more people crawling on their hands and knees towards the ship. Weakly he gestured to them, trying to signal them. To do what? Attack the ship? Run for help? What could they or any other lokies do?

But his gestures made no difference. Certain that God had at last acknowledged their worthiness, the jubilant Daniks only pressed their noses further in the dirt as they crawled to the spaceship. Loper said to Vanity, "Your slime friends have come to say goodbye."

Hump ran forward to fling himself at Loper. Immediately Vanity freed herself from the seat and started kicking and punching. But it was hopeless. Weak, Hump could not get up again after a single shove knocked him on the floor. He watched Loper slap Vanity's face, once, twice, until she froze, giving him no more excuses. With one hand Loper tore her loose low-necked dress down the middle. He spun Vanity around, stripped her, then shoved her aside to open the doors and throw the dress onto the sand. Bitterly Hump thought of the Daniks' confusion when they would run to catch the relic and find it one of their own sundresses.

"Sit down," Loper ordered Vanity. She didn't move. He ran a fingernail down her breast to her nipple, erect with fear. The sharpened nail left a red line on the dark gold skin. Calm, curious, Loper watched Vanity like a half bored child. "Sit down," he repeated softly. Vanity took her seat.

"Hump," she said without looking back, "get on the couch." Hump limped to his giant leaf.

The ship took off more smoothly than Vanity's; whether from better equipment or a better pilot, Hump didn't know and didn't care. He heard the same dull roar as before, though again he felt nothing but a mild pressure and a soothing vibration. "The ship absorbs most of the acceleration," Vanity had told him. "Don't ask me how." Dimly he thought he heard cries and screams from the people outside, caught in the flame of the crawl drive. But of course, he only imagined it. Or maybe, he heard himself and Vanity.

The sun got brighter and brighter, then oddly dropped away. Flying on the night side, Hump realized and thought of alien vampires. The acceleration pressure got worse and worse, until suddenly it rose like a ghost from Hump's body. He sat up and looked out the window.

There it hung, suspended in nothing, like a blue green Christmas ball without a tree. The Earth. His planet. His home. He gagged, panic convinced him they'd opened the doors and let out all the air. Laughter. They, no, Loper, was laughing at him.

"For burst's sake," Vanity said, "put him to sleep, you bastard."

Loper got up. "Your work-servant friends have contaminated your language," he said as he picked up the tube gun and set a dial on the side. He fired at Hump.

A soft dreaminess replaced the terror. Hump let out his breath and lolled back on the wonderful green bed, miles wide, a world of living bed. Just before he fell asleep he thought: *What happened to us? When did we get so afraid?* The astronauts didn't get so scared when they saw the Earth from space. They would have glided out to Andromeda if they'd known how to do it. *How did we get so afraid? What did they do to us?*

He woke, groggy, confused. As soon as he groaned, Vanity rushed over to pick up his head and slide an arm around his shoulders. "Are you all right?" she asked and, before he could answer, held out a blue beaker of some hot liquid. "Here, drink this."

The sweet caramely syrup had hardly slid down his throat before the pain in all his muscles eased, replaced by a giddy floating sensation. He felt absurdly healthy. The sight of Vanity's anxious face made him grin. Except—he squinted at her. An eye had swollen and she looked bruised. Her breasts (she was naked) were red with what looked like insect bites, and her sides and thighs were black and blue. "Holy Jesus," Hump said. "What did he do to you?" He tried to sit up but Vanity held him down.

"Stay here," she urged. "I'm all right. He's hardly started on me yet."

"But you're—"

"I told you it's nothing," she said savagely, then softened and whispered, "Besides, when it gets bad enough I can always escape."

"What? Where?"

She shushed him. A moment later a *presence* in his mind said soundlessly, "Got room for a hitchhiker?" Abruptly the presence was gone and Vanity was grinning at him. He moaned.

When Hump tried to look past Vanity for Loper, she held him down on the couch. Something odd—he blinked, stared to the side. The giant window was blanked out. Instead of the expected star field he saw a dull red wall. "Where are we?" he said.

"Just be quiet. Drink some more." She held out the beaker.

Hump shook his head. "No, I want to know where we are."

His voice sounded absurdly piping. He heard laughter from behind Vanity.

"Hump, please be quiet."

"No. You promised me the truth. Where are we? Why are the windows sealed?"

"We're nowhere."

"What?"

"Non-space. Nothing. Loper's decided to keep us here for awhile."

"Oh god." Wetness touched his face, his own tears or Vanity's.

A large figure loomed in front of him. "Since you insist, I'll clear the windows."

"No," Vanity said. "You told me you wouldn't."

"He insisted, Golden Vanity. You know what a talent he's got for forcing terms on me." Loper strolled to his instruments. A moment later an awful greyness flooded the front of the ship. At once infinitely deep yet flat, it pressed the window like a great wind or a living creature, driving the ship backwards; and yet it didn't move at all, just hung there, nothing, the end of life, of space, of all existence. Hump stared, transfixed with horror that such emptiness waited for them outside the universe. He heard Loper's laughter, as cold and empty as the Greyness. Numbly he let Vanity open his mouth and pour some other liquid down his throat.

When he closed his eyes the grey wind beat against them, and he tried to squeeze Vanity's arm, but his fingers came loose as he fell back against the couch; even his dreams opened the way to nothingness, monstrous nightmares of a fake world collapsing to reveal the grey emptiness hidden in the center of life.

Hump woke to find Loper shouting something unintelligible as he slapped a limp ragdoll Vanity. Dimly Hump sensed a crowding inside his head. He tried to get up. *Stay down* came a soundless command. He fell back asleep.

He was looking at Loper's hand raised as if to slap him. Pain, terror, and frustrated anger from days of humiliation ran through his naked body. But something was wrong. His body— Forgetting Loper he jerked his head to the side and there lay Hump, stretched out on the couch. He looked down at his thin gold arms, the bruised swell of his breasts.

Vanity, he thought, *I'm inside your body*.

I know, came the soundless answer. *You won't like it here.*

Loper grabbed Vanity's shoulder. She—they—winced. "What are you doing? Why are you looking at him?"

Before Hump could hear Vanity's answer, his mind vanished back into the darkness of his own body.

Hump never remembered how many times he woke up groggy and dazed before Vanity finally retrieved him from the haze. He never found out what things he dreamed and what actually happened. Vanity would later never talk about it.

Twice, he thought, they actually landed on a planet, the first a violent new-born world of volcanos and constant earthquakes, rivers of molten metal, huge chasms, great jets of fire gushing into the air. Loper stayed just long enough for Vanity to think he might actually let the fires flood them away, for her to beg him to raise the ship.

The second landing took place on a humanhome, one of the worlds exploited by the companies. It looked as alien to Hump as the fire planet. Though he later couldn't recall leaving the ship or even his couch, he did remember a brown sky and an abrasive wind that burned his skin. They walked across a bare dirt plain, past huge windowless box buildings and derrick-like machines that mostly stood motionless, like neo-functionalist sculpture. At first Hump thought that the squat grey shapes scuttling about were machines or maybe work animals. Only when Loper led them into a long cold office in one of the buildings did Hump discover that the creatures were humans with "altered" squat bodies and stumpy legs encased in plastic "enhancer" suits grafted to their bodies like new skin. While Hump and Vanity shrank in fear from the scarred pitted faces, Loper negotiated something with a stooped white-faced woman, the only ordinary human.

The three travelers trudged back to the ship, Vanity and Hump weary, Loper tense and angry, while the altered people loaded something into the hold. And then Hump lay on his leaf couch again as the ship streamed elegantly through space and non-space, and he wondered in his dreams if the brown world hadn't been a dream as well.

Someone was shaking him, vibrating loose the fog surrounding his head. "Whose body?" he mumbled until a hand clapped on his mouth silenced him.

"We're going to land soon," Vanity said. "Try to wake up."

He squeezed his eyes shut, opened them wide. Vanity sat next to him wearing a long mud-colored dress, gathered at the waist, with green metallic loops like fish scales down the sides. Folds of pink material at the breasts and thighs made Vanity look old and wrinkled, an impression not challenged by her face, puffy from lack of sleep and from crying. Though the bite-like marks were gone, her bare arms looked in places like she'd been rubbed down with wire brushes.

More than her raw skin, Vanity's eyes and posture disturbed Hump as he drank the hot broth Vanity had given him. She sat stiffly, like a soldier or determined athlete, and her eyes shone with furious intensity, burning away her fear. Hump had seen that look in his schizzed lover Kate, before she ran screaming from his house long ago. His mind flooded with pain for Vanity. He hoped she wouldn't do anything to get them both killed.

He asked, "How long since we left? Left Earth?"

"Can't say. We've spent most of the time in non-space, where time doesn't count. Maybe two days outside."

"Did you say we're going to land?" She nodded. Hump sat up straight to look at the star-specked blackness beyond the window. "I can't see anything," he said.

"We're not there yet. But you won't see much."

With a nod towards Loper, Hump whispered, "Isn't it dangerous for him? To land, I mean."

He winced at Vanity's laugh. "Do you think he's taking us to a spaceport and a luxury hotel?"

"Then where?"

"He's got his own place. They all do. Here." She gave him a drink.

They sat for awhile silently, Vanity's arm around Hump who stared at the floor, his mind blank to anything but the pulse-like vibrations of the ship as it maintained the artificial gravity. He imagined the ship as an animal, and himself and Vanity and Loper as food. "Probably get indigestion."

"What?" Vanity asked.

He shook his head. "Nothing."

"Can you stand?"

"I think so." He got up shakily.

"Good. Shower time." She led him to a booth more disguised with decoration than the one on her ship. Hump hardly noticed the blasts of air and revitalizing juices; his glowing body might have belonged to somebody else.

He waved away Vanity's offer of some green and yellow pleated overalls. "I'm still a lokie," he said, and pulled on his filthy jeans and tee shirt and sandals.

"Go sit down," Vanity ordered. Timidly Hump walked to an empty seat behind Loper who took no notice of him. The huge man stared sullenly out the front of his ship. Vanity sat down next to Hump.

The Worker turned some switches and somewhere underneath the ship, intense lights fanned out against the darkness. Far ahead of them a heavy mass loomed. No, Hump realized, as it rushed towards them, it was actually close and fairly small, no bigger than a medium size mountain. Roughly cylindrical, the moon, or asteroid, displayed such a bumpy surface that Hump couldn't imagine where they could land. Maybe the ship could reconstruct itself after an accident but what about the people? He began to sweat.

The landing went so fast Hump hardly noticed it. The rock cylinder spun around, revealing a smooth face at the end of the tube. Triggered by the light, doors opened, and an instant later closed again after the ship had darted inside.

They came to rest at the end of a tunnel, only a few feet before a smooth metal wall. Hump let out a long breath. Ignoring him, Loper got up from his seat and turned around to yank Vanity off her chair.

She pushed him away. With a crooked smirk she said, "Do you think you can crack me open in your rock hole when you couldn't do it in space?"

For the first time Hump noticed the tight fury in Loper's face. "I'll get what I want," he said. "I've got all the time I need."

Vanity laughed. "You don't have the first idea how to get me, no matter how long you work at it."

Clumsier than when he'd first captured them, Loper shoved them through the ship's air lock into the docking tunnel and then through a side door into an elaborate chamber with a cloudy red glass floor and walls made of some material that gave the illusion of constantly shifting sand inlaid with jewels and bits of colored liquid light. Miniature sculptures of strange creatures simply hung in the air, singing or chanting in various languages as the trio passed them. Hump whispered to Vanity, "Did he design all this himself?"

Vanity laughed loudly. "Him? He stole it. Somebody, probably Jaak, once made this hole for a hideaway, then got sick

of it. So Loper moved in, like a balul nesting in a dead bork."
Loper said nothing.

The asteroid reminded Hump of a railroad flat with the
rooms arranged in sequence. They passed through a bathroom
with elaborate devices, hot pools whose steam formed misty
illusions of people playing silent music. More rooms followed,
one of them decorated in deep blues and purples with pink
life-sized marionettes performing impossible sex acts. A trio
blended themselves into one thrashing unit then burst apart into
five new ones. "Metasex," Vanity said to Hump's stare.
"Invented on Arbol."

Vanity's arrogant smile vanished the moment the wall parted
for the next chamber. *Nothing* waited there. No light, no
elaborate fantasies, *no walls*, just a bumpy rock floor and
beyond it the darkness of space. In the dim light thrown by the
doorway they guessed that the floor continued for possibly
twenty yards; beyond that lay the stars, light years away.

Panic flared in Hump's mind. He tried to run back but
Loper's hand held him so he couldn't even turn. He squeezed his
eyes shut, found that made it worse, looked and made a noise
while his hands seized the door edge as if they'd crush it.

Loper laughed. "Don't empty your insides. The air and
gravity won't vanish. Just make sure you don't lean over the
edge." He peeled away Hump's fingers from the door.

Vanity stood rigid, hands clenched, shoulders pushed high,
"Jaak didn't design this," she said.

"Of course not," Loper agreed. "Jaak hates space almost as
much as you do. You're throwbacks, the two of you. You belong
on a sweaty little market world like your pet here. All that slime
back there, Jaak's pathetic fant of being some Arbolian art lord,
that had nothing to do with space. This is the only reality."

Through her trembling Vanity said, "Loper's very own
spacehole. You see yourself as some new step in evolution, don't
you? Founder of the new kurois. What a twisted little fantasy."

"I couldn't care less for your market world aesthetics, Golden
Vanity. But let me give you some advice. I wouldn't try your
little trick of slicing consciousness. You might fall off the edge."

"Do you know something, Loper? All you're doing, this
place, your clumsy tricks with me, you're just trying to copy
Jaak. You don't care about me. You didn't even care about me
when you raped me. You didn't know what to do with me then
either; you just wanted to copy Jaak. Except your filth mind

couldn't come up with anything but slime. And then when Jaak kicked you out like an old huun you had to get whatever *he* owned that you could sneak away from him."

"You're right about one thing. I didn't want your work-servant body then, and I certainly don't want it now. Contaminated filth. I'll crack you open for one reason, as a way to break Jaak. He and I are natural enemies. Didn't he ever tell you that? We stayed together as long as we both could get what we needed, and if Jaak hadn't blinded himself with greed he would have known the time had come to attack. He's crumbling, Golden Vanity. Without his precious toy, you. And when he sees the tapes I'll send him, he'll shatter all over his blood filthy empire. Think of it, his dearest possession diseased, crippled, blinded. I've got plans for you, a whole range of experiments. Have you ever seen anyone licked by a Mmlian acidbeast? The skin comes off like dried mud. Whether you stay in your head or not. But first—first Jaak has to see you give yourself to me. Beg me to touch and stroke you."

"Ripping me won't break Jaak. Nothing will. He'll just come after you and tear your cold snaking insides out."

Loper looked her up and down like a surgeon deciding on the best place for an incision. Suddenly he grabbed each of their shoulders and spun them onto the rocks. While Hump clawed at the ground, Vanity screamed, "You bursting borkson sonofabitch!" The wall slid shut in front of them.

"Oh god," Hump wailed. He crouched on all fours, his hands convulsively holding the rock face.

"Shut up!" Vanity shouted at him. Muted laughter came up from speakers under the rock.

Acutely aware of Vanity whimpering beside him Hump thought, *I've got to help her. Look how scared she is. I've got to do something.* Only when Vanity reached up to touch him did Hump realize that he too was crying uncontrollably.

"It's all right," Vanity half whispered, half croaked. "It can't harm us."

"Where does it start?" They both stared at the rock, needing to know the exact limits of their dark world. With one hand Vanity reached around for pebbles. Carefully she tossed them at graded distances until they no longer heard the dull clunk of pebble and ground. Hump imagined he could see the tiny piece of reality glide away in an endless arc. He gripped the ground harder.

"There's plenty of room," Vanity said unconvincingly. "Try to relax."

"Relax?" His voice sounded like it could break a wine glass.

"Please," she said and looked over his shoulder at the rock wall.

"Oh," he said. "Shit. He's listening." Okay, he thought, relax. Act normal. Pretend it's Jones Beach at night. He imagined the tide pulling them out. Forget Jones Beach. Make it Central Park. At night? Oh, forget it.

The more Hump tried to think of something brave to say, the more his mind froze on him. At last he wailed, "What are we going to do?"

She made a noise. "Pray to the zodiac?"

"For god's sake, can't you ever be serious?"

"I'm always serious. That's why—"

"I wish I'd left you. Oh god, I wish I'd left you. Right there in the desert. I really wish I'd left you." The gravity cut caught Hump shifting position. The movement proved enough to propel him off the surface, slowly turning in the air, while his arms and legs flailed and his throat screamed.

"Hump!" Vanity shrieked. Holding tight with one hand, her own legs floating out like a flag, she reached up to grope in the dark until she found his ankle and grabbed hold. At that moment the gravity came on again. The two of them thudded to the ground.

They didn't even notice their bruises. Scrambling for a secure hold Vanity changed. "Just hold tight. As long as we hold tight we're safe. Hold tight."

Slowly at first, then faster, like an electric coil, the ground heated up. "Take your shirt off," Vanity ordered. "Put it around your hands." She struggled to remove her dress without taking both hands off the ground.

"No." Hump shook his head. "I can't." He smelled his skin smoking.

"You've got to."

Hump half sat up and tugged at his shirt.

Right then a wind came on. Blasting them from hidden blowers in the asteroid wall, it bore them steadily backwards across the still burning surface, pushing them towards the edge.

Vanity shouted something in her own language. She shouted it again and again. Both the wind and the burning stopped just before Hump and Vanity reached the end of their tiny world. A moment later, the door opened, and Loper walked out to them, the slightest smile distorting his lips. Ignoring Hump's weeping body he put out a hand to Vanity.

With a wild scream she leaped forward and butted his stomach, hoping to push him over the edge. Surprised, he staggered back a few steps, but then he caught Vanity's shoulder, yanked her upright, and slowly, carefully, began to claw her cheeks.

Hump was all set to launch himself at Loper when suddenly *something* entered his mind, and a soundless voice ordered him, *Stay here.*

Vanity? he asked inside his head.

No. Rocky Jones. Shut up.

Acutely conscious that Vanity was looking with him, Hump looked up at Loper shaking Vanity's slack body. The huge man roared something in his own language.

Vanity smirked with Hump's mouth. "See? Didn't I tell you only I could handle her?"

If you want to provoke him, Hump mind-shouted, *get out of my body.*

Loper dropped Vanity's body and in two steps had grabbed Hump. "How does she do that?" he shouted. He raised his hand to slap Hump's face, but now the Earthman's body fell limp as Hump discovered himself, with Vanity, inside Vanity's body. While Loper stared at Hump, Vanity crossed her arms and said, "Surprise. He can do it too."

Enraged, Loper flung down Hump's body and started for the mocking girl. Suddenly he stopped, cleared the anger from his face, then turned and walked back to raise Hump's mindless body over his head.

"No!" they both shouted with one voice, and then Hump found himself back in his body, staring up at nothing.

Loper called, "Say goodbye to your souvenir, Golden Vanity."

"Loper," Vanity pleaded, "I'll do whatever you want, just put him down."

They never got to hear his answer.

An explosion filled their universe. Loper spun backwards, dropping Hump, caught his balance, and turned a stunned face to the open doorway. A fantastic robed figure in a wide brimmed hat stood there, an ancient engraved rifle raised to his shoulder. Loper put a hand to his own shoulder and touched blood.

Enraged, he took a breath to attack when the rifle boomed again. And again. Loper stumbled, fell, and was rolled across the ground by yet another bullet, until—

For more than a second he kicked and whirled his arms at nothing. For more than a second he screamed soundlessly. And then he simply blew apart. The darkness accepted the fragments.

Hump collapsed on his back, trembling. But Vanity, on all fours, pointed with her head like a dog at the grinning wizard who posed with his cannon in the doorway. "AAri?" she whispered.

Chapter Eighteen

"Jaak's really not coming behind you?" Sitting on a gently rocking silver cushion, Vanity looked suspiciously at AAri.

Their unexpected savior had half led, half dragged them to a long narrow room crammed with curios: splashing fountains, what looked like long windows open to a group of musicians playing softly in a garden (Hump could actually smell the flowers, and when he gingerly poked his hand at the window it passed into clear air), an ornate box containing wild animals who appeared and disappeared from the box's flat walls, and most startling to Hump's terror-weary eyes, a bright blazing ball hanging in the air, giving off warmth and light like a miniature sun. After setting them down on cushions that looked like engraved metal but were actually softer than foam, AAri had scooted off to return a moment later with ointments that all but healed their burns and bruises.

"No Jaak, no SA, nothing," AAri said in a voice more harshly accented than Loper's or Vanity's. "Me alone." He crossed both hands at the wrist. "I swear by the fiery breath."

"What does that mean?"

AAri nearly blushed. "That's an oath from my homeworld. It's very sacred."

Hump could see Vanity fight a snicker. "Are those clothes sacred too?" She herself had changed to a close-fitting purple dress with giant bat sleeves that constantly blew behind her as if they carried their own wind. Hump had again refused an offer to replace his rags.

AAri said, "These are the traditional ceremonial robes of the picture tellers." He sat up deliberately straight, refusing to be embarrassed as the too big robe angled off his shoulders. Beside him lay the engraved rifle and the red wide-brimmed hat. "They don't fit all that well," he said apologetically, "because I grabbed them in a hurry from the museum room."

"You look wonderful," Vanity assured him. "But what's happened to you?"

He was silent for a moment, trying to find the right words. "I realized the truth," he said.

"About what?"

"About a lot of things. My people on G'GaiRRin, Jaak, and the companies. Center did things to me, Vanity, it twisted my head, my whole life, in ways that I never really understood. Do you know that I was terrified for years to take a fant course? I thought about it all the time though. If you knew anything about my home world you'd understand the absurdity in that. On G'GaiRRin the whole community was spinning visions while the people at Center were killing each other for piss-sticks."

Vanity licked the tip of her thumb, then scowled at the salve's bitter taste. "Poor Jaak," she said. "Everyone's deserted him. First Loper, then me, and now even you."

Hump decided the conversation needed a less elegaic note. "How did you find us?" he asked.

"Oh, I've known for years that Loper used this place. Luckily I made it my own secret. I was never foolish enough to tell Jaak everything."

"But how did you know that Loper had taken us?"

"I didn't. I figured that out when I went to look for you on Earth and found you gone with your ship still there. Who were those odd people, by the way?"

Vanity laughed. "The Daniks? What did they do?"

"Well, they've draped your spaceship with rows of ugly streamers. When I tried to speak to them they all ran away."

"Maybe your costume scared them."

Hump said, "More likely Loper scared them so much they've decided to worship the aliens from a safe distance."

"Worship?" AAri repeated. His eyes gleamed.

"Listen," Hump said, "I'm sorry to press these mundane matters, but you were saying how you found us."

"Oh yes. Typically Jaak put me in charge of the search, so all information came to me. Including the results of the atmospheric tracer search we did for Vanity's ship. Instead of giving the information to Jaak or one of our agents, I decided to follow it myself. And when I discovered you had vanished, I guessed Loper had gotten to you first and taken you here."

"How did he find us?"

"Stoops most likely. Does it matter?"

"It does if Jaak could still find us."

"Not here. I told you, he doesn't know about this place. Even years ago it occurred to me I might want to contact Loper on my own."

"So we're safe?" Hump asked. "We're actually safe?" He couldn't believe this bizarre alien place could really shelter them; at any moment he expected the musicians beyond the "window" would attack with blowguns or the miniature animals would leap out and bite their necks.

Vanity said, "But AAri, why *did* you come after me? I mean, if you've sliced from Jaak."

AAri looked down. "I thought you'd ask that sooner or later." He fidgeted with his hat. "Actually, you see, I didn't come to rescue you. Oh, I did, that is, once I realized Loper had taken you I suddenly saw who my enemies were."

"But before that?"

He looked at the rifle. "Well, before that I planned to kill you."

"What?"

"Jesus Christ," Hump said.

"You've got to understand—" AAri pleaded.

"What do you mean I've got to understand? Why would you want to kill me?"

"Just listen a moment. I gave my whole life to the company, to Jaak. I even thought of us as partners filling out each other's skills. Then all of a sudden everything collapsed. The company fell apart, my mind was falling apart. And Jaak wouldn't make any decisions or even listen to me. He didn't care if the SA burned us out of the galaxy, he didn't care if the shrieker ate up half of space. And he certainly didn't care about me. When I tried to talk to him he ridiculed me. And all because of you. At least that's what I thought. Until I realized that what Jaak and the company had done to me went back long before you were born. That's when I decided to rescue you."

"But why? How did I become so important to you?"

"You hate Jaak as much as I do. It just took me a longer time to realize it. And maybe, if it wasn't for you, I never would have realized it."

Vanity wandered over to the animal box where she adjusted some dials. A miniature rainstorm scattered a herd of giraffe-like spotted beasts. "AAri," she said slowly, "what did you mean before about the shrieker eating up space? What shrieker?"

"The one Loper told us he'd killed."

"Didn't he?"

"He sent it into non-space. By some quirk or other, it came back."

"And Jaak hasn't done anything?"

"He refused even to talk about it."

"What'll happen to it?"

"The SA's trying to handle it. The last I heard they've already sent out one team that had to pull back. Too big. Burst knows what'll happen to it. Or what'll happen to the company when the SA finds out how the shrieker started in the first place."

Vanity went off to sit by herself in the corner, hunched over, her elbows on her knees, her mind far away. For awhile the two men stood around awkwardly with nothing to say. Pretending to look at the curios (he was much too weary to marvel), Hump wished he could get some time alone with Vanity, figure out what to do next. He wished he could get home.

When Vanity came back to them, one look at her excited zealous eyes told Hump his troubles had far from ended. "Tell me about the shrieker," she said.

"What about it?"

"How do you kill a shrieker?"

"Well, first of all, the ship does it."

"Of course. Go on."

"Yes. Well, a shrieker, as far as we know—" He glanced at Hump.

"That's okay," Vanity said. "He knows how little we know. I told him about the kurois."

AAri looked at Hump with new respect, then turned back to Vanity. "A shrieker consists of energy patterns. It starts when a ship explodes, and then it becomes a self-sustaining process. You know that what we perceive as empty space is really an energy pattern feeding on itself. The Arbolians had proved that even before we, before Center, contacted them. Well, a shrieker breaks into that pattern and simply devours it." Despite his newly found religion AAri appeared to enjoy a more business-like discussion. "Now, a killer ship contains damper devices. These are actually energy alterers themselves, but by acting just beyond the shrieker's fringes they take away the available energy so the shrieker can't feed on anything."

"Back fires," Hump said.

"What?"

"On Earth, when a fire gets out of control, we light a small fire, just beyond the big one, so when the big fire reaches that area it's got nothing to burn."

"Yes," AAri said, "that sounds something like the first step. But only the first. Because then the ship has to go in and start cutting down the shrieker itself by altering the shrieker energy pattern, pecking away at it until it gets smaller and smaller and finally the ship can damp out the core. And that's the really tricky part."

"Why?" Vanity asked.

"Because of the energy involved. Remember, the shrieker starts because the original Worker couldn't hold onto the wave patterns. So the Worker in the damper ship has got to hold onto even trickier structures. That takes a very strong head."

"But does the shrieker get too big for the ship?"

"As far as we can figure out and the robots will tell us, no. A killer ship contains more than enough power to damp out any shrieker short of galactic proportion. The *Golden Vanity* could handle any shrieker I ever heard of. But not without Loper. It's the Worker that's the problem."

"Because of the skill needed to work the dampers or just because of the pressure?"

"The pressure. The ship does all the technical parts."

"Let's think about that Worker a moment," Vanity said. "Is it just the raw power that overwhelms him?"

"I don't understand." Hump didn't understand either, but he knew he didn't like it.

"Well, look," Vanity said, "the Worker's head collapses because it can't handle the constant pressure of the battle. His fants snake and he gets sucked into the shrieker. But suppose he could release that pressure?"

AAri shook his head. "I still don't understand. Can't we speak *****."

"No, Hump's got to understand too. I'll try again. What makes the Worker's head snake is the intense pressure of matching huge wave structures over a long period. Well, suppose the Worker could relieve all that pressure. Suppose he or she found a way to drain it off, say into some other person."

"Oh shit," Hump said. "Oh mother. You stupid bitch! I won't do it, Vanity."

"Hump, shut up. You don't even know what I have in mind."

"I don't have to know. I can guess. And my answer, Captain Vanity, is fuck you." He bent over to cover his face with his hands.

AAri said, "Will somebody explain what's going on?"

Vanity said, "I'm trying, if Rocky Jones will shut up. Think about what happens just before a Worker collapses. He starts to broadcast. Telepathically. Have you ever thought about that? What it means? He's trying to drain off the pressure. Trying to get other minds to take some of that excess energy over for him."

"It's possible," AAri agreed. "But so what? He still collapses. The two Workers who escaped to tell us about the shrieker said that the collapsed Worker broadcast all over the points before he blew up."

"Exactly. He was trying to find an escape route. Another mind that would take over the pressure. Now suppose he had that all along?"

"Had what?"

"Another mind to take the pressure. Someone who could follow the fants, follow the battle, everything."

"Two Workers?"

"No, no. One Worker, but two minds. That's the whole point. The second mind is not attached to the ship, it's attached *to the Worker.* Don't you see? The second mind can handle all the excess energy because it doesn't endanger the ship at all; it's just got to take up the overflow from the Worker. So the Worker can keep going endlessly and never reach a crisis point."

"Do they both feed their heads?"

"No, only the Worker. The other keeps himself blank, or rather he monitors the Worker's fants, even participates in them as a kind of helper, or protector, or something. But he doesn't grow his own fants because what he's really doing is draining off the energy. You can call him a dummy."

Hump said, "He's not dumb enough not to know when someone is screwing him."

"Hump, please."

"I thought this whole thing scared you so much. Something new in the world. You wouldn't even talk about it."

She shrugged. "I guess I found more important things to be scared of."

AAri tugged at his robe. "What's the point of all this? Maybe what you're saying would work, but since it can't happen what's the difference?"

"See?" Hump said. "A man of sense. Why don't we just scram the idea. Slice it. It can't possibly work." Immediately that presence entered his head, like someone bumping into him. *Can't work, huh? Hello, dummy.* Back in her body she said, "It has worked, Hump. When you were snaking under the image maker, I jumped into your fant and pulled you out again. You could do the same with me. I know you could." She turned to AAri. "This shrieker. The SA's already lost some ships on it?"

"I didn't say that. I don't know."

"But they probably will?"

"There's a good chance."

"Well, suppose someone took care of it for them. Do you think they'd appreciate that?"

"Yes, of course."

"And suppose that person used a startling new technique, never before heard of, even by the kurois themselves? Would they be interested?"

AAri nodded his head slowly. "Oh yes, I think that would interest them very much indeed."

"And suppose that person then offered to teach the new technique. How would they like that?"

"They'd probably like that best of all. For burst's sake, Vanity, do you really mean—"

Vanity laughed and took his hands. "AAri, I know that you've begun a new life. But do you think you can bring back some of your old talents?"

He looked at her suspiciously. "Such as?"

"Such as your wonderful ability to bargain. I want to make a deal with the SA, and I need someone to do it for me."

"Deal?" Hump said. "What could we possibly get that's worth setting ourselves up like that?"

AAri said, "Yes, what exactly *do* you expect to get for this discovery of yours?"

"Three things," Vanity said. "First, immunity from any SA

charges against me and Hump. Two, I want Jaak kept away from us. For good. I don't care what the SA does with him as long as they guarantee that he never goes near me or bothers me in any way ever again. I don't want him dead, you understand, just out of the way."

"I don't think the SA will object to that demand at all. Especially when we let them know this particular shrieker's history."

"What's the third?" Hump asked.

"This one's in exchange for teaching. The other two go for killing the shrieker." She took a breath. "I want Earth established as an SA protectorate. No companies, no auctions, no manipulations. They get ships, 'mitts, but no companies. For good. Can you do that, AAri?"

"I don't know. If you've got something genuinely new, and so powerful—*if* you do, I can't see how—I don't know. The SA won't like the idea, but that's just bureaucratic habit, and there's always been a more activist faction that wouldn't mind whittling down the companies a little. You're not really asking very much."

Hump had been staring at Vanity, but now he shifted his face to AAri. "Not much? You're crazy. Both of you. You're out of your minds. She's asking for a whole planet."

AAri shrugged.

Vanity said, "But Hump, it isn't much. Really. It just isn't."

Hump opened his mouth, closed it. Maybe—maybe it wasn't much after all. As he sat down an awareness pushed itself on him, a knowledge he'd been fighting for months. To a people whose territory covered a hundred worlds, one little backward planet simply didn't count for much. It just didn't, no matter what the natives thought about it. This fact, and the refusal to recognize it, had paralyzed Earth since the first moment the aliens arrived. The aliens hadn't done anything to Earth, not yet anyway. The aliens hadn't made Earth xenophobic. Oh, they'd undoubtedly counted on that reaction, waiting for it to set in before they made any serious moves. But they hadn't done anything. Earth had done it to herself. Leaving Earth had terrified Hump because it made Earth so trivial. He could do it so easily. Like leaving your home town.

But now a new thought struck him. So what? What difference did it make? If he simply accepted Earth's insignificance, why, then it didn't have to bother him any more. He, and all the other lokies, could join the big wide galaxy. After all, you've got to leave home sometime, don't you?

When he looked up, AAri was already speaking into the transmitter.

They stopped to rest just before their goal. Hump could see it as a throbbing bright ball filling half the view window. Flashes at the edges sent out arms or tentacles that sometimes stayed alive, but most often burned out like the tail of a firework. At first, Hump saw only the angry white fire, but after a moment of staring he thought he detected, deep in the center, a dark core. A greyness. "That's the real shrieker," Vanity said when Hump pointed it out to her. "It mixes up space and non-space. The explosive part's just an effect."

"That effect can still blow us up."

"The ship can handle it. Remember, we're the problem, not the ship."

"Great. How far away are we now?"

"In lokie measurements, around five hundred kilometers."

"What? How big is that thing, anyway?" He didn't wait for her to answer. "Look, Vanity, this whole thing can't work. I can't help you operate one of these things. I don't know anything about them."

"You're not supposed to." She turned and touched his face. "Hump, you've got to believe me, it's not as dangerous as you think. We'll know pretty early if we can do it, and if not, we can back out while the ship's still nibbling the edges. It's perfectly safe."

Hump sighed. "The galactic optimist."

She was walking barefoot, no, naked, no, wearing only a cape of green light that flew out behind her to mingle with her flame-like hair. She walked along a road paved with jewels that burst open with perfumes as she stepped on them. She grinned. "Hey Hump," she said to the air. "Not bad, huh?"

A sour voice came from the ground. "Yeah, lovely."

Vanity laughed. Beside her ran or hopped her lul, the bug-eyed, tube-shaped little yellow creature who'd followed her on all her adventures. At road's end she could see the grove of trees and the victory feast, where the representatives of all the worlds were already cheering her safe return. "Liberator!" they shouted. "Teacher." The lul bounced happily.

Of course they worshipped her. Hadn't she brought something new into the world? Hadn't she proved humans could still create? Hadn't she freed them from history?

Briefly she saw, beyond the ecstatic crowds, a more somber gathering, men and women, ancient, wise, sadly beautiful, their faces shiny with blood. *No*, she thought, *get them out of here.* She fixed her eyes on the cheering mob as they waved symbolic flower swords. Suddenly she saw that the swords were real; light glinted off the edges. And then she saw, hidden in the grove of trees, the mouth of a cave, and knew that when she got there they would push her back into the tunnel.

"Hump," cried her fantasy voice, "it's no good. You're right. The energy's too wild for me even to get a structure going at all. We've got to pull out."

For just a moment they glimpsed the *Golden Vanity*'s cabin filled with harsh light and, beyond the window, bursts of fire. With Hump's eyes they saw Vanity's trance-like body fixed in her seat. When they jumped back into that body, the road came back and the shadowy blood-spattered figures. "I can't get loose," she cried. "Hump, help me."

And then the strange thing happened. And though he and Vanity thought and talked about it for years (and psychologists from Arbol to G'GaiRRin interviewed them consciously and subliminally) Hump himself never really understood it. Thrilled at Vanity's retreat he meant to answer, "Great. Let's go home." Instead, his voice, from the sky, called down, "We'll just have to go forward then. Keep moving."

"Hump, what are you talking about? We'll explode."

"I'll anchor you. Discharge it all into me and keep on going." What *was* he talking about? "Just don't try to control anything. That's the key. Let it all come out whatever way it wants."

"But you've got to control a fantasy. Otherwise it'll snake on you."

"You've got me to take care of that. Just follow the road wherever it goes. The road's the fantasy, Vanity. It doesn't matter if it snakes. As long as you keep going, the structure stays intact. I'll handle the problems."

Vanity got to her feet and walked timidly down the road. The crowd had vanished, and the landscape had changed from hills of green and pink and gold to a flat dirt. Only the grove of trees remained at the road's end. Odd constructions, small machines, no, miniature wrecked spaceships littered her path. A chill wind licked her bare body. "Hump?"

"I'm here."

"It makes no sense," she whined, but kept walking. Bird-like spaceships were landing farther down the road. From the first emerged a black cloud, which, as it approached her, changed into thousands of insects swarming, hissing, and clicking all around her.

"Don't stop," warned Hump's voice, hardly audible through the buzz. She looked up and saw him sitting on a mountaintop. As soon as she took a step, the flies deserted her. In a thick line they flew up the mountain to surround the fantasy Hump who sprayed some mist at them from a yellow can. Vanity's eyes moved to the next spaceship.

A flood burst open the door, hot oil boiling down the road. Vanity stopped, looked to either side, only to discover the ground beyond the road covered with a network of hot sharp wires. "Hump," she cried. "We've got to get out of here."

This time the voice came from under the ground. "Didn't I tell you to keep walking?"

"But—"

"Come on."

The sickly smell of the oil contorted her face. The heat was already scorching her skin, but she managed to put a foot forward. At that moment she heard a crack, and the ground beneath her heaved up into a hillock. Like a diverted river the oil flowed on either side while Vanity stood safely, grinning down at the ground. "Good work," she said.

But when she jumped down to the cool green road and looked ahead to the grove of trees, she saw, hidden among the branches, the ancient faces, watching and waiting for her. Shaken, she slowed her pace.

Three more times the spaceships tried to stop her with squat "enhanced" women firing laser stones, with a thin mist that covered her body in sores, and finally with a squad of android SA police, led by a robot caricature of Jaak, begging her to come home. Each time her invisible protector intervened with a light shield, with a healing rain, with a robot Vanity to lead the androids off the track, so that finally Vanity had made it past the spaceships. Finally she stood before the dark grove, where the wind brushed the dry leaves together in a slow song. Vanity stepped forward.

And immediately found herself back in the tunnel, the damp stone corridor of all her snakes and dreams. "You tricked me!" she shouted.

"Keep walking," ordered the voice; barely recognizable as Hump, it carried a distant metallic quality like an ancient recording.

Defiantly she tried to sit down, but immediately the cold settled on her. It came from the floors and the smooth walls to force her to her feet and march her down the long stone corridor towards the red door.

"Hump?"

"I'm here. Don't get scared."

"Scared? You stupid borkson. Of course I'm scared. You'll get scared too when the ship blows up."

Slime began to ooze from the walls, thick, with an awful smell like—like what? Rot. Decay. She clenched her fists in useless fury but kept walking.

Now the noises began, the constant roar, then screams, the shriek of metal being ripped apart. Vanity covered her ears, pounded her head, shouted in pain and fury. But she didn't stop.

Suddenly she was running, at incredible speed; the walls flashed past her, the red door leaped forward. Her chest heaved, pain shot up and down her body.

She was running so fast that she simply couldn't stop when the naked men and women leaped in front of her. Their bodies glowed, their muscles rippled, their genitals, gigantic, monstrous, burned like the sun over the Danik desert. Great masks with grinning demon faces covered their heads and shoulders. When they held up their hands, the fingers changed to knives.

They'd come to stop her, keep her outside the door. The knives cut off her hands. She kept going. They slashed her stomach until her insides burst out upon the ground. Her legs kept pumping. They hacked off her feet, her thighs, but when they finally sliced through her neck, her head shot through the air like a comet, until with a great boom like an exploding star, Vanity's face struck the red door and burst it into as many pieces as Loper's shattered body.

They waited. Quietly, women and men, faces sad and joyful, bodies made beautiful by a million years of conscious evolution, they gestured with their eyes and hands to Golden Vanity's recreated body.

"Come inside," the kurois said. "Sit down with us."

Chapter Nineteen _____

Outside, the *Golden Vanity*—an organic entity, misnamed a spaceship, constructed or grown by robots under the "direction," more properly "request," of two megalomaniacs named Jaak and Loper—continued to whittle down the shrieker. Energy dissipated energy in patterns too intricate for any human mind to consciously follow.

Inside, two naive humans sat in motionless oblivion. The lights of the battle splashed across their faces, mildly scorching the skin despite the heat shields; they didn't notice. One of them, a Center woman named Golden Vanity, occasionally moved, short convulsive jerks, akin to the after-reactions of electric shock. The other, an Earthman named Humphrey McCloskey, never moved at all.

Further inside, in Golden Vanity's mind, wave structures joined and complemented the mechanisms of the ship. The union wasn't necessary; the ship could have handled all its functions by itself if it had been designed slightly differently. But such a creature would have excluded humans from playing any role in the universe other than passive objects carried like stones from place to place. And that was never the purpose of the ship's long dead creators.

Golden Vanity was learning about those purposes even while her ship fulfilled them. Did she actually speak to the kurois or

209

only to a solipsistic fantasy of them? In later years rationalists would argue that the brain had taken energy caused by Vanity's fears and formed wave structures which Vanity subjectively experienced as her confrontation with history. Spiritualists would claim that the kurois themselves, in their transformed state, perceived this woman's lifelong obsession with them and chose this moment to answer her. Those given to synthesis would suggest that the kurois implanted certain information in all the ship's memory systems, as well as in the human genetic code, to be conveyed to the right mind at the right moment. Whatever the explanation, one fact remained; it happened when Vanity's and Hump's minds joined together.

Vanity sat in an open space like a rocky plain, under a reddish sky, and faced these creatures whom she'd viewed in holos a thousand times. Years of love, hate, envy, and guilt swam inside her.

"You're fake," she accused them. "A trick of my mind. I let my fants get carried away and ended up with you. It's all Hump's fault. I made you up from all those holos I used to watch." Her voice dissipated into the windless sky.

Strange events punctuated that dull sky and ground. Flashes of light exploded in the air, silent clouds of dust erupted from the cold rock. The clouds and light came together in bright swirls, formed tiny nebulas, star systems, planets. In minutes, these miniature cosmos passed from chaos to order to entropy, and then vanished into the blank sky. Vanity paid no attention. She watched the enemy and nothing else.

A woman leaned forward. Light appeared to shine from behind her cheekbones, giving her skin a translucent goldenness. "You didn't create us," she said, "any more than we created you." Though she didn't speak in any special way, her voice vibrated Vanity's body like a silver hammer striking a bell. "However, we did anticipate you."

"No." Vanity shook her head. "This is nothing but a fantasy. I've thought about you so long I've got you stuck in my head." They said nothing. "What do you mean, anticipated?"

"We knew that eventually someone would discover how the ships were meant to work. Of course, we never intended them to function under one person's isolated direction."

"You're lying," Vanity said. "I invented it and now you're trying to steal the credit."

The woman paid no attention. "Not only does the

individualist strategy limit the ship's capabilities, it also distorts the Worker's mind. It makes breakdowns inevitable."

A man added, "Your friend Hump saw that immediately."

"Hump?" Vanity said. "He doesn't know anything. He's a loudmouth lokie idiot."

"Do you remember when you tried to teach him? He said that fantasies should liberate what he called the unconscious. Take it beyond the ego."

"But he was just talking. Because he didn't want to do his lessons."

"That talk came from a deeper place than he himself realized. The basic wave structures of the imagination are diagrammed so that what you call the lower ego always wants to take you beyond the conscious mode. Your fants all snake on you because they're trying to break free of the upper ego. On Center you make the upper ego so dominant the imagination perceives it as an enemy and resorts to terror."

A woman who hadn't spoken before said, "Remember, Hump didn't grow up on Center, while you, happily, lacked the technique to train and fortify his upper ego. When you took him into your fantasies and gave him the energy generated by your wave structures, his own imagination took that energy and used it to break loose from conscious direction. That release generated a great deal of free energy which then fed back to *your* imagination, pushing it to revert to its natural free state. It's a chain reaction caused by the linkage of two minds to one set of wave structures. Whatever prisons you construct for yourself, the addition of someone else's mental energy will collapse them."

"You've got it all wrong," Vanity said. "*I* forced *him*. Hump!" She spoke to the ground. "Are you there? Tell them how I made you do it." No answer. "Burst!" Tears spouted in her eyes. Angrily she wiped them away. "You're taking everything away from me. I thought I created something new. Me and Hump. But now you're telling me I didn't create it after all. You people planned it all along. Just like you planned everything else."

"We knew it would happen," the first woman said, "we didn't plan it. Originality, you should understand, doesn't demand exclusivity. Just because we once developed these techniques, and probably others developed them before us back through the history of the universes, doesn't diminish the originality of each fresh creator."

"But I wanted to bring something completely new into the world."

"You have. We're dead, have you forgotten? Between our death and this moment the techniques of unified awareness did not exist."

"You didn't die. We killed you. Oh, what's the use." Just to Vanity's right a vast fleet of tiny spaceships took off from a miniature world. Did they see her? she wondered. Could people see anything so huge and monstrous? "You don't understand," she said tearfully. "I wanted to make something you never had, so I could free people, cut them loose from you. You're killing us. Oh filth, what difference does it make if Hump and I developed the slimy techniques all by ourselves? What good is it?"

A man with fine white hair floating delicately around his face said, "You're looking at everything the wrong way. Why can't you appreciate that you've turned your people away from self-terror and isolation? You've started them towards conscious evolution."

"Evolution ended when you returned."

"Nonsense. Evolution continues for each species in its own place."

"So what do I do? Tell the SA I've invented evolution?"

"Tell them exactly what you planned. That you killed a shrieker and invented a new technique. You'll impress them. They'll ask you to teach them. And once they've learned and tried it in some difficult situation, they'll discover, like you and Hump, exactly what they have learned."

"But I can't teach anyone. I thought I could, or maybe faked it, to give Earth time. But I don't even know how it happened."

A woman so thin and supple she looked like a waving branch said, "It happened as a combination of your own weakening structures and Hump's demand that you open your mind to him. It happened because you, and your time, were ready for it. As for teaching, you'll know what to do. Believe us, you will. It's not very complicated after all. The readiness is all that matters. With Center people that readiness may take longer to mature, but it will happen. And of course, the fant teachers and the companies will oppose you, but not effectively. They can't. The new techniques mean freedom."

"Freedom from what?"

"You should understand that. From themselves, from history."

"History? You filthy arrogant—" She jumped as an explosion filled the sky with red dust. "It's you that holds us down. It's you we've got to free ourselves from. You're the ones who made us so afraid. You!" She was screaming at them.

One of the women, naked, yet draped in slow moving swirls of colored liquid, leaned forward with snake-like suddenness. "Because we didn't tell you the truth? Would you prefer that we had taught you the entire system? Then you could have discovered nothing for yourselves."

"You've still left us nothing, not if you've thought of it first. But I'm not talking about techniques. You know I'm not. I'm talking about what you made us do, just because you couldn't do it for yourselves."

For the first time their confidence wavered. "We had to do it that way," a woman said. "We needed you to help us."

"By killing you?"

"Yes. We were frightened. We tried; there was simply no alternative. But don't pretend you received nothing but guilt. We gave you starships, the transmitters, the entire structure of your civilization, in exchange for one moment of violence. How can you claim we didn't give you anything?"

"I never claimed that. I don't care what you gave us."

"Only because you've grown up with it. Ask Hump or Marilyn about the value of our gifts. Look at how their people scramble for them."

Jets of flame shot up from the ground; the world prepared to blow itself apart. (*What's happening out there*, Vanity thought; for just a moment she saw the ship again, the window filled with explosions. Then her reality returned to the scene in front of her.) She said, "Hump doesn't care about your great slimy gifts. He just wants everyone to leave him alone. That's what you couldn't do for us. You couldn't just leave us alone. You tricked us."

Angrily the white-haired man shook a finger at her. "We didn't force or trick your people into murder. They conceived and executed the whole plan themselves."

"Exactly. Exactly. You gave us something much worse than guilt. You taught us the truth about ourselves. You carefully gave us just enough freedom to put the whole burden on us."

"Would you rather we'd stated clearly our desires? Would you rather we'd openly offered you knowledge in exchange for death?"

"Yes. Definitely yes." The ground was shaking; she became

scared a crack would open up and swallow her."

"They might have refused."

"Right, right. That's why you never really gave us the choice. Not a conscious choice."

They all edged forward, hungrily. "Suppose we gave you that choice? Now?"

Vanity shrank back. Smoke obscured their faces. "What do you mean?"

"We'll give it to you all over again. Kill us freely. Now." A weapon, an absurd multi-barreled rifle, appeared in Vanity's hand. Horrified, she dropped it on her foot. She kicked it away.

"I don't understand," Vanity wailed. "If you're already dead—"

"Yes, physically," a woman broke in. "But didn't you say you couldn't get us out of your minds? We've trapped ourselves. We thought we could get free if we could abandon our bodies. Instead, we just trapped ourselves inside our children."

Vanity thought, *None of this is real. I've made it all up. But they're right. I've got them in my mind, and I've got to find some way to get rid of them.*

"Kill us," they begged. The sky flashed brighter.

Vanity picked up the weapon. All her emotion pressed her to pull the trigger: hate, envy, resentment, even love, for didn't they claim this second death would free them? She looked down the sights at the figures huddled together. And then she lowered the gun.

"What are you doing?" Lava burst from the ground.

Vanity shook her head. All around her, the miniature worlds blew apart. "I'll never get free if I kill you," she said and threw down the weapon.

"Don't you understand?" they cried. "We're the shrieker, your enemy, you've got to kill us." Golden Vanity got shakily to her feet. The figures coalesced, became a long scaly beast which Vanity recognized as an Earth creature, a dragon. The lizard mouth grinned at her, and she almost dove for the weapon. Instead, she turned her back and stepped away.

The dragon roared. Vanity kept walking. She wished she could laugh defiantly, but she was too scared. So she just kept walking. Until the burning ground opened up in front of her.

Unable to stop, Vanity pitched forward into the darkness, falling into nothing, into blackness.

She sat in the cabin of the *Golden Vanity*, her body scalded

and covered in dry sweat. Her eyes blinked open painfully; she'd
been squeezing them shut with all her might.

Darkness. Cool black darkness, pricked with stars. *We did it*,
she thought, grinning stupidly despite the pain of her cracked
skin. *We really actually did it*. "Hump?" she cried, turning her
head. "Look. We did it."

He didn't speak, he didn't move. He just sat slumped in his
seat, his hands limp, his head dropped forward. When she shook
his shoulders the head snapped back and forth like a rag doll.
"Hump! For burst's sake, wake up, you slimy borkson."
Weeping, she pressed her head against his shoulders. "Please,
Hump. Wake up."

Deep in Vanity's mind Hump's voice said, *Why don't we give
him a bowl of Vita-flakes*? An instant later, consciousness
stirred his face, and his cracked lips whispered, "How'd we do,
Rocky?"

Closing Acts ——————————

1

Through the long days the puppets dutifully acted out the simple movements they'd repeated for years. The trapeze artist ran through his meager repertoire of spins and flips, the three-armed Lukmii labored up Mt. Drosso, then leaped down to the vibrating carpet and started all over again. Only one group of puppets had vanished: the milk boys and their cows, reminders of Earth. Even that change hadn't come from Jaak himself; the SA had done it as a "delicate courtesy." Now and then, in a fit of helpless fury, Jaak would snatch one of the puppets from its obsessive task and fling it across the room. They only groped their way back and started all over. Sometimes he thought of pulling down the trapeze and smashing the mountain; but then he'd have to humiliate himself by asking the SA to replace them.

If the puppets' routines didn't vary from the old days, other things in Jaak's playroom-prison had certainly changed. The six projection windows no longer showed real-time events on other worlds, but simply tapes, at first histories of Jaak's one time triumphs, then projections of what he might have achieved if he'd stayed in power. A vast team of men and women worked constantly on these tapes, developing themes, keeping inner consistency, in short, developing an alternate life for the entire human galaxy. The fantasy company faced and solved its own crises, discovered new worlds, opened new markets. It didn't take long before this group of artists developed their art for its own sake with trends, motives, artistic fashions. Soon they forgot Jaak completely.

The prisoner hardly noticed. Sometimes he looked sadly at the projection, wishing he could surrender to their persuasive realism. His sanity never allowed it. The depiction of him as ruler of the galaxy (doing things totally alien to his character) only demonstrated his total helplessness. Their elaborate succession of events only reminded him that every day was exactly the same.

So he turned away from the windows, though he never dared demand them erased (as if they'd listen to him), and instead spent his long dead days with *her*—stubbornly ignoring the fact that she was no more real than the glorious events splashed across the walls.

She never left him. She danced and sang for him, she applauded his weak attempts to play any of the scattered instruments from different worlds, she exercised beside him or discussed their "future plans," and when he went to sleep she sat beside the bed. Probably they kept her there all night, because he always found her in the same place when he opened his eyes.

Once or twice Jaak had tried to explain (talking absurdly to the air on the not so certain assumption that someone was listening) that the real Golden Vanity hardly saw devotion to Jaak as her single goal in life. It made no difference; *she* still followed him loyally about the room.

She could hardly have done anything else. Keyed with all the hundreds of tapes of Golden Vanity from Jaak's collection, plus whatever information the designers could gather from Vanity's fant teachers, servants, and anyone who had known her, this new invention, the "responsive hologram," still depended on Jaak for its immediate reaction and new memory input. Sensors throughout the room registered Jaak's statements, actions, and emotional responses, fed them through computer channels attached to the hologram projector system, and then the channels instant-programmed the holo-Vanity's behavior in accord with its memories and fundamental laws of "character." A masterpiece, its creators assured each other and the SA functionary in charge of the project. Understandably, their enthusiasm ignored the one disturbing flaw.

Over the months, as the machine added all of Jaak's slightest intonations to its memory routine, the holo-Vanity became more and more divorced from its original inspiration, more and more a projection of the ex-chairman, rather than his daughter. Jaak saw this; he couldn't stop it. No one else cared.

"You're not her," he grated.

"Of course I'm her," she laughed. "Who else could I be?"

"Nothing. A trick to magnify my solitude."

She looked pained. "I just want to make you happy."

He shook his head. "Would *she* ever say that?"

He tried not speaking to her. It never worked. She pleaded for attention until he ordered her to leave him alone, and then she sat stiffly in the corner, robbed of any responses, like a deactivated robot. So Jaak let her prattle on, while in the sanctuary of his mind he constructed elaborate plans of revenge, takeover, control. *When I get out*, he thought. And stared at the playroom door.

What happened outside there? Did the company still function? Did people chase each other frantically along the corridors, trading information, assignments, directives? Or had the SA destroyed the company completely, draining the ten thousand rooms of all the workers, machines, children, sensors, mistresses male and female, communicators, treasures, teachers? For all Jaak knew they'd razed the building to the ground, leaving this solitary room with its projectors and life supports, surrounded by slowly eroding rock. How could he possibly know? He never saw a single other human being. Alone forever, Jaak watched his holo-Golden Vanity, laughing and dancing, but never eating, talking constantly but never touching him with even a tip of a finger or a single strand of hair.

2

The prophet woke up early that morning, hoping to get some time to himself before the disciples would mob him for yet another picture story. He splashed water on his face, chewed the remnants of his late-night supper. Cold cheese and meat. Some breakfast. Still, better than going down to the kitchen and having to make up some parable or other when he just wanted food. He laughed. His parents' legends never explained the drawbacks of the prophet occupation.

A scowl contorted his face as he stared at the lightening sky. Another visciously hot day. Soon, he promised himself. Soon they'd leave this filthy desert for some cool forest. The various pseuds had certainly offered him enough locations. He just needed a little more time to consolidate the myths and doctrines. Business, he thought. Stay with a good market until you're really sure of it.

He dusted off his robe, then set his hat on his head and slipped out the door. His followers spotted him before he'd even got to the end of the corridor between the buildings. One of the younger ones (he didn't recognize her, but so many new ones had come he hardly recognized anyone except his inner disciples) was chanting some prayer (what an awful reedy voice. Why couldn't lokies sing?) by the corner of the food hall. She opened her eyes to catch a breath just as the teacher was tiptoing past her. "Lord AAri," she burst out, as if she'd caught him trying to escape. "Where are you going? Can I come with you?"

"Of course," he said wistfully.

She stood up nervously, like a virgin alone with a famous seducer. "It's all right?"

He managed a smile. "I'm not god, you know. That's the first lesson, remember? No gods, only Spirit, infecting lokies and alies together."

The girl nodded. "We've just got to open our minds to it," she chirped.

"Yes," he said, thinking how he could just as well have eaten breakfast. "That's the hard point."

"You have to kill the past."

"Kill? No, of course not. Not at all. You've just got to release it. The past always wants to get away from us. But the harder we try to destroy it, to kill it, the more we hang on to it. It's a trick."

"Just release it," the girl repeated solemnly.

AAri nodded. Over his shoulder he saw the "gang," as Judy called his followers, lining up along the path. He sighed. It always struck him as so eerie—the way they stood there silently waiting for him to speak. About time to tell another picture denouncing reverence, he thought. With the easy expertise of months of practice he began constructing the bare lines of a story in his head. A ship in space, maybe, using obsolete star maps, something like that.

A voice cut in. "Hi. Getting an early start?"

AAri turned to see Judy grinning at him. "Sure," he said.

"Hit the shrines before the sun gets too strong."

"Lord AAri walks to the shrines," Judy called out. "Do we follow him?"

"No," someone answered according to the ritual. "We walk together. With the Spirit."

They marched in a rough line, four or five across, like an Arbolian softworm oozing across the desert. Judy stepped up alongside AAri. "I saw you slip out, but I thought you could use some time alone. Sorry it didn't work out."

"Thanks anyway." As he looked at her with a mixture of fondness and lechery, he remembered how he and Vanity had sneaked up on the Danik camp late at night and virtually kidnapped Judy. Once she'd gotten over the shock—and that filthy reverence—she'd listened delightedly to Vanity's plan; she'd even made a few suggestions about how she could fake her miraculous revelation. By the time the Lord Prophet made his grand entrance, Judy had primed the market so well with her prophecies and divinations that AAri might have been a beloved grandfather visiting his family.

"What do you hear from the Queen of Virtue?" Judy asked when they'd gotten a few steps ahead of the others.

"Vanity? Her classes are going all right. She says she doesn't really know how she does it, but she somehow gets the partners to merge. Of course, Cixxa joining her has helped a lot, politically as well as practically. And they've got the image makers to induce Crisis."

"One of these days I want to join one of those classes. Then maybe you and I can go exploring."

He grinned at her. "And give up religion?"

Judy shrugged. "I don't know. From what you tell me of Vanity's ideas it doesn't sound that different from what we're doing."

"It shouldn't. The Queen of Virtue designed both systems, remember?"

They fell silent, AAri squinting against the already bright sun as he thought about that peculiar title Vanity had given herself. Queen of Virtue. It sounded so absurd, but the Daniks loved it. Just as they'd loved the entire picture she'd devised for him (how could her instinctive brilliance have gone unnoticed all those years with Jaak?). The Spirit taking an alie form and visiting Earth. The "lokie consort" (Hump as a god!) sharing her burdens and oppression. Then came the Ghost of Fear, Loper, to kidnap the Queen. And finally, Lord AAri the Prophet, killing the Ghost to release the Spirit into the world. Perfect. Balanced, solid; no one on G'GaiRRin could have done a better job. He laughed out loud.

Judy raised her eyebrows. "What's the joke?"

He squeezed her hand. "I'll tell you later."

By the time they'd reached the shrine AAri was dripping sweat from his scalp to his toes. If they didn't leave soon, he'd start preaching a doctrine of release your mind through nakedness. Puffing, he mounted the small wooden platform they'd constructed so everyone could see him. At least the plastic canopy gave him some meager shade. The gang sat on the ground and looked up like obedient loopies at feeding time.

The shrine consisted of the two spaceships, his own and the one Vanity had left behind, with the story platform strung between them. Though the Daniks had painted Vanity's ship with glowing symbols of the galaxy's different religions (the library had greatly expanded since AAri's arrival), the prophet had instructed them to cover his own ship with mud, a symbol of irreverence. Both ships gleamed in the sun. Lord AAri looked over his silent disciples.

"Before the planets and the stars," he said, "there existed only one creature in the entire universe. A great black bird flying round and round in the darkness with no place to rest. The bird's name was REE-awk, from the sound it made when it couldn't stand its weariness."

Sitting in the front row, Judy winked at him.

3

The spaceship weaved drunkenly through the pink and turquoise blossomed trees to land with a lurch against a grassy hill. Not far away an ancient mound temple lay under clumps of purple moss. Inside the ship, the driver looked ruefully at the woman sitting next to him. "Sorry," he mumbled.

"Sorry? Is that the best you can say? Oh, my sorrowful stomach."

Hump jerked himself loose from the seat. "Your stomach could survive an earthquake."

Vanity waved a finger at him. "You talk back to your teacher and you'll never get your captain's license."

"You know something? You're even more obnoxious as a teacher than when you were hiding everything."

She smiled at him. "You're just upset because Ann and Marilyn have both got their licenses already."

"License? Hah. A slimy little piece of paper with your signature on it. Besides, Ann and Marilyn get to merge with each other. I'm stuck with you."

"You love it."

"I could land much better if you'd shut that damned teev off." He tried to reach past her to snap the switch on the small television fixed to the instrument panel.

Vanity slapped his hand away. "You leave Errol Flynn alone. I didn't go to all that trouble arranging a hookup through the 'mitts from Earth just for you to switch it off."

"God, what a use for black holes. Well, you and Errol can stay here. I'm going outside." He snatched the picnic basket full of Jewish delicatessen ("Believe me, Hump, even the Ktanerians can't stand Ktanerian food") and strode past her before she could grab it back.

"Oh all right," she said. She followed him outside.

Hump sat down with his back to a tree and tilted up his face to the sun. "Feels good. Hard to believe it's not the same one we've got back home."

Marching around like a child investigating all the trees and flowers, Vanity said, "This place smells a lot nicer than Earth." She peered at some insect buzzing through the lower branches of a tree.

Hump stretched out with his hands behind his head. "Come down here next to me," he said.

She saluted. "Yes sir. As soon as I watch this spider thingy."

"Spiders don't fly," he said sleepily. Eyes closed, he stroked Vanity's hip when she lay down beside him.

After a moment's silence Vanity said, "You know, I've been thinking of demanding that the school always include a certain quota of Earth people."

"In the student body?"

"Teachers too. Ann could teach. And I'm sure I could find some others."

"The SA won't like it. They want you to concentrate on their people."

"Of course. That's why AAri told me to insist they locate the school on Earth. It'll make this new demand much easier. If they fight it, Marilyn and I could probably arrange some harmless guerrilla attacks by resentful lokies."

Hump sighed. "When are we going to slice all this political stuff? You promised me the grand tour, remember? I want to see the World Tree on Arbol."

She snuggled against him. "Believe me, I'm as sick of it as you are. That's why I want to get these changes through. Once we give Earth a permanent place we can leave everyone else to work things out. What are you laughing at?"

"I was just thinking of sending Gloria a picture postcard from Lurittii."

"Yech. Lurittii." She reached in her shirt to scratch her stomach. "Hey, I've got an idea."

Hump grinned. "Yeah? I'll bet I can guess what it is." He relaxed his mind and body, and a moment later sensed that soft pressure in his head. A soundless voice said, *Howdy.*

Howdy yourself, he answered, while together they looked through Hump's eyes at Vanity's limp body.

Vanity said, *She sure looks nice, doesn't she?*

Yeah. Innocent. Together they reached out Hump's fingers to unbutton the shimmery blue Center blouse and the Earth jeans. When the light gold body lay naked on the hillside, they stroked the thighs, the breasts, and pressed Hump's lips softly against the belly and then the nipples.

Your turn, Vanity said. A moment later Hump's body fell limp while Vanity's sprang to life.

Hump said, *He feels good. Warm.* They removed his Ktanerian tunic and mirror bright Dlurstan trousers, bought the day before in a subterranean market on the other side of the planet. Directed by Hump, Vanity's long thin fingers ran along the tan body.

Briefly they separated minds to kiss and stroke each other, but as soon as Hump reached full arousal he abandoned his body to join Vanity's as she climbed on top of him. With a quick easy rhythm they began switching back and forth between the two bodies.

Fantasies welled up between them, an explosion of images and actions. They became animals, changing form constantly until they settled for a moment into long-legged sleek cats, their fur a rainbow of stripes as they ran effortlessly under a pink and orange sky. Abruptly they lifted into that sky, becoming silver eagles with white beaks. They exulted in the heat of a summer sun, the smell of flowers drifting up from the ground, the tight pull of muscles as their black tipped wings rose and fell, shifting with the wind. Their cries shook the trees, rang echoes in the rocks.

With no change, the lovers lay again upon the damp Ktanerian grass, Vanity aware of Hump's weight moving against her and his arms and legs clasped around her sweating naked body. For an instant the world wavered, and the eagles returned, only to vanish as their bodies thrust together and their real shouts overrode all imagined cries.

ABOUT THE AUTHOR

Rachel Pollack lives in Amsterdam, Holland, where she lectures and reads Tarot cards as well as writes books. Born in Brooklyn just before the Japanese surrender in World War II, she grew up in Poughkeepsie, New York, and went to NYU and Claremont Graduate School. While writing she has supported herself as an IBM production planner, a university lecturer, a dishwasher and bar cleaner, a squirter of patchouli oil in little brown bottles, and a maker of cheap jewelry. She has traveled through most of Western Europe and before moving to Holland lived in London for a year.

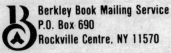